THE CHAMPION

A Series of Worthy Young Ladies
Book Four

Kate Archer

Dragonblade Publishing, Inc. is an imprint of Kathryn Le Veque Novels, Inc.
P.O. Box 23
Moreno Valley, CA 92556
ceo@dragonbladepublishing.com

Produced in the United States of America

First Edition August 2022
Trade Paperback Edition

ARE YOU SIGNED UP FOR DRAGONBLADE'S BLOG?

You'll get the latest news and information on exclusive giveaways, exclusive excerpts, coming releases, sales, free books, cover reveals and more.

Check out our complete list of authors, too!

No spam, no junk. That's a promise!

Sign Up Here

www.dragonbladepublishing.com

Dearest Reader;

Thank you for your support of a small press. At Dragonblade Publishing, we strive to bring you the highest quality Historical Romance from some of the best authors in the business. Without your support, there is no 'us', so we sincerely hope you adore these stories and find some new favorite authors along the way.

Happy Reading!

CEO, Dragonblade Publishing

Additional Dragonblade books by Author Kate Archer

A Series of Worthy Young Ladies
The Meddler (Book 1)
The Sprinter (Book 2)
The Undaunted (Book 3)
The Champion (Book 4)

The Dukes' Pact Series
The Viscount's Sinful Bargain (Book 1)
The Marquess' Daring Wager (Book 2)
The Lord's Desperate Pledge (Book 3)
The Baron's Dangerous Contract (Book 4)
The Peer's Roguish Word (Book 5)
The Earl's Iron Warrant (Book 6)

PROLOGUE

Grosvenor Square, 1812

T HE SOCIETY OF Sponsoring Ladies had been called to Lady Redfield's drawing room with very little notice. As they filed in, each of them hoped they would discover something different about the room, but the lady of the house had not yet redecorated. It was beginning to seem as if she never would.

Lady Redfield's long-dead husband had, late in life, become an admirer of all things Indian and had made purchases and changes to the London house with reckless abandon. Lady Redfield stood helplessly by as imported pieces came in and her staid English furniture went up to the attics. She had even had some sort of attack when the six-foot stone statue had been wheeled into the house, necessitating three days abed with calming draughts. Still, the baron's preferred furniture and objects d'art remained precisely where they had been since he'd departed the world. Lady Redfield did not like it, but she could not see her way clear to disappoint her baron, even in death.

Lady Heathway glared at the looming stone statue of Ganesh standing guard in the corner. The statue stared implacably back at her, his expression enigmatic and refusing to avert his gaze.

Lady Mendleton shifted on an ornately carved ebony chair whose velvet cushions were found rather too thin for her comfort, despite the lady's own generous padding.

Lady Featherstone squinted at the dizzying pattern of the carpet as if she were searching it for clues.

Lady Easton glared at a small but fierce warrior arrayed in gold armor, who stood on a table and bravely peered into the distance as if he might spot an enemy on the other side of Lady Redfield's drawing room.

The duchess surveyed it all and said, "The baron continues to have his way, I see."

Baroness Redfield hurried into the room, having had to chase down her servants so they might provide tea. Nobody else in the room would countenance having to chase down their own servants, but the lady was rather a marshmallow and all her staff knew it.

"Do sit down, Cecilia," Lady Heathway advised. "If those rascally servants of yours do not attend you, I will hunt them down myself and they will regret the encounter."

As if all who worked in the house heard the ominous threat and nobody wished to be faced with the fearsome Lady Heathway, Hemmings came in with a tea service. He was followed by a smirking footman carrying a tray with a rather thin assortment of biscuits on it.

They laid the tea and retreated, averting their eyes from Lady Heathway's doleful expression.

After the door had closed, Lady Redfield said softly, "It's not Hemmings' fault, my butler does try, you know."

"I am certain it is not Hemmings' fault," Lady Heathway said, looking meaningfully at Lady Redfield.

"In any case," Lady Easton said, "here we are and here is tea, and I have an appointment with my modiste at four. I do not care to be late."

"Now, Cecilia, your note was mysterious indeed," the duchess said. "At least the one I received was. It only said, *I have dared and I have prevailed. Come to me on Tuesday at two.*"

"Precisely what mine said, too," Lady Featherstone confirmed. "I studied it backward and forward for clues, but could discover nothing. Unless," she said, tapping her forefinger on her chin. "Could Tuesday be a clue? Or the time itself, two o'clock?"

Lady Easton and Lady Heathway sighed in unison.

"As for myself, I cannot stay long," Lady Mendleton said. "Georgiana quite depends upon me to be by her side at this important moment in our history. She's had the baby, you know."

"She had the baby four months ago," Lady Easton said, "as we have all been informed of by more than one letter on the subject. And by the way, Louisa, do not expect me to believe the child is showing signs of genius."

Lady Mendleton was not at all put off by the swipe, but rather, looked at Lady Easton sympathetically, as if to say—*too bad you don't have your own granddaughter to think about.*

"You'll never guess," Lady Redfield said, pouring the tea with a shaking hand.

"We certainly will not," the duchess said. "Out with it, Cecilia."

"It is only this," Lady Redfield said, putting the cup down. "Lady Arabella Berestock, daughter of the late Earl of Westcott, who was a second cousin of mine, has been relegated to one of Lord Skeffington's estates in Cornwall. She's his ward, you see. Oh, I never did like him being named guardian. I did say as much to the baron once…"

"And the baron told you it was none of his affair and that was that," the duchess said.

"That *was* that, I'm afraid," Lady Redfield said.

"But now, Cecilia," Lady Featherstone said encouragingly. "What's happened now?"

Lady Redfield smoothed her skirts as if straightening them were a sign of courage. In hurried tones, she related her encounter with Lord Skeffington. The scenes played out in her mind as if they were happening all over again.

Until just forty-eight hours ago, Cecilia Finch, Baroness Redfield, had never done a daring thing in her life. She'd thought about no end of daring things, she'd admired her friends' daring, but when it came to it she found herself a basket of quaking and shuddering nerves. At such moments, she was in the habit of looking for open doors and hurrying through them to be away from whatever unpleasantness was brewing.

But two days ago, she felt herself driven forward. She thought and paced and thought and paced and finally, she called the carriage. Then she canceled the carriage. Then she called it again and got in. Then she ordered her coachman to drive hither and thither, making circles around the town. Finally, she directed him to Lord Skeffington's residence. She attempted to get out of the carriage for a full half-hour, to no avail. Her legs simply would not move. Then the lord's own coachman drove his carriage to the front of the house, waiting for his master to depart. She must act or go home.

She'd stumbled out of her carriage and climbed the steps. Somehow, the knocker had been knocked, she supposed with her own two hands, or maybe it had been her groom. Her state of mind had not been conducive to thinking and remembering.

A rather thin and serious butler had answered, and she *did* remember him—he'd looked at her as if she were a peddler arrived to the wrong door. Reluctantly, he'd led her into Lord Skeffington's drawing room to await the terrible man's arrival.

In near blinding terror, she kept one idea in her mind. Lord Skeffington must be convinced to hand over his ward. She wished it with such fervor that her feet had carried her there, despite the frantic beating of her heart and the feeling that there was not enough air in the room.

She dared, and she hoped she did not faint in the middle of it.

It would have been so much less terrifying had it not been Skeffington that must be overcome. He was stern and standoffish. He was, well everyone knew him to be, that was, Cecilia was *certain* he was a rogue and seducer. There could not have been so many rumors about him unless at least some of them were true.

She glanced nervously around the room, wondering if the

actress that was purported to be living in his house just now hid behind a sofa. It would be very like an actress to leap out at a person.

The door opened and Lady Redfield steadied herself on the arm of a chair. Lord Skeffington strode in, looking slightly annoyed to find her there.

"Lady Redfield," he said with a short bow. "I was just on my way out. Is there some matter I can assist you with? If it's a charity, leave the details with my butler."

Lady Redfield clutched the arm of the chair and stared at him in horrified fascination. She could not think when she had last broached a conversation that was anything other than pleasant and cheerful. She briefly wondered if the windows were unlocked and if she might dive out of one of them. Why had she come?

"Madam?" the lord said, his voice full of irritation.

She could not run. No, she really could not. Poor Lady Arabella could not be left to be ignored in the countryside.

She'd taken in a deep breath. "Yes," she said, her voice quavering. "I mean, no. Not a charity. It is, well, I demand you hand over Lady Arabella Berestock. To me. To bring out this season. Lord Westcott was a cousin."

There. She'd said it. Now she waited for the roof to fall down around her ears.

Lord Skeffington considered her. He straightened a cuff and said, "You *demand* it?"

Had she said the wrong thing? Should she have said she only requested it?

With a small smile, which was really very unpleasant, Lord Skeffington said, "Very well. Save me the trouble of writing to Lady Arabella regarding the details, if you would be so kind. My butler will provide you with the address."

"Certainly, oh yes, of course!" Lady Redfield said, rather stunned that she'd prevailed. "I can assure you that Lady Arabella will be cared for, and guided, and naturally we hope there may be a match…"

"Your hope could not possibly exceed my own. I'll thank you to get that girl and her trustee out of my life once and for all. She comes into her majority next year, a year I have eagerly anticipated. She is an ingrate and the trustee is tightfisted. He refuses to let go of any money to make repairs to the house in Cornwall, despite the fact that I could be renting it out were it not occupied by the girl and her companion. I will send over the details of her dowry. Do not trouble me with any expenses incurred while she is in Town, that will be *your* responsibility."

He turned to leave and said over his shoulder, "And by the by, I could not care less who she marries."

The door shut behind him and Lady Redfield sank into a chair. She had dared and she had done it.

Now, as she gazed round at her friends' various looks of surprise, she finished her breathless story of overcoming Lord Skeffington. "So you see," she said, "I gained my point. Goodness, I practically staggered out of that house. My legs could hardly hold me up."

"But you persevered," the duchess said. "There is something noble to be said about perseverance."

"Goodness, Cecilia," Lady Easton said, "I do not ever remember you having the temerity to demand anything from anybody."

"I never have, I do not think," Lady Redfield said.

"Yes, well done, brava," Lady Heathway said. "But what are the plans? When will she come? Has Skeffington sent over the details of her dowry?"

"Lady Arabella's dowry is very generous—twenty-thousand pounds," Lady Redfield said.

"Heavens, that ought to do it," the duchess said.

"It may well do it a bit *too* well," Lady Heathway said. "We'll need to be on our guard against rogues and scoundrels."

Lady Redfield fanned herself, not having considered that aspect of it.

"Never mind that," Lady Featherstone said. "Have you

communicated with Lady Arabella?"

"I have written the dear girl a letter explaining everything that has happened, and that will happen," Lady Redfield said.

"Was the letter clear, though?" Lady Easton asked. "I only say that sometimes your missives are very charming and cheerful, but I am not always certain what they actually say."

The other ladies nodded in agreement, having received such letters themselves.

Lady Redfield was thoughtful. Then she said, "Oh, I am certain I spelled everything out. I must have."

The duchess set down her teacup and murmured, "Let us hope."

"Though," Lady Redfield said, "I find I am rather frightened of going to collect her on my own with just my maid. Could not one of you come on the trip? As soon as tomorrow?"

Lady Easton shook her head. The duchess was prior engaged. Lady Heathway tapped her finger to her chin as if she were mulling it over. Lady Mendleton only murmured, "The baby, you know…"

"I will go," Lady Featherstone said. "I've never traveled to Cornwall and knowledge of its countryside may prove valuable if I'm ever asked to solve a case in that neighborhood. One must collect information when one can."

Lady Redfield nodded gratefully, if not confusedly. Of course, everybody knew that Anne was a keen member of Lord Ryland's criminal society and if one were to forget that fact, they would be reminded by her emerald brooch. It had been won at Ryland's mystery supper and was the constant companion of all of her gowns and dresses. Lady Redfield had not thought Anne would be called *anywhere* to solve an actual crime and then Cornwall seemed rather far afield. Though, she knew so little about how crimes were solved she supposed it was possible.

"Then it's settled," the duchess said. "My frie s, we prepare to launch Lady Arabella Berestock this season. Cec. I will fund her wardrobe as I do not imagine you would like to go to your son over it."

Lady Redfield nodded gratefully, as she had been wondering how to convince her seventeen-year-old boy that he must part with a lot of money to dress a lady he'd never met. He was at school, and she'd already tried to write a letter about it with little success.

"I would suggest," the duchess went on, "that just as a practical matter, we make every effort to ensure this introduction into society goes smoothly. So far, we have had a few too many…bumps in the road."

"I am certain it will all go smoothly," Lady Redfield said.

"Cecilia," Lady Heathway said, "if there is one thing I've learned from our experiences over the past two years, it is to be certain of nothing."

Lady Redfield nodded, but she would not dwell on Lady Heathway's advice. It was very unlikely that her nerves could hold up against any further upset. Her trip to Lord Skeffington's house had taken her to the edge and back. Now was a time for calm.

In any case, Lady Arabella was dear Lord Westcott's daughter. She could not possibly be any trouble.

CHAPTER ONE

L ADY ARABELLA BERESTOCK had been an orphan and a ward of Lord Skeffington's for as long as she remembered. Who her guardian was mattered little to her, as she had always had Mrs. Weston by her side. That good lady had been her nursemaid, then her governess, and now her companion, ever since coming to Cornwall from her late father's estate in Derbyshire. Mrs. Weston had been a childhood friend of her mother's and had gone to Lord Skeffington and insisted it be so. She would not allow her friend's daughter to be turned over to strangers. The dear lady had not, at that moment, known they were to be exiled to a remote corner of Cornwall, but she'd stuck by Arabella regardless.

Mrs. Weston was a comfortable sort of person and tended to be indulgent in everything except Arabella's schooling. There was no room for indulgence there—Mrs. Weston was a bishop's daughter and had been raised well-read and mannered herself. She had equipped Arabella to enter any drawing room in London, should she ever get there to enter one, and to speak creditably on a suitable variety of subjects.

Arabella had turned twenty and should have gone to London already, but it seemed Skeffington could not be bothered. Her guardian had made clear that if she was not to be of any use to him, and she most assuredly was not, then she was free to rot in Cornwall.

She was not certain of her opinion on the matter. In a year, she would come into her majority and could make the decision for herself if she liked. But on the other hand, could she really bear to leave her beloved animals behind? She had recently been mulling over the idea of taking everybody with her, though it would be a most difficult matter to arrange. How to convince the likes of Mrs. Twitch-nose to pack up her family and get in a carriage? And then, all of her rescues were meant to go back out into the wild. What would Sir Slippery do when he was so moved to answer the call from the out of doors and take his rightful place in nature? Where would he go in London?

So, there she and Mrs. Weston were, still in Cornwall, with only Mrs. Penrale doing the cooking and housekeeping and Freddy acting as man of all work to keep the place going. Crookhill Manor was located in a lonely place, set on a hill overlooking mostly wooded land, the only interesting thing about the view was the river that ran through it. Neighbors were few and mostly farmers. They were friendly enough, but Mrs. Weston did not encourage anything over-friendly.

There were days when Arabella longed for adventuring to London and parts beyond, but then other days when she was quite satisfied to regard her current circumstances.

Just now, she re-read the letter that had most unexpectedly arrived from a certain Lady Redfield.

"What does it say, my dear?" Mrs. Weston asked, knitting another scarf for nobody knew who, since everybody in the house was well-supplied with them. Even Mr. Prickles had dragged a few under a table in the drawing room to use as bedding.

"That is what I am trying to determine," Arabella said. "It seems she is a cousin of some sort and knew my father. Aside from that, she's had some dust-up with Skeffy."

"Does not everyone who encounters that wretched lord either have a dust-up, or want to have one? He is most unpleasant. Though, I wonder why the lady felt compelled to inform you of it?"

Arabella handed over the letter. "Perhaps you'd better read it, you might make more sense of it than I. I hardly know how to answer such a communication."

Mrs. Weston perused the paper, her eyebrows marching toward each other like two battalions preparing to meet on the field of battle.

My dear Lady Arabella,

You will not know me, or know of me, I suppose. Your father did know me as a cousin and what a wonderful man he was. I recall a particular circumstance where a carriage wheel broke and I was certain he should be in a temper about it but he carried on with supreme equanimity. I was very comforted by it.

I write to you now to inform you that I have dared and pre-vailed on your behalf. I have gained the point and Lord Skeffington has lost the point.

You will be as surprised as I was, as this is the very first time I have ever attempted to prevail. (It may very well be the last as I was quite shaken by the encounter.)

For now, rest assured that I HAVE dared and I HAVE pre-vailed.

We shall have such fun!

Cecilia Finch, Baroness Redfield

"Fun doing what, I wonder?" Mrs. Weston said.

"I cannot be certain, but I feel the fun is in whatever she's dared and prevailed," Arabella said.

"I suppose she means to come to us at some point," Mrs. Weston said, "unless the fun is to be writing muddled letters back and forth."

Arabella nodded as Mrs. Penrale brought in the tea tray. She smiled at the black nose poking out of the bottom of the tablecloth covering a side table. It was the hedgehog's preferred housing, as it was dark and contained, covered on all sides, and conveniently near where tea was generally had. Now, Mr. Prickles had heard the tea coming in and was anxiously waiting for some little tidbit to drop to the floor.

"I think I know what's happened," Mrs. Weston said. "Lady Redfield has dashed off a note and intends to write another, longer letter that will say if she will come, and when. And, hopefully, why."

"I am sure you are right," Arabella said. "Now, though, Mr. Prickles' heart shall be broken if I do not casually drop a piece of biscuit next to his residence."

PEREGRINE HADLEIGH, MARQUESS of Blackwood and eldest son of the Duke and Duchess of Stanbury, had finally purchased a house in town. He'd been looking for ages, but anything he would prefer was only for rent, not for sale.

Suddenly, an opportunity had arisen. Lord Gasper had kicked off and his only son had interests in America. The fellow would keep the country estate, but he had no use for Town.

The house was on Grosvenor Square and was precisely what he'd looked for—commodious, well-built, a sizable garden out back surrounded by a tall stone wall to contain his beast of a dog, and mews leading to ample stables. If there were anything at all to criticize about the place, it was only that his new neighbor to the left was Lady Redfield, one of his mother's cabal of matrons.

Still, if one were to be located nearby any one of the duchess' intimates, it was preferable it be Lady Redfield. She was an ineffectual sort of lady, rather like a fluttering bird. However, she was also unflaggingly cheerful and he'd never heard of her giving anybody any trouble. He could not say the same for the likes of Lady Heathway and Lady Easton. Or his mother, for that matter. The Duchess of Stanbury could be quite the typhoon when she liked it.

He'd not informed the duke and duchess of his purchase yet, though he must do it soon as the furniture was being moved in this very day. He'd only avoided it so far because he could already hear his mother's views on the subject—*My dear boy, how fortuitous that you will be a neighbor to one of my friends. You must call on Lady Redfield, and of course I will drop in to see you whenever I am in the neighborhood, which will be often.*

His mother was a dear old girl, but he could not be quite comfortable never knowing when she might suddenly descend upon his house. He was in his prime, as were his friends, and they could perhaps involve themselves in things the duchess would not approve of. Wild oats were felt, and wild oats were sowed.

All he could hope for was that his mother's time would be entirely taken up with that society the ladies had cooked up between them. Though it had, when he'd first heard of it, sounded like the most staid thing in the world to sponsor a girl coming into society, it had since taken some surprising turns.

Miss Wilcox had somehow saved Langley from footpads and now they'd become a rather dashing couple, always seeming to be headed into Buckingham Palace.

Gresham had married a lady known to have clung to the outside of a house via drainpipe and been shot at by the butler of the premises. Peregrine had yet to hear of why Miss Yardley felt compelled to scale Lady Heathway's walls like a housebreaker.

And now, the strangest news of all. Pierrepoint swore that buttoned-up Bertridge had married a lady who had managed to scandalize Brighton. Bertridge, of all people. The man had been a hundred-years-old since he was twenty and Peregrine had been certain he would wed the most silent and boring lady he could dig up, not one who sent tongues wagging.

The matron's society looked to get these girls married and they had certainly done that, but it had not been the dignified process that he was certain his mother wished for. Or *noble* process, as she would prefer to call it.

Whatever trouble his mother's society would fall into next,

he would steer well clear of it. The season was ready to begin in full force and there would be no end of balls and parties.

Peregrine had perfected his mode of operation through it all—he happily engaged with charming ladies who he knew to have set their caps elsewhere or had made clear they were not struck by him.

He strenuously avoided any person who may have set their cap in his own direction. There seemed to be enough of them, though he did not take it as a compliment to his person. He knew himself to be rather lanky and not everybody appreciated his coppery hair color or his equally coppery eyes. But he also knew himself to be the heir to a dukedom, and it seemed there were ladies who would overlook what they might consider his middling personal charms for a chance at duchess.

He often delighted in thinking of finding a lady he actually wished to pursue, and who might think his person held some sort of appeal. Though, this wonderful lady should not come to London so soon. Two years from now would be the perfect time to think of such things. She ought to be at home just now, practicing her playing or whatever young ladies did before they were out. He had no sisters of his own to know much about it, though his friend Rendridge had three and said they were confounded creatures who were either laughing or crying. If his dear darling wife was out there somewhere, he hoped for her sake that she was mostly laughing.

For now, though, thanks to his mother's ideas regarding how a marquess should be funded, added to a delightful streak of gambling wins, and a prosperous estate given him by his father, he had plenty of money in his pocket. He also had plenty of energy in his person, and there was plenty of adventure to be had.

LADY REDFIELD AND Lady Featherstone had set off in the carriage four days ago. Neither of them had really thought through how long and arduous a journey it would be, though Lady Redfield had been told outright by her coachman. They had not brought their lady's maids, and this had proved problematic. They had made attempts at doing each other's hair with little success and had taken to keeping their bonnets on except for sleeping. They were surprised at how rumpled their clothes had become and not exactly sure what to do about it.

Lady Featherstone had some idea that wetting her skirt overnight might straighten it out but all that came of it was a silk skirt that was water-stained, damp, and still wrinkled. The lady had begun to wonder if silk were really the right fabric for traveling. It had seemed so when she had her maid with her, but perhaps when she went soldiering off on her own a sturdy cotton might have been best.

At least Lander was a Cornwall man and knew the route sufficiently well. The reliable coachman took them to inns that were well-appointed. Once there, he delivered strong words to the innkeeper about how they were to be cared for, despite their disheveled persons giving them the appearance that they were running from the law.

Lady Featherstone had passed the time by making note of all she observed out the window, which seem to occupy her well enough. Though, Lady Redfield was at a loss as to why a particular old oak at a turning was vital to remember, or why the presence of a farmhouse with an uneven set of windows might prove important at some later date.

As for Lady Redfield herself, she spent most of the time daydreaming of the coming days. She was finally to be a mama to a daughter! And how fortuitous it was that there was not even an original mother to leave behind. It was sad that Lady Arabella was an orphan, but did not an orphan wish for one thing? Did not they yearn for a mama? And here she was, on her way to be just that.

At the last inn, they had hired a local girl to do something with their clothes and their hair. The girl had taken one look at them and said, "Goodness gracious." Four hours in her capable hands and Lady Redfield thought they at least looked presentable.

The carriage trotted down a forested lane, old oaks hemming them in on either side.

"A rather perfect place to hide a murdered body," Lady Featherstone said, scribbling in her notebook.

Lady Redfield shivered at the idea. Thinking to turn her friend's thoughts away from murder, she said, "I believe we get very close to the house. Lander said it was not two hours from the inn and I believe we must have been going that long."

Lady Featherstone closed her notebook and said, "Well, this is exciting. I feel we have been to the moon and back and now finally we will arrive."

They came around a turn and a house with a short winding drive was just ahead. It was a lonely looking sort of place, surrounded by trees as its only neighbors.

The carriage stopped and Lander called down, "That's it just ahead, my lady. Give me the signal when you want to proceed."

Lady Redfield felt her nerves rolling over her like a wave of water. Suddenly, she was afraid. What if the girl did not like her? She always tried so hard to be agreeable, but that did not mean she would be liked. What if dear Lady Arabella did not wish to come to her in Town? Should she have waited for a response to her letter?

Just then, the front doors of the house flew open and a young lady strode out with sleeves rolled up and something brown squirming in her arms. She promptly dumped the thing in the fountain, there was a lot of splashing, and then it slipped out and ran back into the house as fast as its short legs would carry it, its long tail swishing behind.

"Sir Slippery, really! You are such a goose," the girl shouted after the creature, chasing it back into the house.

"I do believe that was an otter," Lady Featherstone said, snapping open her notebook and scribbling at full speed.

The doors to the house closed behind the girl while Lady Redfield sat in stunned silence. An otter in the house. What on earth went on in Cornwall?

Lady Featherstone opened her window and said, "Well, Lander? We won't find out anything if we don't go in."

The coachman drove the horses forward.

CHAPTER TWO

I N TIMES OF stress, Lady Redfield often found she had a rather threadbare memory of what had been said or done. This seemed to be such a moment.

She could not recall getting out of the carriage, but she could recall the door being answered by a middle-aged lady who she would come to know as Mrs. Weston. She also came to know that aside from Mrs. Weston there was an individual named Freddy who acted as man of all work, and a woman named Mrs. Penrale who was both the cook and housekeeper.

Lady Redfield was certain Mrs. Penrale had too much to do, as the good woman was at a moment's loss to decide whether she ought to make tea first, or go above stairs and fetch Lady Arabella first. Mrs. Weston pointed out that she already had water on the boil and directed her toward the kitchens to arrange a tea tray.

Now, the tea had been brought in and Mrs. Penrale trudged toward the stairs, not looking particularly enthusiastic about where she was going.

Mrs. Weston poured and said, "Lady Redfield, Lady Featherstone, how did you find the journey?"

"Oh, very pleasant," Lady Redfield said.

"It was grueling," Lady Featherstone said, "but I've filled a crime-solving notebook, so that must be my recompense."

Lady Redfield found herself very grateful that Mrs. Weston appeared to have enough sense not to inquire what went into a crime-solving notebook. She would not wish to converse on the subject of murder and she certainly did not wish the lady to be informed that her local wood was an excellent place to hide a murdered body.

Rather, she kept glancing at the stairs, waiting with great anticipation laced with terror to see Lady Arabella upon them. She equally hoped that when she did see the darling girl, it would be without an otter in her arms.

"Now, I must ask, Mrs. Weston," Lady Featherstone said, "why is there an otter in your house?"

Mrs. Weston nodded, as if she had been expecting such a question. "He is one of Arabella's rescues, I'm afraid. Abandoned as a pup."

Lady Featherstone murmured, "I see," as if she were committing the circumstance to memory.

Just then, there was a clatter on the stairs and Lady Redfield turned to see Lady Arabella racing down them.

Her sleeves had been rolled back down and her hair straightened from her recent encounter with the local wildlife. She was very petite, which Lady Redfield had not initially noted, and she had the most lively mass of blond curls. She was lovely.

"Lady Redfield," she said, hurrying into the room. She curtsied and said, "Goodness, we did not expect you. Lady Featherstone, pleased to make your acquaintance."

"Dear me," Lady Redfield said. "I wrote a letter informing you of it. It must have got lost somewhere."

"Oh no, we received your letter," Arabella said. "But it didn't say…"

"Did it not?" Lady Redfield asked.

"No, I am afraid not," Mrs. Weston said, "though we are delighted to be surprised."

"Of course we are," Lady Arabella said. "And naturally, while we could not know how it was you prevailed over Skeffy, we were delighted to be informed that you had."

"Skeffy?" Lady Featherstone said.

"Lord Skeffington, Arabella's guardian," Mrs. Weston said.

"I call him Skeffy because he does not like it," Lady Arabella said. "Though, we have not seen him in over a year and presume we will never again see him."

"Over a year?" Lady Redfield asked.

"Oh yes, grim Lord Skeffy attempted a foray last year," Lady Arabella said. "He thought he'd marry me off to some old fellow—I suppose he owed some sort of gambling debt and thought to use me as the settlement."

"He could not force Arabella, of course," Mrs. Weston said, "but I suspect he thought he might come in as the great lord and frighten her into it."

"You poor dear! I did not know! He really is so frightening, too," Lady Redfield said.

"It was no matter, Lady Redfield," Lady Arabella said laughing. "I ran him off quick enough."

"You ran him off? Lord Skeffington?"

"Well, I should not say *I* ran him off, but rather *we* did," Lady Arabella said, seating herself beside Lady Redfield and helping herself to tea. "You see, Lord Bushwick was in residence just then and I can assure you, while he tolerated me and Mrs. Weston, he did not tolerate Skeffy crashing in here. And then Mr. Prickles heard the ruckus and very helpfully nipped one of the horse's ankles. The last I saw of my guardian, he'd wrestled his coat out of Lord Bushwick's mouth and was chasing his runaway carriage down the road."

"But, who are these men? Why were they here?" Lady Redfield cried.

"What I would like to know is why a lord has got another lord's coat in his mouth and why should a man bite a horse?" Lady Featherstone asked. "Is Lord Bushwick senile? Is this Mr. Prickles in the habit of nipping horses? Is it some sort of Cornwall habit? Or are they both mad?"

"Men?" Lady Arabella said, laughing. "Goodness, no. Lord Bushwick is a badger, since gone off to live his life, and Mr.

Prickles is a hedgehog. Pricky darling, come out and say hello and you shall have a piece of biscuit."

To Lady Redfield's horror, the fabric covering a table down to the floor shifted as if of its own accord. A hedgehog came lumbering out from underneath it, walked across the room, and settled at Lady Arabella's feet.

Lady Redfield lifted her own feet up lest the creature wish to come any closer.

Lady Featherstone peered down at it. "Lady Arabella, I find this fascinating. Have you never considered more usual pets? Like a dog or cat?"

"These are not pets, Lady Featherstone," Lady Arabella said, breaking off a piece of biscuit and feeding it to the creature. It took the bit and waddled back under its table with it.

Lady Redfield watched it disappear and slowly put her feet down as Lady Arabella went on. "These are injured animals that require assistance. We go out looking for them, you see. Now granted, Mr. Prickles has been loath to leave though his sore paw is perfectly well healed, but most of them decide very sensibly when they are ready to venture out. I had hoped Sir Slippery would see the charms of the out of doors today, but he is not quite ready. He will be though, any day now."

"That would be the otter?" Lady Redfield asked.

"Yes," Lady Arabella said. "I did not hear you arrive as I was busy settling him back into his bathtub. I had to read him a story to calm him."

Both Lady Redfield's and Lady Featherstone's eyes drifted toward the stairs.

"Do not worry though," Lady Arabella said. "You will not encounter him, he's in the west wing next to the room the Nightly family occupy."

"The Knightlys?" Lady Redfield asked. "I am acquainted with Mr. Knightley and his lady. I believed them to be on their estate in Surrey. They so rarely leave Donwell Abbey, I wonder what could have brought them here."

"Nightly as in nighttime. Bats, I'm afraid," Mrs. Weston said.

Lady Redfield worked very hard to put all these facts into a cheerful light. Despite her efforts, she was rather shaken. It seemed they were to spend the night in a menagerie.

MR. CECIL HEMMINGS had been butler to Baron Redfield since before the lord had married. He had got on with Lady Redfield exceedingly well throughout the years—the mistress was rarely out of sorts and never put up much of a fuss about anything. But then the baron had died, and Hemmings knew he was in for a troubled road ahead.

Precisely the thing that had made the baroness so pleasant had now become a sticking point. She could not be forceful, she could not make difficult decisions, and she could not support him in his own.

The staff that had once been regulated by the presence of the baron began to be lax. Worse, if he dismissed one of them, they promptly went to Lady Redfield to plead their case and were reinstated. He had no real power, and therefore no authority.

The habits of the house were a shambles—one of the footmen, Oscar, was inclined to work, but the other, Clive, was always trying to get in his way. Clive had been dismissed twice and somehow got back in again. The housekeeper had not actually been on the premises for above six months, claiming she was caring for a sick relative. The maids had to be harried into doing their work. The baroness's lady's maid, Flora, was a saucy creature who flirted with the footmen though she had not the least intention of anything serious by them. The cook was lackadaisical and did the bare minimum required.

Aside from Oscar, the only other person he could actually count on was Lander, the coachman. On occasion, when he'd felt he had really had enough, he would visit Lander in the stables of an evening. Lander, having no patience for nonsense, kept his grooms in good order by explaining to them that if they ever approached Lady Redfield with a complaint he'd horsewhip them. Lander also kept a bottle of brandy on hand for just such visits from a harried butler.

And so, he'd gone along, wondering what to do. Should he look for other employment? Should he try for a better-regulated house? But then, why would he say he was leaving Lady Redfield's employ? Should he tell the truth? *I am afraid, my lord, that Lady Redfield has no more spine than an earthworm and I cannot manage a staff without a spine at the top of the ladder.*

Nobody would hire him if he were to insult his current employer.

Further, he was fond of Lady Redfield and shuddered to think what would happen if he left her alone with these idiots. They'd probably burn down her house for want of care.

Then, five days ago, she'd called him to the drawing room and they'd had a most unusual conversation. A certain Lady Arabella Berestock was coming to stay and everything must be perfect.

He had stared at Lady Redfield, rather incredulous. Nothing in the house had been perfect since the baron died. He had been forced to speak and lay out the facts.

He'd thought the lady might collapse in a heap as she was wont to do, but she'd only shook her head and said that Lady Heathway had told her just the same. Further, Lady Heathway had said that if she did not allow Hemmings to lay down the law and fire the miscreants, she would get nowhere. Lady Heathway had capped the whole lecture off by explaining that she was a marshmallow and must turn herself into a brick.

Hemmings had begun to have rather fond feelings for Lady Heathway.

Daringly, he'd pointed out that Mrs. Redmond had not been in residence in above six months. Though the housekeeper had been sending regular letters on the progress of her sick sister,

Hemmings thought it all a ruse to be paid to do nothing.

It had been agreed that Hemmings must have his way in things. He'd since been composing his speech in anticipation of lighting a fire under these rogues.

Now, he regarded his staff and said, "Everything in this house is about to change. You can change with it or be shown the door. No amount of crying to Lady Redfield will do you the least bit of good. She has faced down Lord Skeffington, received guidance from Lady Heathway, and she brings the daughter of an earl here. She is determined that the house be well-regulated, as am I."

The only face staring at him that looked at all pleased with the news was Oscar, who had no doubt been waiting quite some time to hear it.

"Clive," Hemmings went on, "if I see you lounging about for even a minute, you are out. Mrs. Beltrain, start cooking meals as they should be, not the pathetic offerings you have been. I suspect you have been buying cheap ingredients and pocketing the difference. Do not let me catch you at it. Flora, step carefully and keep your inane thoughts to yourself; you are a lady's maid, not the Queen of Sheba. You maids, I want this house cleaned top to bottom as it should be. Raise your standards or get out. Further, you are all to know that I have written a letter to Mrs. Redmond and she has one week to return from what has been, I am certain, an extended holiday. I doubt we will see her, and so you should expect a new housekeeper to be hired. I will do the hiring and I intend on hiring a dragon. Now, get to work."

As his staff scattered in all directions, Hemmings felt a great sense of peace. He had said everything that had been in his mind for years. He would bring this house back to standard if it was the last thing he did on this earth.

God bless Lady Heathway.

SUCH HAD BEEN Lady Redfield's inscrutable letter, and such had been her sudden arrival, that it had taken some time for Arabella to fully understand why the lady had come.

Now, she had been apprised of *The Society of Sponsoring Ladies* and its stated purpose of assisting worthy young ladies of distressed means.

"But Lady Redfield, I am not in distressed circumstances," Arabella said. "I shall have access to my own money in a year."

"You are twenty, my dear," Mrs. Weston said. "It really is time. I could not let down your mother in allowing you to closet yourself in the countryside when it has very happily become unnecessary."

Arabella glanced at the little side table under which Mr. Prickles had made his home. "What about Mr. Prickles, and Sir Slippery and Mrs. Twitch-nose?"

"Mrs. Twitch-nose?" Lady Featherstone asked. "I do not believe we have yet heard of her."

"A mouse and her no doubt rapidly growing family," Mrs. Weston said, glancing toward a hole in the baseboard in the corner of the room.

"And Mrs. Murder!" Arabella cried, ignoring the horrified stares at Mrs. Twitch-nose's front door. "Goodness, I nearly forgot poor Mrs. Murder as she spends so much time lurking around the Nightlys' door. And her children, too!"

Lady Redfield and Lady Featherstone turned to Mrs. Weston. The lady sighed and said, "A cat and her two kittens, always hoping to get at the bats."

Lady Featherstone erupted in laughter. "Goodness, after everybody else we've been told of, I had been expecting a lion or tiger."

"I do beg you to come, Lady Arabella," Lady Redfield said in a rather plaintive voice. "I really do. I have fretted over the years that I did not do more, but then, I was so frightened of...Skeffy, as you call him."

"Arabella," Mrs. Weston said, in her voice that said she meant business, "I know what holds you back. How will all these creatures be cared for? Freddy will do it, you know he is quite capable of it."

"Yes, I know he can," she said. "It is just that, well, I think they will all miss me. Do you not think so?"

"No, not really," Mrs. Weston said. "I do not suppose their memories go back more than a week. As long as they are fed and housed, they will be quite content."

That idea did bring Arabella some comfort.

"And do not forget," Lady Redfield said hopefully, "I do not live in China. We only go to London and you may write Freddy as often as you like. And then, Mrs. Weston will come with you, will you not?"

Mrs. Weston nodded.

"So you see, Mrs. Weston can accompany us to all the balls and parties," Lady Redfield said.

Mrs. Weston held her hand up. "I will come to settle Arabella as it will be a vast change for her. But once that is done, I would prefer to go to my sister in Lambeth. It has been many years since I have seen her. I will not be so very far away and you might call me back to Town if there is a need."

"Oh, do say you will come, Lady Arabella," Lady Redfield said.

On the one hand, Arabella was loath to leave her dear animals. But on the other, London would be an adventure. There would be real balls to attend, not the dancing in the drawing room with Mrs. Weston acting as the gentleman. And then, Mrs. Weston had been so careful of her all these years and had worked so hard to prepare her for society. The poor lady had relegated herself to the middle of nowhere when she could have been all along with a sister in Town.

That was the real reason to go. Mrs. Weston had made so many sacrifices. It was time for her to make her own sacrifice and submit to being parted from her darling creatures.

"Freddy can do it," Mrs. Weston said, well-knowing what was

on her mind.

"Yes, of course," Arabella said. "I have been a goose. Of course I will come. Mrs. Weston must be given time with her sister. I will supervise Freddy from afar and it shall be quite all right, I think."

There was great relief all around the table and the party settled down to making plans to depart in two days' time and eating the rather simple fare Mrs. Penrale had prepared.

LADY REDFIELD SURVEYED her drawing room. It was still in the Indian mode, which was always distressing to observe, but she had been surprised to find everything a deal more shined than it had been when she left. She'd given Hemmings leave to straighten out the staff and it seemed he had done. She felt rather stupid for not doing it years ago. Though, she might not have even done it now, but for Lady Heathway's dire prediction—*How shall the daughter of an earl be comfortable in this haphazard house?* That idea had spurred her on.

The trip coming back from Cornwall had been no less arduous than the trip going there, though the pleasures and challenges had been entirely different.

On the one hand, Arabella, and she insisted to be called so rather than *Lady* Arabella, had provided no end of interesting conversation. Despite the privations of her upbringing, she had an engaging manner full of optimism and rather a large and soft heart. Lady Redfield felt a real kinship toward her growing day by day.

On the other hand, that large and soft heart seemed alarmingly apt at seeking out every needy animal on the route.

First, there had been the mangy dog she'd collared, demanding soap, vinegar, and a tub, and scrubbing him down at an inn's stable yard. She had only narrowly been convinced not to track down its owner and demand answers.

Then, there had been the cat found at the next inn who was afflicted with an infection of the eye. This was cleaned with a damp cloth and the innkeeper was advised to provide a meat diet to support healing.

Finally, they had almost got to the outskirts of London when they encountered a goat with a rope tied round its neck. The goat had apparently got away from its owner and grown bigger in the process, and now the rope was digging into the creature's skin. Lander had provided a knife and Arabella had chased the creature clear across a field, tackled it, and cut off the rope. She had returned to the carriage triumphant, and also terribly stained and dusty.

It had all been exceedingly alarming, but at least they were home now and there were no creatures in her own house that must be wrestled.

They had arrived late in the day yesterday and dear Arabella was just now out in the garden with Mrs. Weston, dictating a letter to Freddy. Soon, her friends would come to meet the girl and Lady Redfield did indeed feel like a proud mama. Wait until they all saw how lovely she was, in both person and manner!

Lady Redfield jumped as the drawing room door crashed open. Clive ran through it, the footman appearing as if he were being chased.

"Goodness, what—"

"Lady Redfield, Mr. Hemmings has gone and sacked me again for no reason whatsoever. He just don't like me, is what it is. Please do tell him I'm to stay on."

"Well, I—"

Hemmings walked into the room, seeming out of breath. Lady Redfield supposed it had been him chasing Clive.

"Lady Redfield," he said, in a serious tone.

He said no more than that, but then he did not have to. She'd promised him he would have his authority and now she was being put to the test. The house seemed so very much in order since she'd returned. She must stand firm with her butler.

"Mr. Hemmings must have his way," she said resolutely. "You must go, Clive."

She waited with trepidation to discover what would happen next. She'd been approached by staff and asked to overrule Hemmings often over the years, and Clive himself had asked twice. This was the first time she'd not given in to a plea to stay on.

Clive seemed rather incredulous to hear it. Then his expression darkened and he picked up a clay figurine and threw it at the fireplace; it shattered on impact. He turned on his heel, pushed past Mr. Hemmings, and took himself out the front door.

Mr. Hemmings stared at the shattered ceramic. "Thank you, my lady, and I apologize that the scoundrel has broken a valuable item."

"Oh, that?" Lady Redfield said, feeling rather elated now that the danger had passed. "That was something the baron had brought in, I never liked it."

PEREGRINE HAD BEEN walking his garden for no more than a minute before he overheard a spirited conversation going on in Lady Redfield's garden next door. He peered through a chink in the garden wall to view a rather pert young miss pacing back and forth. Her petite person was the owner of a charming pile of blond curls peeping out of a blue silk bonnet and she had a very adorable little nose. An older, comfortable looking matron sat on a stone bench with a paper in hand and writing instruments laid out beside her.

As the girl paced back and forth, she began to dictate while the matron took down her words.

"My dear Freddy: Naturally, I was alarmed upon leaving the house so precipitously when we have so many dear ones that require attention. I must depend upon you to provide me regular news of how everybody gets on. Foremost, I fear Mrs. Murder is teaching Rogue and Scoundrel to hunt mice, as I noticed the night before I left that they had abandoned their watch over the Nightlys' door. Please be certain that Mrs. Twitch-nose understands the situation and does not fall prey to their claws. You might slip some cheese into that hole in the wall that leads to her cozy home so she does not need to venture out so often. I believe she will understand the hint."

"But, my dear Arabella, as to Mrs. Twitch-nose," the matron said. "Mice, they do, you know, replicate rather rapidly."

"Oh yes, I suppose they do. Excellent point, Mrs. Weston. She must have a large and lively family by now. It's quite lovely to think about, really."

"Is it?"

"Certainly. Now, let us carry on with our instructions for Freddy. I will not rest easy until I know this letter is safely in the post. Please write: Freddy, make Mrs. Twitch-nose's cheese a rather large piece, as she is likely caring for an extended family.

"New paragraph, Mrs. Weston. Freddy, I am of course eager to hear how Sir Slippery does and whether he has graduated from the bathtub to the fountain. Do not rush him as I did! It occurs to me that any otter with the least sense will come downstairs of their own accord when they are ready. Until then, see that the tub water is changed daily and he is well-supplied with fish from the market. And do tell him a story every evening, he quite enjoys it. Mr. Prickles, I am afraid, has quite made the drawing room his home for the time being. I suspect he will at some point get wind of a prospective Mrs. Prickles nearby and be on his way. For now, see that he has everything to make him comfortable, including a quarter of a biscuit at teatime. As for our dear family of bats, I pray you have kept that end of the corridor quiet, as they do like to sleep during the day. New paragraph, Mrs. Weston."

Peregrine suppressed his laughter. Poor Mrs. Weston was writing out a veritable novel to Freddy, whoever that poor fellow was.

"I count on you to keep a constant eye out on the grounds. If you spot an injured animal, or one that merely looks confused or hungry, go right to the rescue, Freddy! You know what to do and I have full faith in you. In case you are wondering, Town is very promising. There is a family of squirrels outside my bedchamber window and I believe we will be friends."

"My dear," Mrs. Weston said, "should you like to provide any direction to Mrs. Penrale on keeping the house?"

"Mrs. Penrale – do help Freddy with the animals!"

"I'm sure she will be delighted," the matron said. "Now, we'd best go in. Lady Redfield has invited her friends for tea."

"Ah yes," Lady Arabella said. "As far as I could gather, Lady Heathway is a dragon, Lady Easton cannot abide lateness, Lady Mendleton will take no note of me as I am not a recently arrived grandbaby, and the duchess likes things noble."

Peregrine slapped a hand over his mouth and moved away from the wall. He must assume this Arabella, as the matron had called her, was the latest project of his mother's society of sponsoring ladies. If her letter to Freddy was anything to go by, she was quite the handful. The poor duchess, she probably did not know it yet, but another season's games had begun for the ladies.

CHAPTER THREE

A RABELLA HAD BEEN presented to the ladies of the society determined to sponsor her, and how different they were from Mrs. Weston!

Mrs. Weston, herself, had been all calm and graciousness and rather unperturbed over being introduced to such an august company. She had not even blinked when the duchess had pronounced her noble for accompanying Arabella through the lonely years in Cornwall.

Lady Heathway looked Arabella up and down as if she were thinking of buying a horse. She said, "Very pretty, in a blond sort of way. Of course, my Grace is gifted with very dark hair. Her coloring is exceedingly striking."

"Lady Heathway speaks of Miss Yardley," Lady Redfield put in for Arabella's benefit. "She is now Lady Gresham, married to Lady Heathway's nephew. A...spirited lady, and very devoted to her sickly mother."

"She is equally devoted to *me*," Lady Heathway said. "Perhaps more, if we're going to be direct about it, and there has never been a thing wrong with Lady Barlow but inertia."

"Lady Arabella," Lady Easton said, ignoring the debate over who Lady Gresham was most fond of, "do you consider yourself an impetuous sort of person? Or in the habit of calling out of carriage windows to grooms?"

Arabella was not quite certain if she were impetuous or not, though she was rather certain of the lady's opinion of that shade of temperament. She suspected it had been born from a prior experience she did not look favorably upon. "I don't believe I am impetuous, Lady Easton."

"And the calling out of carriage windows?"

"I have never yet done so."

Lady Easton seemed satisfied with her answer, and Arabella pretended she did not notice Mrs. Weston's small smile over it.

Lady Mendleton did not ask Arabella anything at all, but rather spoke of her granddaughter. By all accounts, the baby was exceedingly advanced for only having come into the world four months ago. At least, by Lady Mendleton's account, she was rather astounding.

The duchess finally interrupted her and said, "Louisa, I will not believe an infant of four months is on the verge of talking."

"She is very advanced, though," Lady Mendleton said.

"I suppose she's planning to net a purse or play the pianoforte next," Lady Easton murmured.

There was a moment's silence as everyone considered the chances of Lady Mendleton's granddaughter fumbling with purse silk or somehow dragging herself to the pianoforte and banging her tiny hands on the keys.

Lady Featherstone broke the silence, and that lady chose the moment to outline all the different animals that could be found in a recently visited Cornwall house.

Until that moment, Arabella had not considered there was anything terribly unusual in caring for sick and injured animals. Or animals that were not sick and injured any longer but taking their time to get going out of the house. It was what country people did, was it not?

The ladies were fairly horrified and disease was brought up more than once. Lady Featherstone regaled the party regarding her sleepless night in the house, on high alert lest an otter or a bat or a hedgehog or a mouse make a visit to her in the darkness. She was even rather afraid of the cat and her kittens, though she had not set eyes on them.

"This is to be laid at Skeffington's door," the duchess said.

Lady Heathway's eyes had drifted in Mrs. Weston's direction, as if she might want to also take up the mantle of fault.

Mrs. Weston, not one to be intimidated by the likes of Lady Heathway, said, "It is a lonely house in the middle of nowhere with no neighbors to socialize with. I thought it entirely appropriate that Arabella be allowed to occupy herself with caring for injured animals. A young girl can only do so much sewing and practicing on the pianoforte in a day."

"Quite right," the duchess said.

"Though we did find the badger a step too far," Mrs. Weston admitted.

Arabella, eager to defend her companion, said, "Indeed, we did. Even I was forced to admit that a badger on the mend ought to be a badger out of doors."

"Thank heaven for small mercies," Lady Easton said. "But, of all the creatures mentioned, I have not heard anything about a horse."

Arabella was forced to admit she'd never ridden a horse, though she'd longed to. Lord Skeffington would not fix the stables on the estate, though they were in great disrepair, and so there had been nowhere to put one. They'd made forays into town by paying a neighboring farmer to borrow his cart. Freddy drove the contraption while she and Mrs. Weston did what they could to remain comfortable in the back of it.

Arabella had suggested they might use the drawing room as a stable once, assuming they got a fairly small horse. Not surprisingly, Mrs. Weston had closed the topic with, "I think not."

"She must have riding lessons at once," the duchess said. "There is nothing so attractive as a young lady in a smart habit upon a horse in the park. I'm sure my duke thought so when I passed him by all those years ago. I will arrange it, Cecilia."

Lady Redfield nodded gratefully.

"Peregrine will know somebody," the duchess continued, "he

is very knowledgeable about horses. I'll pop in to see him when I leave here, as he is now very conveniently living at the next door. He does like it when I surprise him with a visit."

"That is Lord Blackwood," Lady Redfield said to Arabella. "He is a marquess and Her Grace's son. He's taken Gasper House and I am delighted. Lord Gasper was always so…well, he seemed always annoyed. Though he is dead now, which I am sorry for."

"Peregrine will no doubt be instrumental in introducing you to the right sort of gentlemen," the duchess said. "He is a devoted son and there is no end of efforts he will put in to please his mother."

Lady Easton cleared her throat. "As to that," she said, "I only say, have a care, Theodosia."

Arabella did not know what the duchess was supposed to have a care about, though the other ladies seemed to comprehend it easily enough. There was head nodding all round.

"I know what you fear, but this is an entirely different situation, Clara," the duchess said. "Peregrine has told me and the duke that he has no intention of marrying for another two years. I rather think he has somebody in mind, and I rather think it is Lady Constance Melberry. She is to be out either next year or the following and they have known one another since they were children. It will be a brilliant match."

"Theodosia, what Clara hints at, if I am not mistaken," Lady Featherstone said, "is that Bertridge was set on waiting for the Duke of Clayton's daughter and then he wed Miss Upton."

"The difference, though," the duchess said in supreme confidence, "is that Peregrine would never go forward with such a thing without my approval, and I am quite set on Lady Constance."

With this speech, Arabella grew to understand that the hint Lady Easton had posited had to do with her setting her cap on Lord Blackwood. And, that this idea was to be instantly dismissed.

She blushed deeply and was certain she was not pink, but red.

She had the sort of complexion that was set afire by embarrassment and though she'd attempted to control it in the past, it was no good. Her skin had a mind of its own and it was very contrary—she did not bloom with charming pink cheeks, but rather burst in flames with an entirely red face. Freddy had once said her blushes made her look like a middle-aged gentleman who indulged in too much port.

When she had been younger, it had been no trouble at all for Mrs. Weston to understand that she'd told a fib about some infraction or other. She'd say, *Dear girl, do not bother claiming you do not know what happened to the last of the biscuits, the red of your face tells me very clearly what happened to them.*

Lady Redfield patted Arabella's hand. Lady Featherstone said, "My deductive skills tell me that you have embarrassed the girl, Theodosia."

"For the love of heaven," Lady Heathway said, "a nearsighted fellow at a distance could have deduced that. She's as red as an apple."

Lady Featherstone sniffed at the remark.

"There is nothing in the world to be embarrassed about, Lady Arabella," the duchess said. "It is well that one understands the lay of the land when venturing into new territory. Never fear, my dear, there will be plenty of gentlemen you will meet who *are* ready for marriage."

Arabella nodded, though she felt as if she had been accused, convicted, and exonerated all in an instant. Whoever this Lord Blackwood was, she wished she had not been so directly informed of his plans. Or warned of his plans, as the case might be.

Now, the interview having been over for some hours and there being a lull before dinner, she and Mrs. Weston were to go for a walk. It had always been their habit to venture out for exercise before dining, as Mrs. Weston was of the opinion that it encouraged a healthy appetite.

Though they had often ranged over hill and dale in Cornwall, they had promised Lady Redfield that they would not venture beyond the square. Arabella thought that it would necessarily be a half-hearted sort of ramble, but then Lady Redfield was likely right—she and Mrs. Weston did not yet know Town well enough to go sauntering off in any direction.

They had just come out of doors when Arabella noted a carriage standing outside the next house, with four horses being constrained in the most awkward position. Their heads and necks were held up high and the poor creatures were nearly looking at the sky. It seemed an odd sort of rein ran over their heads and across their shoulders, preventing them from lowering their heads to a natural angle.

"What on earth?" she cried.

"What is it, my dear?" Mrs. Weston asked, looking all around her.

"The horses," Arabella said. "Look at the angle of their heads and necks. They cannot be comfortable."

Mrs. Weston looked where she was directed. She said, "They wear bearing reins. Quite usual in Town, though we do not see them in the countryside."

"But why have they done it?" Arabella asked. "What purpose could such an awful thing have?"

Mrs. Weston hesitated, knowing her charge so well and knowing how she might view the explanation.

"Please, Mrs. Weston, I must know why these poor horses are treated so."

"Well, it is to, you see, it holds the horses' heads high…"

"Yes, I can see that," Arabella said, looking at Mrs. Weston earnestly. "But for what purpose?"

"To…improve the look of them, their bearing, you see."

"It is for appearances? *Appearances*?" Arabella cried.

Peregrine had spent approximately twenty-six hours peacefully enjoying his new status as master of a London house. He had not imagined that his peace would be shattered so rapidly and in such quick succession. One blow followed the next like a trebuchet hurling boulders at his equanimity.

Earlier, he'd seen the line of carriages arrive to Lady Redfield's door and he'd very cleverly closed the curtains to his front facing rooms. The house now looked suitably shut up and anybody passing by would assume he'd gone out, probably for a long time. The particular anybody he was most keen to convince of his being far away was his mother. One of the carriages lined up outside was her own, and she had promised to visit him whenever she was nearby. Which she had also shudderingly informed him was often.

He should have known that just looking like he was not at home would not be sufficient to put Her Grace off. After she'd rapped on the door with her walking stick for some minutes and Mr. Sindu had stared first at him and then the door disapprovingly, she'd marched down the mews and checked his stable. Noting all his horses and his carriage present, she'd then gone to the back of the house and let herself in through the servants' entrance.

Seeing he was trapped, Peregrine sent Mr. Sindu above stairs and he made a great show of coming down them, just as the duchess entered the hall.

"There you are, my darling," she said, as if she had not just been prowling round his premises and letting herself in like a housebreaker.

"I did not expect you, Mother," he said, lightly kissing her cheek.

"Of course you did not, I did not expect myself. Now where is Mr. Sindu? I rapped on the door for ages."

"Afternoon off," Peregrine said, glancing at the stairs.

"Never mind, I'm sure there is a footman lurking about who can get us some tea. Though, I always do find them rather scarce in your house."

Peregrine was well aware that he was not lacking footmen, it was just that they seemed to melt into the shadows when the duchess was nearby.

"I'll find somebody, do make yourself comfortable in the drawing room."

The duchess set off for that room, still talking to him. "You'll *find* somebody. Goodness, Peregrine, do not become like Lady Redfield, she is forever having to search for her servants. It is not a sensible way to go on."

Once she was out of view, he found somebody easily enough. Back in the drawing room he wondered how long she planned to stay and if he would get through it without her bringing up Lady Constance. His mother had somehow leapt to the conclusion that he was waiting for that lady to be introduced to society so that he might pursue her. Nothing could be further from the truth—they were childhood friends and that was absolutely all. He had not disabused the duchess of the idea, though. It had kept her from wondering why he was not attempting to marry himself off presently.

Linus hurried in and laid the tea, studiously avoiding the duchess' eye. It would not be unknown that the duchess might choose that moment to interrogate the poor fellow about where he'd been hiding. It was a relief to the boy, and to Peregrine himself, that she did not.

After Linus closed the door behind him, the duchess said, "My dear, you know all about our society, of course."

Peregrine nodded dutifully and attempted not to laugh. He knew about it, and he also knew that this year's young lady was likely just as much trouble as the last three had been.

"Lady Redfield takes the reins this season," the duchess went on. "Lady Arabella Berestock, daughter of the late Earl of Westcott, has come to her. It is well she has, as Lord Skeffington has kept the poor girl holed up in some rustic location in Cornwall. He's her guardian, though why anybody thought that rogue should be guardian is quite beyond me."

That Skeffington was involved was something Peregrine had not known. He got along with the fellow well enough, though he could not say he liked him. Skeffington was always putting on some interesting opportunity for betting—boxing, a cock fight, or a horse race, usually—and that seemed a good enough reason to be on acquaintance terms. However, Peregrine did not wish to know him more than that. There was something distasteful about the man.

"You cannot imagine how he's neglected Lady Arabella. He did not even purchase her a horse or ensure that she could ride one."

Skeffington may not have bought Lady Arabella a horse, but as he recalled from her dictated letter to that unfortunate person named Freddy, she'd not hesitated to go out and gather what animals could be found for free in her neighborhood.

"In any case," the duchess said, "she must be given lessons, and a horse. You will arrange it, will you not? You must have a suitable horse, just now your stables are very full of candidates. And you will find someone to give her lessons?"

"Well, I, as to lessons…I am not certain…"

"You will find someone; I have all confidence of it. Do so quickly, if you please, this matter really cannot wait. And the horse?"

"But you see, my horses, I am not sure—"

"What about that pretty chestnut mare, her nameplate said Bonny Betsy."

Blast. His mother had made a full accounting of his horse-flesh.

"That would not be at all convenient," he said. "Bonny Betsy is set to travel to Lancashire to be bred with Archduke, who was grand-sired by Highflyer. I expect the resulting foal to be a champion."

The duchess waved her hands. "No romance between mare and stallion will get off the ground until later in the spring. And then, you've most of the summer too. Bonny Betsy will do very well for Lady Arabella."

"But I am not at all sure the mare is trained for a lady rider," Peregrine said. "I only purchased her two months ago and never inquired if she'd had a sidesaddle on her."

"Ah, yes, the saddle. I'll send one of my own over. I very much doubt Cecilia has got one, she does not have the right mental strength to control an animal of any size. Indeed, I have never seen her mounted."

Peregrine was well aware that his mother was an athletic sort of person, though she had reached an age when most would give it up. She took some pride in it and the last time he had dined with the family she'd told some outrageous tale of swimming in a storm off the coast of Brighton. Had anybody else told him it, he would have been certain it was made up, or at least exaggerated. Not the duchess, though.

"Yes," the duchess murmured, "it will be just the thing. Lady Arabella trotting round the park in a smart habit and on Bonny Betsy."

As his mother seemed determined to rifle his stables, he supposed he should be grateful that she'd not set her eye on Alfred the Saxon, or Alfie, as he was called by his intimates. He'd purchased the horse three years ago and never had horse and rider been so in sync. He barely needed to give any direction at all and Alfie understood where he wished to go and how fast or slow he preferred to get there. If there were two beings on earth he loved above all others, it was Alfie and his dog Apollo.

Granted, not everybody loved Apollo as he did. Particularly not his valet, as the beast always seemed to be making off with a shoe or a neckcloth. In fact, his last valet had quit over it.

Apollo was a Danish boar hound and though Peregrine had been well-aware that he would grow to an unusual size, it seemed Apollo had been determined to surprise him. The puppy had grown by leaps and bounds and then kept on. Now, at two years and full size, it was not necessary to bend over if one wished to pat his back. He was enormous and always into trouble. He insisted on making himself at home on Peregrine's bed and sometimes rolled him off it in the middle of the night, but who could resist that ridiculous face and wagging tail? Who could not be charmed when the silly thing sought to sit on his lap, entirely forgetting his size? Who could not love him when he titled his head and looked entirely confused? He was always into mischief, but then he was so enthusiastic about it that it was very hard to be aggravated with him.

Fortunately, he did not see Apollo in the vicinity just now and he supposed Mr. Sindu had corralled him above stairs. Mr. Sindu seemed to be the only person Apollo paid any heed to, his butler ruling over his dog with serious and consistent direction.

If Apollo had a fault at all, it was that he did not understand when people did not wish to be near him. He had already assaulted the duchess with a licked face on more than one occasion and she was not an admirer.

"My own feeling," the duchess said, "is that it ought to be an older gentleman well past his prime. One cannot be too careful. We must keep Lady Arabella well out of range of anybody who would be unsuitable. *Especially* with the size of her dowry."

Peregrine realized his mother had been nattering on while he'd been thinking about his horse and his dog.

"I'm sorry, who?" he asked.

"Lady Arabella's riding instructor. For lessons on Bonny Betsy. Please, darling, do keep up."

"I really do not know of anyone fitting that description."

"Find somebody, Peregrine. You are a resourceful young man who finds that his mother, the duchess, is counting on him. Lady Arabella's riding habit ought to be completed in a week. Let us say the lessons commence on Tuesday next."

She had kissed his forehead and left him then, off to terrorize somebody else's house.

The duchess had been shatterer of his peace number one. If only there had not been more to come.

Above stairs, he'd found Turnbury in a wretched state and

Apollo wagging his tail with a neckcloth hanging out of his mouth.

"Just starched and ironed," Turnbury said, staring at the shreds that were left of it.

"Yes, I see," Peregrine said.

"Mr. Sindu said I must look after him while the duchess was downstairs. Mr. Sindu said he needed to check on how the housekeeper was getting on with the setting up of the other bedchambers. Furniture was delivered yesterday and he must see to its placement. Mr. Sindu said he shouldn't be long. Mr. Sindu *knows* nobody but himself can control this dog. The creature wrestled the cloth from my hands as if it were some kind of game! And where is Mr. Sindu now?"

Apollo dropped the ruined fabric and helpfully licked Turnbury's hand.

"Calm yourself, Turnbury. I already had to part company with the last valet over these kinds of mishaps, do not be the second."

Turnbury lifted his chin and said, "Oh no, my lord. I will not be defeated by that beast. He and I will have a reckoning one of these days. We will come to an understanding. I will convince him that he is to leave your things alone. And leave me alone too!"

Apollo apparently thought this speech some sort of commendation to himself and took to hopping from paw to paw and licking Turnbury's hand with abandon.

"While you're waiting for that great day of reckoning, order more neckcloths," Peregrine said. "We really cannot have too many in the house."

Shatterer of peace number two—his hysterical valet.

He had, in the ensuing hours, turned his mind from the chaos in his house to the evening ahead. He would be off to his club for a long night of cards.

Turnbury having found a neckcloth that Apollo had somehow missed, Peregrine was dressed and his carriage waited outside. The carriage was necessary on such a night, as he would likely leave White's far too worse for drink to ride Alfie. He went down the stairs as Mr. Sindu looked on. Fortunately, Linus hurried to open the door, else he'd have had to open it himself. Mr. Sindu, for reasons only known to himself, did not open doors.

"Please keep everything in order, Mr. Sindu," Peregrine said.

"By everything, you mean Apollo."

"Yes, you understand me perfectly," he said, "you are the only one capable of it as far as I can see."

He turned and left the house. Then he stopped at the top of the steps.

His coachman was being berated by Lady Arabella, the little miss who'd come to stay with Lady Redfield. The same person he was to give over a horse to and somehow find an instructor for by Tuesday next.

Bullford looked helpless against her as she shook her finger at him. The matron that accompanied her only looked exasperated.

"What's all this fuss?" he asked, jogging down the steps.

She whipped round to him, her little person very red in the face. "All this fuss, sir, is about your horses. All this fuss is regarding the medieval torture devices you have trapped them in."

CHAPTER FOUR

PEREGRINE STARED AT the incensed lady. "What on earth are you—"

Before he could finish his sentence, the lady took her forefinger and lifted his chin to the sky. What was she doing? He'd never had a lady touch his person. Not a proper lady, anyway. What was he to do about it? How could he get her away without assaulting her?

"Now you see what your horses see," she said, pushing his chin ever higher. "The sky is in front of you rather than the road. Is this comfortable? Can you imagine going on like that for an hour or even a minute?"

She dropped her hand and the matron stepped forward. "Arabella! That really is enough!"

"But it is not enough," she said defiantly. "Those horses are being mistreated so that their owner may look more grand. It's criminal!"

"My horses are in no way mistreated," Peregrine said, stepping back from her.

"Then hold your head up again and see how long you can do it before you feel the pain of it," she said. "If you do it long enough, the muscles in your neck will begin to atrophy and you will lose range of motion. You will be in pain all the days of your life, for the sake of appearances."

Peregrine was rendered speechless. It was true that when

she'd held up his chin it was not very comfortable, but he was not a horse! Certainly, it would not be such an accepted practice if it caused any real harm. His horses did not look as if it pained them. Did they?

"Bullford?" he said, looking at his coachman. "What do you say to this?"

Bullford did not look very comfortable himself. He muttered, "Well, as to the muscles shrinking a bit, by the time it comes on they'll be ready for farmer's work and then it don't much signify."

"The cruelty of it!" the miss said, stamping her little foot.

Peregrine felt his own face go red. On the one hand, he would never intentionally be cruel to one of his animals. On the other, he'd like to pick up this feminine Tartar and throw her back inside Lady Redfield's door.

Lady Redfield herself came hurrying down her steps. "Goodness, what's happened?"

Nobody answered her. The young lady looked away, Peregrine stared at his coachman, and the matron bit her lip.

"Well, Arabella, Mrs. Weston, it seems you've met Lord Blackwood. Lord Blackwood, Lady Arabella Berestock, daughter of the late Earl of Westcott, and her companion, Mrs. Weston."

"It's about the horses," Lady Arabella said.

Peregrine felt as if his head might explode in a thousand bits. "Bullford," he said, "take the carriage back to the stables and make the necessary adjustments so that I may leave my own house without being accosted!"

He turned on his heel and marched back into the house, slamming the door behind him.

Shatterer of his peace number three—the very highhanded daughter of the late Earl of Westcott.

"Accosted?" Lady Redfield said, looking back and forth

between Arabella and Mrs. Weston.

"I had a responsibility to speak out, Lady Redfield," Arabella said. She'd rather not say more than that, as she found herself shaken over her boldness. It had been right to speak out, of course it had. But perhaps not as right to push Lord Blackwood's chin up in the air.

"It was about the bearing reins on Lord Blackwood's horses, Lady Redfield," Mrs. Weston said. "But it is of no account, the whole matter has been sorted out to everybody's satisfaction."

"But I cannot say that Lord Blackwood seemed very satisfied..." Lady Redfield said in a fretful tone.

"He will be, though. Now, I really must take Arabella on a walk or she will not sleep well tonight," Mrs. Weston said hurriedly.

"Well, of course," Lady Redfield said, "we would not wish that..."

"We shall return in a half-hour," Mrs. Weston said, marching Arabella by the arm toward the nearest gate into the square.

Arabella did not look back and so could only assume Lady Redfield went back inside the house. She did not wish to look back, nor to look forward to where she was going. She knew very well that Mrs. Weston was quite incensed.

"My girl, what in the world were you thinking?"

"You know what I was thinking," Arabella said quietly.

"Arabella, you are in Town now. You cannot go off shouting at lords and ladies who do or say something you do not like. They are Lord Blackwood's horses, not your own. And do I even need to mention how wildly inappropriate it was for you to touch his person?"

"Yes, I know you are right, Mrs. Weston. That was a step too far."

"The entire encounter was a step too far."

"I did gain my point, though. He is to take the bearing reins off. That must be something, is it not?"

"You will encounter bearing reins all over London," Mrs.

Weston said. "What do you propose? Do you imagine yourself a lady crusader?"

"No, of course not. I will just have to avert my eyes, I suppose," Arabella said, considering the problem.

"And avert your eyes from Lord Blackwood from now on, too. Heavens, I dearly hope he does not tell the duchess of it. I was to go to my sister on the morrow and now I wonder if I dare leave you here alone."

"Of course you must go," Arabella said. "You have already been parted from her for so long on my account, I could not bear to be the cause of you delaying your visit."

Arabella felt a sudden heaviness upon her. She'd not been in Town a week and she had already caused trouble. She really should have more of a care for Mrs. Weston and all that she'd sacrificed.

And then, what if Lord Blackwood had not made the mistake of using a bearing rein? She had been in such a fury in the moment that it was only now that she thought of his person.

What a coloring he had! That copper-toned hair and matching eyes, and then he was so tall and slim. He was not at all like the stout farmers she was accustomed to seeing. His person seemed more worldly. He was very striking, really.

But then, he was the duchess' son and already nearly engaged to some person named Lady Constance.

Still, it would have been lovely to at least dance with him. Now, the chances of his putting his name on her card were less than zero. She would be the plague and he would be fleeing in another direction.

She must keep her mind on what was important, though. Lord Blackwood had dispensed with bearing reins and those four horses would feel the freedom of it. *That* was what she must consider.

"Lady Redfield will no doubt wish for a clearer explanation than the one we have recently provided," Mrs. Weston said. "Leave that to me and let this be the end of it. With any luck at all, Lord Blackwood will be too embarrassed over the encounter to talk about it widely. Or at all."

Arabella was not certain that she had embarrassed the lord, but she was certain that she'd enraged him.

He'd been very handsome in his temper, she must admit. His color had deepened to almost the shade of his hair and he'd narrowed his eyes and folded his arms in a way that seemed somehow manly. Wonderfully manly.

It was very inconvenient that he was everything wrong—son of the duchess, devoted to the absent Lady Constance, employer of a bearing rein, and avoiding Arabella Berestock like the plague.

PEREGRINE HAD WAITED quite some time before setting off for his club. He did not wish to give Lady Arabella the satisfaction of seeing him set off sans bearing reins.

He'd been in a temper when he'd gone back into the house. Who did she think she was to be lecturing a lord on the street?

Mr. Sindu had got him a brandy and, as was their usual habit, got himself one too and sat with him in the drawing room.

Peregrine had known Amandeep Sindu since he was a boy. It was never clear how he'd come to England, though it was known that his parents were long dead. He'd ended up in an alms house and the duchess had got him out. She'd given him a job as a worker on the home farm, but he'd harangued everybody until he was given the job he wanted, which was junior footman.

Over the years, he'd worked his way up and made three things clear to anybody within hearing range: he intended to become a butler, he would never attend church, and when he did become a butler he would never allow anybody to dispense with his title. He was *Mr.* Sindu and not even Peregrine dared call him Sindu, much less Amandeep, though the fellow regularly called him Peregrine when they were alone. It was Mr. to everybody, even the duchess.

Mr. Sindu had been as good as his word regarding church. According to him, he was stateless and religion-less, having been taken from his homeland as a babe and having received no particular religious instruction. Therefore, he must only follow his own conscience in all matters. His conscience advised him that he need not take spiritual guidance from a vicar who could not hold his wine and who routinely attempted jests that were not at all clever. He was all confidence that God, or the Gods, however it may be, heartily agreed with him on that point.

When Peregrine had come back into the house after his dust-up with Lady Arabella, he thought to outline the situation to his butler. That proved unnecessary, as Mr. Sindu had observed the entire galling encounter from the front doors.

He was in full agreement as to Lady Arabella's hardheaded-ness, her inappropriateness, and her general air of ludicrous superiority. He was also in full agreement with her opinions on the bearing reins. Like so many English habits, Mr. Sindu said, it was barbarous. Forcing an animal into an unnatural position for long periods could only lead to eventual deformity. Nature had its reasons why pigs did not have wings and birds did not walk long distances. Beasts should do as they were built to do.

Peregrine was entirely aggravated to discover that Lady Arabella had been right. He'd been hoping that Bullford would revise his earlier opinion, Mr. Sindu would agree with him, and he would be entirely vindicated.

Mr. Sindu had then pointed out that while Lady Arabella appeared a very great nuisance, she was also exceedingly pretty and so perhaps allowances should be made.

Was that right, though? Yes, she was exceedingly pretty. What a lovely head of hair that lady had. And then, even in her temper and her very red face, she was beautiful by anybody's standards. But, were allowances to be made over a charming countenance?

Mr. Sindu had ended with, *Do not allow your bruised pride to rule your opinion.*

Mr. Sindu often said sensible things like that, but just then Peregrine found it highly inconvenient.

Apollo had then barreled in and leapt upon him, spilling his drink. Mr. Sindu had taken in the situation, stared into Apollo's eyes, and said sternly, *Sit this instant.*

Of course, the dog had sat down. He had never been in control of his dog, or his butler, either, for that matter. Now he was not in control of his horses too.

He'd finally gone off to his club, drank more than he should have, bet more than he should have, and did not have nearly as much fun as he should have.

WHATEVER WENT ON with the family, Hemmings could at least assure himself that the servants were, finally, in good order. Clive had been shown the door and this had seemed to convince the rest of them that their butler meant business. There would be standards kept, and there would be no more running to Lady Redfield for a reprieve.

Mrs. Redmond had not returned and had therefore been dismissed. Hemmings would take his time to hire a new housekeeper. Cook had begun turning out meals of the same quality that the baron had always demanded. The maids now cleaned as it was meant to be done, which was thoroughly, and he no longer found them gossiping in corners. Flora, without the influence of Clive's snide attitude, had quieted her saucy remarks and seemed a deal more rational. Oscar was, naturally, as he had always been—hardworking, loyal, and never shirking his duties.

A new footman had been hired to replace Clive, and Hemmings had made certain he hired a boy younger and less experienced than Oscar. This made Oscar the first footman and gave him an upper hand over William.

Oscar had been tasked with training William on the proper

way to go about things. So far, this had seemed to go well. Though, Hemmings had noticed that Oscar ended every lesson by saying, *Whatever you do, don't be like Clive.* He could not say how illuminating that particular directive was, as William had never set eyes on Clive.

Now, they were attending the family in the dining room and both his footmen were standing by as if they were deaf to the conversation at table. Just as it should be and not at all like the smirks that used to appear on the recently departed Clive's face. Whether William understood it or not, he was very effectively not being like Clive.

It was admirable, he thought, considering the bizarre nature of the conversation.

"You see, Lady Redfield," Lady Arabella said, "it is very cruel to pull the horses' heads up like that."

"Yes, I suppose it would be," Lady Redfield said. "I doubt we use such a thing, else you would have noted it on the way back from Cornwall."

"I can assure you that you do not," Lady Arabella said. "What I noted on the journey was what good care Lander does take of your horses."

"Well, that is a relief," Lady Redfield said.

"Lady Redfield," Mrs. Weston said, "I did caution Arabella that there are to be no more outbursts in the future. She is likely to see bearing reins all over town."

"Goodness, will she? I cannot say I've ever noticed others' arrangements of their horses. I have not even noticed my own arrangements."

"I expect they are exceedingly common," the matron continued. "I wonder if I ought not delay my visit to my sister until Arabella settles in. It is such a big change for her to move from the remote countryside to a busy place where she might encounter all sorts of unexpected things."

"Oh, please do not, Mrs. Weston," Lady Arabella said. "I vow I will not put a foot out of place while you are away. I will be directed by Lady Redfield in everything."

"She is such an agreeable young lady," Lady Redfield said. "It really is very pleasant. I think we will get on together quite admirably."

"Very well," Mrs. Weston said. "I will only be in Lambeth, after all. You may send me a message if you need me. We should discuss one other matter, though. Do you suppose Lord Blackwood will go to the duchess with some complaint over…what occurred?"

Lady Redfield looked thoughtful. "Theodosia does say that her son quite depends upon her and confides everything about his life. One time, she said that Peregrine viewed her as the keeper of his hopes and dreams, and her opinion always remained paramount in his thoughts."

"Goodness," Lady Arabella murmured.

"On the other hand," Lady Redfield said, "my lady's maid told me that she spied Lord Blackwood and his butler closing up all his curtains when his mother's carriage stopped here. Flora had run an errand for me and was just coming in when the curtains began flying shut."

Hemmings would like to have a word with Flora. It was not seemly that she was spying on the inhabitants of the neighborhood. He knew he could not, though. It was a lady's maid's purview to share with her mistress any tidbits of gossip she'd picked up. Even if she were looking around for trouble like any Bow Street Runner.

"I would not like Arabella to have to face Her Grace's wrath on her own, if it comes to it," Mrs. Weston said. "I would be much better equipped to stand up against it and, after all, it was I who accompanied Arabella when the…incident…took place."

Hemmings suppressed a sigh. Young people were such trouble. Lady Arabella had not been in the house for a moment before she'd managed to incur the wrath of the duchess.

"Her wrath, oh dear," Lady Redfield stuttered. She glanced around the room and her eyes settled on her butler. He discreetly nodded. She seemed to take courage from Hemmings' steadfastness, a serious figure standing motionless at the head of her table.

Lady Redfield took a deep breath and said, "I will manage Theodosia, if anything is said. After all, she does not bite. I do not think."

Hemmings worked to keep his features entirely expressionless, though he felt an enormous amount of pride in his mistress. And in himself. She was toughening up. Lady Heathway had provided the spark, and he had fanned the flames.

ARABELLA BEGAN TO be more lighthearted over the days. After all, what had really happened? She'd got the bearing reins removed from the necks of four horses, that was all.

Mrs. Weston had gone off to her sister and already sent a letter from there. Her dear sister Mary Anne, her genial brother-in-law, and their lively brood of children were keeping her quite entertained. Further, Mr. Gentian's brother, the Bishop of Bath and Wells, was to visit with *his* children. He had been a widower these past two years and Mr. Gentian thought he could do with a trip away from his duties. They were going to be quite the party with seven children roaming the house and though the place was quite commodious they would find themselves constantly in one another's company.

Arabella folded Mrs. Weston's letter and put it away, well-satisfied regarding the lady's current situation. Now, if she could just think up a suitable explanation for the bite on her hand. She had been watching the family of squirrels in the tree outside her window for days. They seemed a genial family—a mother and two children. She would guess the kits were four or five months old and had stayed on in the nest to survive the winter, it being common for these solitary creatures to gather for warmth through the cold months.

The two kits were full of fun—biting at each other's wonderful red coats and long fluffy tails. Their eyes were bright, their creamy undercoats nice and thick, the tufts in their ears giving them a charming look of surprise, and their hearts full of vigor and energy. Their mother looked as mothers often do, both indulgent and exasperated.

This morning, she saw one of the kits knocked out of the tree by the other. He did not stay on the ground long, but he came up with a decided limp. Arabella did not think the limb broken, but rather badly sprained.

She had leapt into action. She emptied a hat box and lined it with a flannel nightdress, tearing off a strip of fabric that could be used to keep the limb still while it healed. Then, she'd carefully and slowly opened her window.

It had long been her experience that an animal in need of help will generally take the help that is offered, as long as one did not rush at them or frighten them. They must be assured of their safety and allowed to approach in their own time.

It was some hours, and really growing cold in the room, before the kit ventured in. He seemed very suspicious and the other had retreated into his nest with his mama while she kept watch. Arabella had slipped down to the breakfast room as there were always good things to be found on the sideboard all the day long. She'd filled a napkin with hazelnuts and a pear, and then took a knife to slice the fruit.

She crushed the hazelnuts into pieces and laid them on the windowsill, then cut off a piece of pear and placed it in the hatbox.

The kit came gingerly to the sill. Once there, he began to stuff the nuts into his mouth as fast as he could, chewing as if his very life depended upon it. The mother and the other kit emerged from their nest, they too lured by the nuts.

The injured kit suddenly paused and sat up, sniffing the air. It had caught wind of the pear. The smell of sweetness was irresistible, as it so often was to wild creatures. Arabella had developed a theory that their stomach alerted them to the necessity of such food and drove them forward to it.

The darling thing went straight for the hatbox laying on its side and the piece of pear in it, all caution thrown aside.

Arabella cut off another piece of pear and added it to the sill, along with more nuts. She would not like to think of the poor fellow's family going hungry while he was undergoing treatment.

She'd since named the little squirrel Rusty, and allowed him to stuff himself with hazelnuts and pear pieces. An animal full to the top with food was always calmer and more cooperative than one who was not.

Rusty made a few forays to the since closed window to look at his home and family, that family now in the nest with their beloved slice of pear. The food in the hatbox always pulled him back, though. Eventually, the warmth of the room had its own effect and Rusty began to grow sleepy.

Arabella had carefully picked him up and attempted to bandage the leg.

The little blighter bit her for her trouble, but then seeing that would get him nowhere, he quieted and complied.

Now his leg was wrapped and he was sleeping, his long red tail curled round him for coziness.

She'd wrapped her own finger with a piece of flannel and she supposed it would not show much under her glove, just a little lumpy.

Flora was to come to her soon. It was the evening of Lady Easton's ball and Arabella would wear one of Lady Redfield's dresses that had been taken in to fit, as her own were not yet arrived from the modiste.

She had gently righted the hatbox and laid the top on with just a little crack for air, and now she pulled on her gloves.

A sharp rap on the door, and then Flora bustled in. "Lady Redfield says we are not to be late, as Lady Easton does not like it."

Flora paused and looked at Arabella's gloves. "Most ladies

don the gloves last," she said.

"Oh, well, I did not want to be much trouble so I thought I would do what I could on my own."

Flora's eyes narrowed. "The top of that hatbox just moved and now there's pointy ears poking out it. We don't have mice in this house, what have you brought in?"

Arabella knew there was no hiding Rusty now. She spilled out the story to Flora and begged her not to tell anyone of it. Rusty would only be in her room until he was healed and then he'd go right back to his tree.

Rusty, for his part, seeing a new stranger had arrived, disappeared back into the box.

Flora had seemed to consider the matter. She shrugged and said, "Never mind, I understand country ways well enough, my own da's a farmer. He'd spend all the night in the barn keepin' company with a cow getting ready to calf. Though I don't reckon he'd do the same for a squirrel…"

Arabella had leapt up and kissed Flora on the cheek. "You are a darling," she said.

Flora had harumphed and said, "Tell that to our Mr. Hemmings."

CHAPTER FIVE

ARABELLA HAD NOT had very high hopes for the dress that was to be taken in for her from Lady Redfield's closet. She was rather surprised that it had come out so well. It was a dark green silk and Flora had nipped it in at all the right places. Arabella had not, up until now, worn anything beyond a serviceable white muslin. The feel of the silk fabric was positively divine. She thought the darkness of the shade did something for her too. It did not wash her out like white was prone to do. And then, if she happened to feel her face heat up, it might not be so noticeable. If she was embarrassed and blushed as a result of it when she wore white it was very noticeable. Freddy called her Lady Candle—her white gown the wax and her face the flame.

The carriage had pulled up to the front of Lady Easton's house on Portland Place.

As they were getting out, Lady Redfield said quietly, "Lady Easton will find favor in any comments regarding how wide the avenue is. She quite takes pride in it."

Arabella had nodded, grateful for the hint. She would like to be approved of by all the ladies and was just now quaking over whether the duchess might have something to say to her regarding her devoted son and his horses.

Lady Easton stood in the hall, receiving her line of guests.

"Clara," Lady Redfield said, "you do look well."

Lady Easton nodded as if this was a foregone conclusion.

"Cecilia. How on earth did you get a dress made for Lady Arabella so quickly?"

"I had one of my own taken in. My maid did it for me."

"Clever maid."

Arabella had curtsied. "Lady Redfield was most kind to arrange it. Lady Easton, I must comment that I was so struck by your wide avenue, it is very grand. There cannot be another like it."

Lady Easton flushed with pride. "Indeed, Lady Arabella. My nephew and I prefer Portland Place above all others for just that reason."

Arabella smiled and Lady Redfield nodded approvingly. The lady had hinted that Lady Easton would like to hear praise for her wide avenue and that was apparently very true.

Lord Easton turned out to be a jolly fellow, not at all like Lady Easton. He seemed delighted with the idea that Arabella was to be the ladies' next project and he swiftly introduced her to his nephew, Lord Bertridge, and his new wife, Lady Bertridge, née Miss Upton.

"You see, Lady Arabella," Lord Easton said, "Miss Upton was the *last* project. Now she's gone and buttoned herself up, my nephew has buttoned himself down, and they meet in the middle and go on very happily together."

Lady Bertridge shook a finger at her father-in-law, though the sparkle in her eye belied her delight with Lord Easton.

Lord Bertridge solemnly nodded and said, "And now you know far more than you wondered about, Lady Arabella."

Lord Easton seemed to find this hilarious and roared with laughter until Lady Easton took his arm.

Lady Redfield led Arabella to the cloak room, where she received her card. A real card.

Mrs. Weston had made up such cards as a practice, and Arabella had delighted in filling in Mr. Prickles for the first. But this was a real card and there would be no hedgehogs or otters putting down their name.

A sudden thought occurred to her that had never presented itself while she danced in the drawing room in Cornwall. What if nobody wrote down their name? Mrs. Weston had not said what to do in such a circumstance. Would they take their leave and go home? That seemed the most sensible thing. But, oh, she did not wish it.

As Arabella stared down at the as yet empty card, willing names to magically appear, Lady Redfield said quietly, "There they are."

She looked up and saw them coming. Like a gaggle of geese gliding majestically across a pond, the ladies of the society sailed across the ballroom floor.

Arabella shuddered just the smallest bit. The duchess was at the head of the formation and she would soon hear if there had been any mention of her abhorrence of bearing reins to that lady.

"Lady Arabella," the duchess said, "you look charming."

Arabella curtsied as relief washed over her. That same relief washed over Lady Redfield too, as she heard the lady let out a breath. Whether anything had been said to the duchess, she could not be certain. She thought not and if not by now, then hopefully never. In any case, the duchess had nothing to say to her about it and so all was well.

Lady Featherstone said, "Your first ball in Town, my dear. Very exciting."

"My recently arrived granddaughter will one day be standing just where you are, Lady Arabella," Lady Mendleton said.

"I am surprised she is not standing here already," Lady Heathway said, "considering what you've told us about that baby."

Lady Mendleton nodded, not seeming to take in Lady Heathway's meaning. "It's true, she is *very* advanced."

"Ah, Peregrine," the duchess called. "Goodness, my son does not hear me."

The duchess strode off in pursuit of him and Arabella felt her anxiety rising again. What if Lord Blackwood were to take this moment to explain to his mother that he'd been accosted on the street by her latest project?

She watched in horrified fascination as Lord Blackwood clearly attempted to resist his mother's efforts to bring him over.

He was not successful, though. And they were before her in a moment.

"Peregrine, this is Lady Arabella Berestock, the lady I told you about. Lady Arabella, my son, Lord Blackwood."

Arabella curtsied.

Lord Blackwood said, "We have been introduced."

"Oh excellent, yes," the duchess said, "you would do, being neighbors. Now, it is all arranged, Peregrine will take you into supper. It is quite a tradition for the society, you know. First ball, supper with a gentleman related to one of us. Lady Redfield's boys are still too young, so my own will have to do."

The consternation on Lord Blackwood's face could not have been clearer. At least, it was clear to Arabella though it did not seem clear to the duchess.

Her Grace took Arabella's card and handed it to Lord Blackwood.

He hesitated for a moment, and Arabella wondered if they were coming to the moment of truth. Would he hand back her card still empty and explain to his mother that he would not escort a scold?

Lord Blackwood filled in his name, handed her card back to the duchess, bowed, and marched away.

The situation was ghastly. He had not just been forced to dance with her, but to take her into supper too.

She had the urge to flee, and Lady Redfield squeezed her hand. Blessedly, the duchess and Lady Heathway turned to talk to an acquaintance.

Another gentleman approached. "Lady Redfield, Lady Featherstone, Lady Mendleton."

He seemed a genial gentleman, though none of the ladies appeared over-enthusiastic to see him.

"Mr. Vance," Lady Redfield said. "May I introduce you to Lady Arabella Berestock."

"Lady Arabella," Mr. Vance said with a quick bow. "May I?" he asked, holding his hand out for her card.

She handed it over and he put himself down for the first. Then he turned and said, "Lady Mendleton, I heard you were recently blessed with a granddaughter. You must tell me all about her."

Lady Mendleton nearly swooned over this request and pulled Mr. Vance aside, no doubt to outline all the advanced things the baby had done so far.

"Mr. Vance is to be a baron eventually," Lady Redfield said. "His grandfather was in trade, though. A gunmaker of some sort."

"He seems a very genial fellow," Arabella said.

"Oh yes," Lady Redfield said. "He always has that going for him. Everybody likes him, even if not everybody can go so far as to approve of his lineage. I don't particularly mind it, though you *are* an earl's daughter so…"

Lady Redfield need not finish her thought. Her thought was Arabella would be going down in the world to attach herself to a baron with a grandfather in trade. It was an amusing idea. She might be an earl's daughter, but she'd spent her childhood in circumstances that were probably less elevated than what Mr. Vance was certain to be accustomed to.

Other gentlemen approached. Arabella was particularly interested to meet Lord Ryland, as Lady Featherstone often spoke of him. The lady seemed aflutter to see him now.

As Lord Ryland wrote his name down on her card, Lady Featherstone touched her emerald brooch and told him of some case in Brighton involving stolen fishing nets that remained unsolved. She wondered if this were not the type of thing that could be used at his mystery ball.

Lord Ryland had coddled the lady a bit, but Arabella could see at once that it was *not* the type of thing he would use.

62

"Lady Featherstone won last season's mystery," Lord Ryland said to Arabella. "The prize was the very brooch she wears this evening."

"It is lovely. I have often noticed it," Arabella said, wondering if Lord Ryland was aware that she never took it off.

"I certainly hope you will attend and take your chances this year, Lady Arabella."

"Of course we will come," Lady Redfield said. "Though I am always very useless at the game."

"Ryland," a voice said behind Arabella.

"Skeffington," Lord Ryland said.

Arabella turned. "Skeffy," she said. "As you seemed to have made it back to Town, I presume you eventually caught up to your horses."

Lord Skeffington looked as serious and ill-humored as he always did. He did not answer her.

"Lady Redfield," Lord Skeffington said.

Poor Lady Redfield staggered just a bit. "Lord Skeffington," she murmured.

Lord Skeffington moved his eyes away from the lady and said, "Ryland, I was coming to find you regarding the little contest I mentioned. It is set up for a month from now."

At that, Lord Ryland bowed and moved off with Lord Skeffington, though not before Arabella heard Lord Ryland say, "What's this? When did you have to catch up to your horses?"

Arabella could not imagine how Skeffy would answer the question, only that it would not be the truth. No man would admit to being chased out of a neighborhood by a badger and a hedgehog.

"That man is terrifying," Lady Redfield whispered.

Arabella patted her arm. "He only *attempts* to terrify people. If you do not allow it, he is quite powerless. He could have come back after Mr. Pringles and Lord Bushwick drove him away from the house in Cornwall, but he did not."

"You are made of sterner stuff than I, I am afraid."

"No, I do not think so," Arabella said. "I just have more information about his real nature."

Lady Redfield looked enquiringly at her, but Arabella did not elaborate. There might be a time and place to elaborate but this was not it.

She had lived in the house owned by Lord Skeffington for years. Perhaps she should not have snooped in the attics and perhaps she should not have pried open trunks. But she had, and she knew an awful lot about Skeffy.

※※※※

PEREGRINE HAD FAIRLY stomped away from Lady Arabella after being forced to put his name down on her card. For supper, no less!

Oh, he had heard his mother calling to him clear enough when he'd entered the ballroom. He'd pretended he hadn't and made all haste in the opposite direction.

Why must the lady be so fast on her feet? She was upon him in a moment. And then, had she even bothered to ask him what he would prefer? Of course she had not. The duchess was in the habit of telling people what they thought, not asking them about it.

Now he was forced to sit through a whole supper with the scolding Lady Arabella. He supposed he'd hear a great deal more on the subject of bearing reins.

If only she would not scold, she might be very pleasant. He'd thought so when she was composing that delightful letter to the hapless Freddy in Lady Redfield's back garden. And then, did any lady in the room have such a head of hair? Every time she moved her curls bounced up and down like springs. They must be natural.

He'd heard from his friend Rendridge that his sisters regularly used some medieval torture device that was heated up and made to curl what began as exceedingly straight hair. It never lasted through an entire evening though, slowly drooping. They had been furious at him one evening when he'd taken in their drooping efforts and called them a collection of wilting flowers. Lady Arabella's curls seemed in no danger of wilting.

And then, she was such a petite little person. He quite liked that. He did not see the charm others did in women who were deemed statuesque. It seemed to be the fashion and he did not understand why. Though, perhaps it was because he was tall and lean himself—some of these tall women looked as if they could take him in a wrestling match.

If only Lady Arabella's temperament were steadier. She should be all charming back garden letter writing and no haranguing on the street about bearing reins. Then, her disposition would match her captivating looks.

Out of the corner of his eye, he saw Gresham and his new wife, née Miss Yardley, otherwise known as *The Sprinter* and hanger-on of drainpipes, being introduced to Lady Arabella. He supposed Lady Gresham would have her thoughts taken from drainpipes and put firmly on bearing reins.

"What say you, Blackwood?"

It was Lord Bertridge, milling around and talking to his aunt's guests. Here was another one who'd fallen to the matrons' schemes. He still could not get over it—Bertridge had married a lady who'd been in the middle of some scandal or other in Brighton over the summer. Staid old Bertridge. Peregrine felt like he did not understand the world as he'd once thought he did.

He said, "I understand you are to be congratulated, Bertridge. Had you known the lady long?"

"Not particularly," Lord Bertridge said. "Lady Bertridge was the guest of my aunt and uncle over the summer."

"I presume marriage suits you?" Peregrine asked, though he could not imagine it was a very jolly thing to be married to Lord Bertridge.

"Like a well-cut coat," Bertridge said, his eyes drifting toward his wife across the ballroom floor. "I consider it the best thing I've ever done."

It was extraordinary. The fellow appeared positively smitten. Bertridge. He really would not have thought the man had a romantic bone in his body.

"By the by, what do you think of bearing reins?" Peregrine asked.

Lord Bertridge's brow raised ever so slightly. "That is an abrupt change of topic. I don't use them myself."

"Why not?"

"I do not see the point," Lord Bertridge said. "I have quality horses that keep their heads up high enough of their own accord. Attempting to pull them higher seems…"

"Seems what?"

Lord Bertridge was thoughtful. He said, "I do not prefer things whose sole purpose is appearances. In any case, I suppose the horses do not like it. Ah, there is my wife signaling me to come and rescue her from Sir Richard. He's probably waxing on about his spaniels again."

With that, Bertridge strode over to his new bride as if she were in danger of being overcome by news of Sir Richard's spaniels.

It seemed no matter who he asked about it, nobody approved of a bearing rein. So many did use them, though.

He admitted to himself that he was not terribly inconvenienced by the lack of them. He was just terribly inconvenienced that Lady Scold was proved right.

But was not a man permitted to change his mind on a subject without ever having been wrong in the first place? He was certain it was so. *He* had decided to remove the bearing reins. After careful consideration, he had chosen to do it. For his own carefully considered reasons. Neither Lady Arabella nor any other person had forced him to it.

He had decided.

HEMMINGS HAD MADE it a habit when they were in Town to walk the square for exercise. Some days he took the opportunity when there was a lull after breakfast. However, when Lady Redfield went out for the evening he would wait until she'd gone, and take a leisurely stroll through the shrubberies accompanied by the light from the oil lamps that glowed at convenient intervals. The sturdy gates and a number of alert watchmen made it perhaps the only place in London where one might enjoy the quiet of nature after sunset without fearing an encounter with a cutpurse.

Mr. Sindu was also in the habit of taking in the air of an evening. Hemmings and that gentleman had struck up an acquaintance and would often stroll along together. Hemmings found he quite enjoyed conversing with somebody who was equally elevated and understood the challenges of the position. Mr. Sindu often said something he'd never considered and he found a deal of value in it.

Just now, he'd felt he was well enough acquainted with the gentleman to vaguely outline what had been the problems in the household that had sprung up after the baron had died. There had been no firmness at the top of the ladder, though Lady Redfield had seemed to have begun taking steps in the right direction.

"Mr. Hemmings," Mr. Sindu said, "*you* are the top of the ladder. Peregrine, or as you know him, Lord Blackwood, holds dominion over nothing, not even his dog. I lead the house, as you should do, too. That is why you and I became butlers—to run things. Did we have the world handed to us by way of a fortunate accident of birth? We did not. We grasped our power and, therefore, we are not merely servants. We have transcended the state because we are butlers, Mr. Hemmings. Quite equal to a baronet, at least."

Mr. Hemmings found himself very moved by these ideas. Of course, he had always understood that butler was a lofty space to occupy in the world. But to hear it in such terms! Equal to a baronet. And why not? Did he not have an equal discernment in taste? Did he not speak in the accents of a gentleman? Did he not carry himself with a certain dignity? Did he not take care of his clothes and ensure there was never a wrinkle or spot upon them?

"I had never looked at it in such a light," he said.

"The world will treat you how you teach it to. I have known Peregrine since we were boys, and I call him by his given name unless he has visitors. And sometimes even then, depending on who is visiting. Does Peregrine dare call me Amandeep? No, he does not. Does he dare call me Sindu? No, he does not. He calls me *Mr.* Sindu, because I demand it."

"Does he really?" Mr. Hemmings said softly. "Extraordinary."

"That is not all," Mr. Sindu went on. "I am very fond of books and Peregrine only reads when he has absolutely nothing else to do. Therefore, the library has been given over to my use."

"The library downstairs? The main library?" Mr. Hemmings asked, these ideas hitting him hard and fast.

"The only library in the house," Mr. Sindu said nodding.

"I am staggered, Mr. Sindu."

"You must not persecute yourself for not having demanded such courtesies. It is the English way, is it not? Everybody is to know their place and not put a foot out of it."

"I suppose it is," Mr. Hemmings said quietly.

"But the truth is, we are free to make our own place. We make that place by surety of purpose against their half-hearted defenses. And, in any case, these people we deign to serve are not the cleverest souls. Why does Peregrine's dog only listen to me? Because I save it bits of meat from my dinner and I am consistent with my rewards. Very like how I manage Peregrine, himself. Why has Peregrine not figured this out? Perhaps because he does not read much and has been too busy dancing, gambling, and drinking to think very much."

"I find your ideas very original, Mr. Sindu. I am fascinated by them."

"My ideas are original because I am original. I belong to no country and no religion, and therefore must depend upon my own personal judgment. It is a comfortable way of going on, Mr. Hemmings—listen to nobody but yourself."

Hemmings was rather buoyed by that thought. He *did* think he could rely on his own judgment and just might start relying on it entirely. Was he to go along like a lamb while Mr. Sindu was surging ahead like a lion? Was he to blindly follow society's dictates? Who were they, anyway, who had made all these rules?

He had thought for quite some time that he would prefer to wear a cravat, rather than the unprepossessing tie that was his usual uniform.

He just might purchase a neckcloth. A very high-quality neckcloth. He would experiment with some knots. Some very complicated knots.

⟫⟫⟫⟨⟨⟨

ARABELLA HAD FOUND her senses filled with the sights and sounds of a real ball. There were so many people! The sound of the orchestra was near-overwhelming, so used was she to only a pianoforte or Mrs. Weston sometimes playing the harp.

Then, there were the gentlemen. Under the matrons' watchful eyes, she'd been vastly amused by Mr. Vance, who was a lively person with a rather sunny outlook. He claimed he rather preferred having a grandfather in trade than otherwise, as not too many generations had gone by for him to forget his luck.

Lord Ryland was rather odd but had a charm in his own way. If only he was not so interested in his criminal society. Of all the things she might have imagined discussing at a ball, murder had not been one of them. Still, he was so very keen on the subject that she did not mind it.

Sir Richard was an absolute darling, though far too old for her. Nevertheless, she could not be anything but enchanted when he spoke of his love for his spaniels. He claimed they had soulful eyes, and she was certain he was right. She was tickled that he wondered what they thought about while he was out.

Lord Gresham spoke mostly about his wife, she being the lady that Lady Heathway had brought out. He had purchased her childhood home and they were very happy there, as it had enough space that his aunt might blow into the neighborhood without too much disruption to his household.

Lord Bertridge spoke of commonplaces, but it was obvious enough that he was more interested in his wife's dancing than his own.

Arabella might have felt slighted by Lord Gresham and Lord Bertridge, as they hardly asked her a question. In truth, she suspected they would not be dancing with her at all, had not Lady Easton pressganged them into service to ensure that no lady was left sitting out. However, the obvious devotion they had for their respective ladies was lovely to witness and so she could not take offense.

It was all very wonderful. Except that the dance before supper was rapidly nearing.

CHAPTER SIX

A RABELLA REALLY DID not know how to approach Lord Blackwood. Maybe she should not have said anything regarding his treatment of his horses. Or pushed his chin up so he could regard the sky. As well, Mrs. Weston had been right, she'd since seen bearing reins used on other carriages. But then, how could she have ignored it when it was parked right in front of her?

And what to say about it now?

Perhaps they might be put on better footing if she were to come at it just right. That would be very pleasant. He was rather wonderful to look at and it would be comfortable to be on good terms with a gentleman she was bound to encounter often, as he was just at the next door. Further, the bearing reins were gone, so she need not be unhappy with him longer.

Over the past days, it had begun to feel rather silly to peek out a window before setting off on her early evening walk. Flora usually accompanied her now, since Mrs. Weston had gone to her sister. The maid had surmised quick enough that she was looking out so that she might avoid an encounter with Lord Blackwood and was entirely amused by it.

Really, Arabella did not wish to be on bad terms with anybody. Well, perhaps Skeffy was an exception, but other than him, she was determined to be friends with everybody she encountered.

Now, here he was coming. She had noted him smiling all

evening, but that smile had fled. Rather, he had a look of grim determination, as if she were an onerous chore to be got through. Which, no doubt, she was.

"Lady Arabella," Lord Blackwood said, holding out his arm. His tone was stiff, as if he could barely manage to be courteous.

She allowed him to lead her to the set, though she thought they could not possibly go one indefinitely in such a manner.

As they waited their turn, she said, "Lord Blackwood, I know perfectly well why you are so cross. There you were, just getting ready to order your coachman to remove the bearing reins, but I could not even wait a moment to see it done. No, I was very rude in not understanding your intentions to begin. Of course I know it to be the case, as you *did* remove them and no gentleman would be directed by me on how to treat his horses. Therefore, you had the plan of it all along and it is very aggravating to be told that which you did not need to hear. You were very gentlemanly to refrain from pointing that out."

Lord Blackwood's expression underwent several transformations. At first, it seemed as if he were attempting to follow her logic. Then it seemed he did grasp that she claimed removing the bearing reins from his horses had always been his intention. Finally, he looked entirely vindicated and a deal more sanguine than he had done.

Arabella silently thanked Freddy. Among other bits of wisdom, he had several times claimed that men did not like to know they were being bossed. You could boss them all day long if you liked, but you had to give them a way to be right, even when you were busy correcting their wrong.

Dear Freddy. Lord Blackwood was looking more cheerful by the minute.

"I am only gratified that you perceived what my intentions had always been," Lord Blackwood said. "I had spent some days giving the matter some serious consideration and had concluded that I would remove them."

"Yes, of course you did," Arabella said. "I see that now."

"Well, it was a bit of a dust-up, but no harm done," Lord Blackwood said graciously.

"You are very charitable, Lord Blackwood," Arabella said, working to keep her expression suitably grave.

"Nonsense, we'll say no more about it."

It was their turn to go forward and Lord Blackwood led her expertly and with high good humor.

Now that he was ever so cheerful, Arabella could not help but note his grace on the floor. He was so tall and lean, as if there was nothing at all extra about his frame but just what was needed to be towering and strong. His clothes were so well-fitting, and his wonderful coppery hair shining in the candlelight…well, he was rather wonderful now that he did not look as if he'd like to murder her.

Peregrine was once again struck by his inability to predict which direction a thing would go. He had marched over to Lady Arabella, prepared for an exceedingly grim time of it. He had intended to be coldly formal, just as he'd seen his friend Rendridge do on occasion. He would make liberal use of the word "madam," even though she was a "miss."

Rendridge had proved himself particularly skilled at the operation. What had been the scene that night at Almack's, two seasons ago, when Lady Jersey had chattered on and on and they both felt as if they would fall over from the tedium of it. Finally, Lady Jersey said, "Rendridge, you seem very dull this evening." Rendridge rather famously answered, "Madam, I pray not, as I abhor silence."

Well, did Lady Jersey understand that he'd made a play on words, mocking her nickname of *Silence*? Indeed she did. She talked a lot, but she was not stupid.

Of course, Rendridge had been blackballed from Almack's

ever since. But what a moment!

Peregrine had planned on taking just the same tone—condemning without explicitly condemning, and then hoping Lady Arabella got his meaning and was struck by it.

He had never imagined the whole problem would be lifted off his shoulders so easily. Before he could even throw in one coldly delivered *madam*, he would discover that Lady Arabella thought herself entirely wrong-headed. She believed he'd already made the decision to remove the bearing reins, else why would he do it?

It was a very comfortable thought—he'd not ordered the reins removed because *she* said he ought to do it. He removed the reins because *he* had decided. She must feel very foolish to have been there, ordering him to do what he already planned to do.

Even though he'd not planned to do it. Which seemed beside the point to mention now.

Well, he would not allow her to feel too badly about it, that would be ungentlemanly.

They had got through the set very cheerfully. Her small person was so graceful, and yet lively. Yes, those curls of hers were really very lively, bouncing along to the music.

Now, they had gone into supper and he found he wished to know more about Lady Arabella. So many questions presented themselves after hearing her dictate that letter in the garden. Who was Freddy? Why was he charged with managing a collection of wild animals? And for that matter, was Skeffington really her guardian? He would not, himself, leave Skeffington to guard his dog. The man did not exactly have a sympathetic temperament.

Though he wished to ask all of those things, he realized he could not without admitting to eavesdropping on her dictation to Mrs. Weston. He could ask her questions about where she'd come from, though, and that might lead to the same destination.

Before he could ask anything at all, Lady Arabella said, "I wonder if it is not too prying to ask you about your dog. I have heard him in your garden before, but could not see him as the wall is too high. He makes a terrific amount of noise when he hears me walk about. He sounds very large."

"He is an absolute beast," Peregrine said, very much surprised that they had landed on one of his favorite subjects. "Over one hundred and fifty pounds, I think. But very friendly, he really does like everybody." Peregrine paused, wondering if he should tell the whole truth about Apollo.

"Goodness, that *is* very big," Lady Arabella said. "Is he hard to manage?"

Now they were at the sticking point. Should he claim he held dominion over his dog and that Apollo followed his every direction? Or should he admit to the real case of it?

"I suspect he must be quite the challenge," Lady Arabella said.

Peregrine slowly nodded. "I will not deny it. He does run rather rampant over the household. I've already had one valet quit because of his over-fondness for my neckcloths."

"Yes," Lady Arabella said, laughing. "It is rather like having a small horse running wild indoors. Well, they are pack animals after all. You must just confirm your status as the leader of the pack."

Peregrine blanched just the smallest bit, as he was well aware that Mr. Sindu had somehow made himself the leader of the pack.

"I once had a badger that was equally troublesome," Lady Arabella said.

Ah, *now* they were getting to the mystery of all those animals and the Freddy left behind to manage them.

"How is it that you came to own a badger?" he asked.

"Oh, I did not own him," Lady Arabella said. "He was very sick when I found him, weak as a baby, though his teeth were still sharp. We had to be very careful about that. He had broken a claw very deep into the bed, and then, of course, it became infected. The injury made it very hard for him to forage and he was terribly thin. Mrs. Weston and I nursed him back to health."

"In the house?" Peregrine said, having been under the impression that they were rather devilish creatures.

Lady Arabella nodded. "It was all right in the beginning, but when he began to get his strength back and could move around more…well, in the end he did us a service on his way out."

Peregrine was charmed. What service could a badger possibly do for a young lady? "I must hear of this service, Lady Arabella. Perhaps it will inspire me to take a badger indoors, should I come across one injured."

"Oh, I do not recommend it," Lady Arabella said.

"But the service?"

Lady Arabella seemed thoughtful. Then she said, "I am not certain Mrs. Weston would approve of me speaking of it widely."

"This is too mysterious," Peregrine said. "Now you must tell me. Whatever it is, I vow I will not repeat the story."

Seeming encouraged, she said, "Very well. Lord Skeffington is my guardian and I do not like him one bit. He has ignored me mostly, but he did turn up one day and attempt to pressure me into engaging myself to some old crony of his. Very old, in fact."

"That is vile," Peregrine said. It was also all too believable of Skeffington. What had the man been thinking, to engage this charming lady to an old man?

"It was exceedingly vile," Lady Arabella confirmed. "Lord Bushwick thought so, too – that was the badger's name – and he set upon Lord Skeffington's coat and ripped it to shreds. Right in the drawing room while Mrs. Weston and I observed. And laughed, for that matter. Meanwhile, Mr. Prickles, he is a hedgehog still with us, marched outside and very helpfully nipped one of the horse's ankles, which set his carriage careening off. Until this evening, the last I saw of Skeffy, he was chasing his carriage down the road. Having done us a service, Lord Bushwick left us that night. He had regained his vigor, and I believe he sensed a Lady Bushwick in the vicinity."

Peregrine could hardly make out how he viewed the story. He at once felt like roaring with laughter, and an outrage at Skeffington, and an admiration for how brave Lady Arabella had come through it. Another lady so young and without any real protectors might have felt she must do as she was told. That was probably what Skeffington had banked on. Apparently, he did not know Lady Arabella. Or Lord Bushwick.

"Just now," Lady Arabella said, "though he is far down the table and out of hearing, Skeffy gives me looks from time to time. He attempts to catch my eye with a warning expression. I presume he does not wish for me to ever say anything of him, dreadful guardian that he has been. He would be very put out to know that his encounter with Lord Bushwick has been spoken of."

Peregrine followed Lady Arabella's eyes. It was true, Skeffington looked very determinedly at her. The man quickly looked away when he met Peregrine's gaze.

"It is not right that he attempts to frighten you," Peregrine said, wondering if the duchess knew of the circumstance.

"He does not frighten me," Lady Arabella said. "He only tries."

Peregrine nodded, though he did think Skeffington looked rather threatening. A sudden thought occurred to him. "My mother told me that he would not even buy you a horse."

"We never got that far, actually," Lady Arabella said. "The stables were falling down and he would not repair them, thereby saving himself the expense of a horse, and a conveyance too. I did used to long for my own gig."

He had been very aggravated with his mother that he would be forced to give over Bonny Betsy to the lady, and he'd done nothing at all about finding her an instructor. Now, he began to think it was not such a hardship after all.

"Well, as to that, the difficulty will soon be removed. The duchess recommends you ride one of my own mares—her name is Bonny Betsy."

Lady Arabella seemed mightily surprised to hear it. "That is exceedingly generous, Lord Blackwood. Of course the duchess had mentioned she would call on you to assist, but I had not thought...in any case, I will take good care of Bonny Betsy and you will see she is returned to you without harm."

"As to that...well it seems that there is no riding instructor available just now and my mother insists that you must have your first lesson on Tuesday next."

"Dear me, that is a problem. Well, if it is to be delayed, there is nothing for it."

"Delayed, no, she would not like that at all. There is only one thing for it—I will be your instructor. Until an instructor can be found, of course."

They went on very merrily after that, occasionally turning to their other dinner partner to exchange pleasantries, but then coming back together to discuss the proposed riding lessons.

Now, he had very gallantly followed Lady Redfield's coach home, though he did not really think they needed extra protection. Lander was a brute of a fellow and Peregrine was certain the coachman was well-armed.

He tipped his hat as the ladies were let in their door, and just as he had suspected at the beginning of the evening, Lady Arabella's curls had not drooped one bit.

He jumped off his horse and handed Alfie over to Linus, who would hand him over to a groom. He went into his own house feeling more cheerful than he had in some days. Mr. Sindu met him in the great hall.

The second footman, Dale, took his hat and coat, as Mr. Sindu considered tasks such as that entirely beneath him. His butler would allow his coat to fall to the floor before he would take it with his own hands.

"Well?" Mr. Sindu asked.

"It was an aberration!" Peregrine said. "That blasted bearing reins situation was only an aberration. The lady is very pleasant. Very pleasant, indeed."

Mr. Sindu nodded. "I had inquired about the general circumstances of the ball, but I assume you refer to Lady Arabella. It is just as I thought."

Peregrine could not say whether Mr. Sindu had been a clairvoyant, but it did not matter. The lady was very pleasant. Really, exceedingly so.

He looked around him and said, "Where is Apollo?"

Mr. Sindu straightened his cuffs and said, "I directed him to go to sleep, and so he has gone to sleep. In your bed. Whether there is room yet left for you, you will have to negotiate for yourself."

Peregrine shrugged. There probably would not be and he'd end up sleeping on the floor again. But what matter? The evening had come off splendidly and the lady was very, very pleasant.

REGINALD TAYBURN, EARL of Skeffington, brooded over a brandy in his library. It was nearly dawn, Lady Easton's ball having dragged on and on. He had not particularly wished to attend it, and the pretty little actress just now living in his house had been of the same mind. He forced himself to go, though, as he was certain Lady Arabella would attend too.

He had been stalling Lord Rendiver for over a year regarding her hand in marriage. All those months ago, he'd thought he might go to Cornwall and badger the lady into it. After all, she'd been only nineteen and had spent her life in the remote countryside. What did she even know about the world? He'd make up some story about the match being her father's dearest wish. He thought it unlikely that she could hold up against it. As for her companion, he'd not given her any thought at all.

The marriage would be, on its face, distasteful. Rendiver was sixty if he was a day, fat, and had more hair growing out of his ears than on his head. However, Rendiver only wanted the money. He would not have relations with Lady Arabella, as he already had three sons from his first wife and would not wish to burden those sons with half-siblings to look out for when he went to meet his maker.

Rendiver would not live too many years longer and Lady Arabella would become a merry widow, free to marry who she pleased. She must only go to live in York for the time being, and then she could do what she liked.

Rather than badgering her into the thing, he'd been accosted by an actual badger. And not before Lady Arabella told him in no uncertain terms that she would not oblige him, and Mrs. Weston had announced that he had no right to attempt to pressure her charge into any marriage.

Once he realized that he had a runaway carriage on his hands and a badger who was intent on ripping his clothes off his person, he had made a strategic retreat. His first attempt at arranging the marriage had failed and he must think of a cleverer idea to push her into the thing. He would keep his thoughts in that direction and not ponder why she'd had a badger in the house in the first place.

And push her into it he did need to do. He owed Rendiver nine-thousand pounds. Lady Arabella's dowry was twenty-thousand. Once the marriage was finalized, Rendiver was prepared to give him back three-thousand from her dowry. That left Rendiver with a profit of eight-thousand pounds, and himself out from under the nine-thousand and walking away with three thousand.

It would suit everybody. Except Lady Arabella, it seemed.

He had thought on it and thought on it, all the while writing Rendiver in York that the lady viewed the venture positively but insisted on waiting until she was twenty. Rendiver had occasionally threatened to visit the house in Cornwall, but he'd put him off and advised patience.

Then, by some miracle, a reprieve had arrived. A month ago, news had reached him that Rendiver was on his deathbed. His heir might be unhappy about the unpaid debt, but he would not do anything about it. He could not do, even if he was so inclined. It was a gentlemen's wager, and entirely unenforceable. He would simply say that Rendiver had forgiven the debt when last they met.

Shortly after hearing the splendid news of Rendiver's oncoming demise, with what delight did he meet Lady Redfield in his drawing room. That fluttering lady had hemmed and hawed and then insisted on taking in Lady Arabella. He'd piled upon her head all the frustration he'd carried over the past year. Lady Arabella might go to live with Lady Redfield, or she might jump off London Bridge. He washed his hands of the whole matter. After all, he had no further need of her.

Then yesterday, he was informed that he had been misinformed. Rendiver had suffered an attack of the gout, but was in no danger of dying over it. Rendiver himself had written and when he'd seen the handwriting on the outside of the letter, he'd prayed it was a last farewell from a dying man.

It was not, though. Rendiver had since made a remarkable recovery and was feeling fit as a fiddle. He'd heard that Lady Arabella had been relocated to Lady Redfield's establishment and he would come to Town after he had concluded some necessary business in York. He would have his London house open in a month and they might finally proceed with their long-held plan.

There had to be a way to save the situation. But what? How to force that headstrong girl into the match?

He took a deep breath. First, what did he have going in his direction?

Her opinionated companion, Mrs. Weston, had not attended the ball, though he had certainly expected her to. Perhaps she'd gone off to her family, her duties done for Lady Arabella. Though, if that were the case, he'd like to know it so he could cease paying her stipend.

Lady Arabella's current chaperone, Lady Redfield, was an entirely ineffectual creature, and that was certainly in his favor.

What ran against him?

Lady Arabella herself. She was obstinate. She was also pretty and came with a sizable dowry. That was the real danger. She was bait to the circling sharks. Of course, he was still by law her guardian, and the sharks would have to get by him first. He would refuse to give his consent to any young buck making a run at her.

But then, she could wait him out. She would come into her majority in a year.

Maybe he should send her back to Cornwall, get her out of the way. Or to some new place, even? He might rent some remote estate somewhere. A miserable place that would make marriage to Rendiver seem preferable.

Yes, that was perhaps his only course. The most miserable place he could dig up. And if Mrs. Weston had not already dismissed herself as a companion, he would dismiss her. He'd hire some old and unpleasant crone to do the duty. Then he would see precisely how long Lady Arabella Berestock was prepared to be obstinate.

CHAPTER SEVEN

A RABELLA HAD FAIRLY danced into the house in those early morning hours following Lady Easton's ball.

It had been everything she had imagined.

No, it had been more. The sights, the sounds, and, she thought very, very privately, Lord Blackwood.

Arabella had been terrified when the duchess had forced her son to take her into supper. She had been avoiding him ever since she'd lectured him on his bearing reins. She suspected he avoided her too, and certainly would have avoided her at the ball if he'd had his way.

But it had all come off so well! Dear Freddy had given her some well thought-out hints on the nature of men and it turned out he'd been absolutely right. All Lord Blackwood had required was a way out of embarrassment, a way to save face, which she had gladly provided.

Then...oh, then! Then, she'd seen his real temperament. So charming and full of fun! With his good looks and his title, he might get away with being brooding or stiff, everybody would forgive it just for the pleasure of regarding him. But he was not brooding or stiff at all. Of course, she could only be struck by his love for his dog, Apollo, and his horse, Alfie.

He had spoken in detail about his favored riding horse, that creature apparently understanding his meanings and moods without him having to provide any direction on them. She'd never had a horse of her own so could only imagine the silent communication between horse and rider. She was determined to find the same with Bonny Betsy.

How kind that he'd offered to lend her Bonny Betsy, and to be her instructor too. Arabella suspected the lessons would be just how she would wish. She was determined to understand any animal that came into her sphere and that included Bonny Betsy. Lord Blackwood certainly understood horses.

She did like him ever so well. Yes, she really did.

She had discovered through the duchess that his given name was Peregrine. Was that not apt? There *was* something of the falcon in his lean looks.

Arabella reminded herself to keep her feelings reined into something sensible. During those long days and nights in Cornwall, Mrs. Weston had told her absolutely everything she could think of that would prepare her for the wider world. As a bishop's daughter and a dear friend of her own mother, a countess, Mrs. Weston had been regularly in society. She had kept her eyes and ears open. There were pitfalls a young lady could fall into, most of them involving gentlemen.

Mrs. Weston had told her a terrible tale of disappointed hopes that she'd been witness to during one particular season. Arabella would not soon forget the viscount's daughter who had set her cap on an earl's son. The young gentleman had danced with her quite often and she became so confident of an impending proposal that she'd had the temerity to speak of her hopes in that direction.

As it happened, the earl's son got wind of the talk and hurried off to Spain on a trip. The girl in question had somehow not considered that the gentleman had danced often with quite a number of ladies, and was invariably complimentary to all of them. She had felt singled out, though she had not been.

The girl positively pined, and very publicly, until her father took her home. The young gentleman then returned and made a quick match with somebody else. The end of it was, the girl ended up drifting through a few more seasons and eventually going home to marry the local vicar.

Arabella would never open herself up to such talk.

But it was perfectly all right to think about things, was it not? She might have any sort of feelings she wished, as long as she did not go blathering about them to other people like the hapless viscount's daughter had done. Certainly that was right. In any case, the feelings she had just now were rather delicious to have. They were different from anything she'd felt before and she was loath to give them up.

Lady Redfield had been so surprised when Lord Blackwood had escorted them home. Of course, they went in the same direction, as they were neighbors. But Lord Blackwood had very determinedly waited until their carriage had been pulled up in front of Lady Easton's house and they had been inside it. Then he had ridden his marvelous horse, Alfie, alongside their carriage all the way home.

Lady Redfield had been quite flattered by the attention and so had she.

Now, she was out in the garden, enjoying the sunshine and dictating a letter to Freddy. He had sent her a good long report regarding how her animal patients fared.

Flora had taken the place of Mrs. Weston as scribe and claimed she did not mind it a bit, as her penmanship was very good and she did like to sit out in the garden on a fine day. Arabella was grateful for it. While her penmanship was perfectly adequate, she somehow could not complete the operation without becoming covered in ink.

Arabella had already dictated a long list of instructions for Freddy. She continued on.

"Now Freddy, you do not say so but I imagine there must be some new creatures you have discovered that require care. Do send me the details and I will do my best to assist you from afar. If you have not brought in more animals, then I must wonder—are you looking hard enough?"

"You want him to scrape up more than what he's got on his hands already?" Flora asked.

"Only if they are injured, Flora. Now, let us carry on. Freddy, I do hope, with the warmer weather upon us, that Sir Slippery has at least made it as far as the fountain. I fear he has not as you do not mention it. Open the window next to his tub so he can smell the spring coming on. That might inspire him. Regarding Mr. Prickles, I am afraid he has grown far too comfortable. Begin leaving his biscuit at teatime closer and closer to the door and then onto the steps to the house. That might get him used to going out of doors. As for my own project, Rusty continues to heal, though I do not dare take off the bandage yet. He has settled in and does not draw blood from me anymore. His family has become accustomed to visiting on the windowsill through my judicious laying out of fruit and nuts."

"Those creatures are never going to leave you at the rate you're going," Flora said.

Before Arabella could contest the idea that she was to live with a family of squirrels forever, she heard the familiar sound of the door in the next garden opening and the wild barking of Apollo.

"My dear Apollo," she called.

The dog suddenly stopped barking at the hearing of his name.

"You hear me and wish to make a great fuss and prove you are an admirable guarder of the house," Arabella said. "Very well done."

Apollo took up his barking again, making quite the racket.

"Heavens," Arabella said to Flora, "he will never be comfortable about who is mysteriously lurking over here until he can see for himself."

Flora shrugged, not appearing too concerned with what the dog was comfortable with.

"I know," Arabella said. "Let us employ the ladder the gardener was using to prune the apple tree."

"Us?"

"We'll prop it right against the wall. Then I can climb up and Apollo can have a look at me. He shall see I am nothing to be alarmed over."

"*He* might not be alarmed, but I think my mistress would be very alarmed over you climbing a ladder," Flora said.

"Nonsense, it is a very short ladder. Goodness, in Cornwall, Freddy and I once went up a very high ladder to climb onto the roof of the house, as we were certain we heard the call of a distressed creature."

"And?"

"Oh, it was only a weathervane that needed oiling, though we did encounter a bees' nest and so it was a very fast trip back down. We were both stung terribly and Mrs. Weston scolded us over it."

"There's your problem," Flora said. "You keep poking at nature and it's going to poke you back sometimes."

"Let us make haste," Arabella said, already moving toward the ladder. "Poor Apollo is wearing himself out trying to scare off the dangers next door."

Flora reluctantly laid aside her writing instruments and followed her to the rather rickety ladder the gardener had hammered together.

They dragged it to the wall and laid it against the stone. Arabella checked that it was steady and secure, or as steady and secure as it could be. She picked up her skirt and scrambled up.

She peered over the wall to find a beast of a dog barking and running in circles. Lord Blackwood had not exaggerated, the dog must weigh more than herself. He was a lovely dark color with dark eyes and a shiny coat.

He stopped and silenced himself upon seeing her.

"Well hello, Apollo," she said.

The dog showed his wild appreciation of the greeting through a wagging backside and a drooly smile.

As Arabella had thought, all that barking was only a bad case of nerves. In Cornwall, a farmer down the road had just such a dog. Every time they passed by in the cart on their way to the village, he would bark and howl until she called out his name. Then it was head down and tail wagging.

Apollo trotted to the wall and jumped up on his hindlegs, putting his forepaws on the wall to keep himself upright.

Such was his size that his head was just underneath the top of the wall. She patted him and said, "It is high time we were introduced. My name is Arabella and I live here. There is no cause for barking when you hear me come out to my garden. Do you understand?"

Apollo licked her hand which Arabella knew perfectly well was an answer in the affirmative.

"Now do sit down and I will tell you all about myself. Go on, sit down this instant, young rascal."

PEREGRINE HAD BEEN out in his garden when Lady Arabella and a maid had come out to their own garden. He'd been delighted to hear that there was to be a further communication written to the mysterious Freddy who'd been left behind in Cornwall.

He'd settled himself on a bench to hear the latest directions to that gentleman and he did not find himself disappointed. Apparently, Mrs. Twitch-nose was doing an excellent job avoiding Mrs. Murder and her kittens. The Knightlys continued on in their room and that seemed to have become a permanent set-up. Sir Slippery was making a cake of himself by refusing to give up the bathtub. Mr. Prickles understood which side his bread was buttered on and very sensibly stayed in the drawing room for teatimes.

He was a bit confused over what Lady Arabella called *her own project*. The only clues were she was leaving fruit and nuts on her windowsill for the creature's relations, and whatever it was did not bite her anymore.

As it did not bite her anymore, he must assume it *had* bitten her at least once before. Perhaps on her finger?

He had noticed that there had been padding on the inside of the finger of one of her gloves when he'd led her in the dance. At supper, he'd even noticed a small pinprick of blood showing through.

He had not called attention to it, as he'd guessed she'd pricked herself sewing and no lady liked to admit a failure regarding one of their accomplishments.

Peregrine smiled to himself. He should have known better! The indomitable Lady Arabella would not come upon an injury so commonplace. Of course it had been an animal that had done the damage.

But what? A bird, a squirrel, a mouse?

He did not know, though he *did* know the creature was named Rusty.

He wondered which window was her own and whether he could spy the mysterious Rusty if he went to the very back of the garden. Then he thought surely not. For one thing, Lady Redfield had likely put the lady into a front facing bedchamber to overlook the greenery of the square. For another, it would not be very gentlemanly to go spying about for a lady's bedchamber window. Though, there would not be any harm in glancing up when he was walking on the street.

As he mulled over these possibilities, one of the footmen opened the back door to the garden and Apollo flew into it.

His dog was delighted to see him, but also looking concerned that he'd failed to comprehend that there might be people on the other side of the wall who needed to be frightened and driven off.

Apollo stared determinedly at the wall and barked his head off. Peregrine attempted to quiet him with no success. He could not say anything, as he did not want to be discovered eavesdropping, and so had taken to shaking a finger. It was all for naught. No amount of shaking fingers would turn Apollo from his purpose.

During Apollo's brief pauses, Peregrine heard bits and pieces of Lady Arabella's conversation. She was getting a ladder.

Good grief, she was getting a ladder.

He must not be caught.

He briefly thought of hiding behind some shrubbery, but Apollo was bound to give him away and he would look ridiculous.

Peregrine strode to the back door and let himself into the house, leaving his dog barking behind him. He jogged up the stairs to a bow window in the corridor that lent itself to a view of the garden.

As it happened, it led to a partial view of Lady Redfield's garden too. He watched Lady Arabella determinedly dragging the ladder with the rather reluctant assistance of the maid. She leaned it up against the wall, disappearing for a moment, and then her bouncing curls rose up into view.

If tail wagging was anything to go by, Apollo appeared delighted to come face to face with the enemy next door. He got up on his hind legs and stretched himself to full height against the wall while Lady Arabella took to patting him on the head and talking to him.

He could not hear what was said, but eventually Apollo got back on the ground and sat down.

Why was he sitting down? Apollo sat for nobody but Mr. Sindu.

Perhaps he was only tired.

That was a ridiculous thought. Apollo was either wide awake and full of energy or dead asleep. There was no in-between or winding down.

Well, however she'd done it, it seemed Apollo was entranced with the lady. The hound sat very still while she nattered on to him.

He supposed he could easily find *himself* entranced with the lady as well. Yes, he really could. She was a very delightful person with that petite frame and those bountiful curls. There was something in her manner. It was not quite pert, it was rather something like it though. Lively? Engaging? He could not put his finger on it.

And then, she was so very original too. He did not suppose there were many other ladies who had nursed a badger or who had recently issued instructions about the various other creatures living in her house. He had guessed Sir Slippery must be an otter or some like creature, and Mr. Prickles must certainly be a hedgehog. He knew Mrs. Murder to be a cat and as Mrs. Twitch-nose was meant to avoid Mrs. Murder, she must be a mouse. Who were the Knightlys? That was a mystery, for all he knew was that they had their own room. He had wondered if they were not people, but then why would a whole family be in one room and why was that corridor meant to be quiet during the day?

He did not know. But it seemed that the lady had acquired a deep knowledge of animals through her experiences with them.

He had felt, when they'd spoken at supper, that Lady Arabella really understood his feelings for his horse. It was not easily expressed, and one might even feel foolish for attempting it, but she did seem to understand.

Peregrine shook himself. His mind was wandering in unwise directions. He was not at all ready to court a lady, he'd very sensibly put it off for a few more seasons. In any case, when he did finally marry, he was not certain he'd like to find a hedgehog in his drawing room. Horses and dogs were one thing but bringing in a whole forest of creatures was another.

Well, in the end, it would not signify. A lady such as she would not be on the marriage mart long. His mother had told him she came with twenty-thousand. Even if she had not such charming looks, she would be vied for.

He did not like the feeling he got when he thought of that. Why could she not have stayed in Cornwall a while longer? That really would have been ideal. If she had, might he have…

Peregrine had a sudden urge to dash down the stairs and out into the garden. After all, he could simply come out like any rational person did from their own house into their own garden.

Before he knew it, he was down the stairs and out the door, and pretending to look suitably surprised at finding Lady Arabella at the top of the ladder.

He bowed and said, "Lady Arabella. I see you have met Apollo."

Apollo, for his part, raced to greet him and ran circles round him, his large tail smacking him in the legs.

Lady Arabella, not at all looking embarrassed to be found peeking over another's garden wall, said, "He is very charming, Lord Blackwood. We've just had a long talk about things."

Peregrine was dubious about any two-sided conversation she'd imagined, but he was far too taken up with attempting to settle his dog to make comment upon it.

"He has very high spirits," she said.

Considering the spectacle he was currently making of himself, throwing himself on the ground and gnawing at his ankle, that was a kind description.

In a very firm tone, Lady Arabella said, "Now, Apollo, stop that nonsense at once. Do be a dear and come here and sit down, just as you were. This instant, if you please, young sir."

Apollo happily trotted back over the wall and sat, gazing up at her.

Peregrine was confounded. She'd got him to sit again! He really must talk to Mr. Sindu about how it was done.

To take her attention away from the fact that his dog had been out of control and was now very much in control through no efforts of his own, he said, "Did you enjoy Lady Easton's ball?"

"Very much so," Lady Arabella said.

He could swear she blushed. But no, maybe it was only the sun. No, but she was far too red for the sun, it had come on too suddenly.

"Lady Redfield holds a dinner tomorrow evening," Lady Arabella said. "I understand you were invited?"

"Yes, yes, indeed I was," Peregrine said. He had not yet accepted. In fact, he had planned to decline attending a dinner with Lady Scold of the bearing reins. Now though...now he would accept before the hour was out.

What was wrong with him? He really must contain his enthusiasm.

"I hope we will see you there?" Lady Arabella asked.

"Oh yes, certainly," Peregrine answered.

"Good, yes, very good," Lady Arabella said.

"Yes, good," Peregrine answered. He knew not what to say next. It seemed they had reached an impasse at his attendance at the dinner being thought good.

As he searched his mind for the next thing to talk about, Lady Arabella suddenly wobbled on her perch. Just as fast, he heard a small cry and she was gone. The decided thump told the tale of her crash to the ground.

"Lady Arabella," he called, pushing Apollo out of the way. The dog had leapt up and stood on his hind legs attempting to see what had happened to his new friend.

"I am perfectly all right," she called. "The grass is very soft and has cushioned my fall."

He felt an enormous amount of relief. Really, more relief than was called for, he thought. She'd only fallen from a short ladder.

"The grass has done more than cushion your fall," the maid scolded. "Gracious, look at the state of your skirt."

"Oh dear, yes, I see," Lady Arabella said. Louder, she called, "I had best go inside now, Lord Blackwood. I will see you at dinner on the morrow."

"Yes," Peregrine said.

Yes indeed. The lady was very interesting. Very interesting. Too interesting, probably. Still, she was lovely to talk to. He must just have a care that he did not allow himself to go too far

There was nothing wrong with talking, after all. People did it every day. There was nothing at all unusual in it.

Talking was perfectly fine. Expected, even.

He glanced down at Apollo who was just now lying in the grass and chewing the leather on his boot.

He really had to get control of his dog.

As he wrestled his shoe from Apollo's jaws, one of his footmen hurried out. "My lord," he said, "the duchess has arrived and been shown into the drawing room. She said that if I claim you are not here she will check the stables to test the veracity of my story."

Peregrine sighed. The poor fellow looked terrorized. He really had to get control of his mother, too.

CHAPTER EIGHT

HEMMINGS FELT THAT he was marching toward a new era, step by step. The staff were, by some miracle, in good order. Mrs. Beltrain had composed an appropriately elevated menu for Lady Redfield's dinner on the morrow, far superior to the middling offerings she had been recently in the habit of. Oscar shined as the senior footman, taking the lead with great surety of purpose. William, the new footman, had been fully indoctrinated into not being like Clive, the not-missed-at-all departed footman. The maids did their work with industriousness. At some point he would advertise for a housekeeper to supervise them, but the absence of Mrs. Redmond was so delightful that he'd not been in any hurry to replace her. He rather liked being in possession of the household keys.

Then of course, his eyes had been opened by slow degrees through his walks around the square with Mr. Sindu. That wise man's advice to trust his own judgment and nobody else's judgment had resonated deep within his soul.

It had moved him. It had moved him to buy a neckcloth.

He'd actually bought two, as a gentleman could never be certain that the first effort would be a success. If it were not, into the laundry to be washed and starched it must go.

Hemmings had experimented through sixteen washings and starchings and had finally settled on his signature knot. He began with an Osbaldeston bow, then added a Gordian, finally ending in an exuberant waterfall. It was intricate and elaborate and he'd never seen the like. Most gentlemen went in for one knot, *he* had gone in for three.

He had risen a full hour early in the morning several times and tied it, but then taken it off before beginning his duties.

This morning, though, he'd put it on and kept it on.

The footmen were, of course, all amazement. Had he chosen this moment to stroll down the street, any person passing him by would take him for a well-to-do gentleman. A well-to-do gentleman who might give Beau Brummel himself a pause. All for want of his usual black tie.

Lady Arabella had not seemed to even notice it when she'd come into the breakfast room, though he supposed that was to be expected. She was entirely fixated on filling her plate. He'd never imagined a young lady could eat so much. And then, when she was finished, it still did not seem enough. She was forever filling napkins with fruit and nuts and taking them to her room as if she were a squirrel hiding things away for winter.

She'd since gone out to the garden with Flora, while Oscar had taken a tea tray into the drawing room for Lady Redfield, as was her usual morning habit.

Now, a letter had arrived by messenger. He would take it to Lady Redfield in the drawing room. Now, he would discover what she would say about his new style of dress.

Walking sedately with the letter on a silver salver, Oscar opened the door ahead of him.

"My lady," he said, "this has just been delivered."

Lady Redfield was at her desk, writing her own letters. "Dear me, I hope it is not somebody telling me they cannot attend my dinner," she said.

She looked up to take the letter from the tray.

He noted it the instant Lady Redfield took in his neckcloth artfully draped, her eyes widening and lips parting ever so slightly.

"Goodness. That is... are you going out, Hemmings? Is

there…a wedding, perhaps?"

"No, my lady," he said.

"You are not going out?"

"No, my lady."

"So then…you are just…here? As you are?"

"Yes, my lady."

Lady Redfield took the letter and said nothing further. She was shaken, that he could see very clearly, but she did not say anything against it.

Mr. Sindu was right! One must just trust one's own judgment and set one's own course without a thought to what was usually done.

Cecil Hemmings was now a butler who wore a neckcloth, just like any baronet.

LADY REDFIELD WAS rather stupefied by what she'd just witnessed. For some reason, as yet unknown, Hemmings was wearing some sort of wildly composed cravat. It was a virtual tangle of ups and downs and arounds.

What was the meaning of it? Had some new style been made popular and she had missed the news of it? Was he trying to impress a housekeeper in the neighborhood? It seemed very unaccountable.

She glanced down at the letter in her hand, but she did not recognize the seal. She pried it open and flattened out the page. What she read next nearly sent her to her bed.

My dear Lady Redfield,

You were very kind in offering to chaperone my ward, Lady Arabella Berestock, through a season. Unfortunately, upon viewing my ward at Lady Easton's ball last evening, I have come to the conclusion that Lady Arabella has not yet gained the maturity to venture into the marriage mart. Therefore, I will arrange transport to a suitable location where she may spend a year gaining in that necessary quality. Next season will be time enough to consider the prospect of returning to Town.

I am just now negotiating the rent for a house situated north of Newcastle that will provide the quiet that must be beneficial in that regard. I will also dismiss Mrs. Weston and hire someone more suitable. I do not perceive that her care has been at all sufficient in preparing Lady Arabella for the rigors of life in the wider world.

As you will, of course, be aware, as her guardian I am tasked with ensuring Lady Arabella's safety and her comfortable future. You have my decision. Expect to hear further instructions within a week.

Regards,
Skeffington

What was he doing? What did he mean? Arabella had conducted herself admirably last evening. What did he think he saw?

Most of all, what was she to do about it?

Her thoughts, never particularly organized to begin with, swirled and jumped and ducked and made themselves incomprehensible.

She could not allow him to take Arabella away. No, she really could not.

But how to stop him?

She must bring the ladies together. Somebody would know what to do. The duchess or Lady Heathway would know what to do. They would tell her and she would do it.

She set Lord Skeffington's horrible letter aside and took a blank sheet of paper from the desk. Her hand shook as she dipped her pen.

Letter writing, as her friends had pointed out in the past, was not her strong suit. It seemed she had trouble making herself clear. But she must be clear now.

She wrote:

Theodosia—

Help now. Emergency. Dire.

Cecilia

She wrote out four more letters of the same brevity to Lady Featherstone, Lady Heathway, Lady Mendleton, and Lady Easton. She prayed they came to her quickly.

The drawing room door opened and Arabella tripped into the room.

If Lady Redfield's butler's attire had not been surprising enough, she was rather taken aback by the state of Arabella's skirts, which were decidedly grass stained.

"Lady Redfield," she said cheerfully, "I've come into confess my crime as Flora says she is not at all confident that the stains can be got out. Something about new grass being particularly difficult."

"But my dear, what happened? Did you fall?"

"Indeed I did, right off the gardener's ladder."

Lady Redfield attempted to work out why Arabella would be on a ladder, with little success.

"You see, Lord Blackwood's dog was making a terrible fuss," Lady Arabella said.

"Yes, he does bark a lot," Lady Redfield said, now more confused than ever. She had begun to think the only logical explanation was that Arabella had decided to prune the apple tree. What did Lord Blackwood's dog have to do with it?

"Of course, I knew if he could only see me he would not bark quite so much. He's got a case of nerves, you understand."

Lady Redfield nodded, though she did not understand at all.

"Well, it's all worked out. Except my skirt, that is. I promised Flora I would change right away so that it might go right into a soak. Though, I did not feel right in hiding it from you. I pray you are not angry with me."

Lady Redfield had determined that she would say nothing about Lord Skeffington's letter until she could consult with her friends. Unfortunately, she took that moment to burst into tears.

Arabella rushed to her side. "Oh no, I am so sorry. I did not comprehend how upset you would be about it. I shall pay whatever you spent for it out of my pin money and I will never fall down again. Really, it will be all right."

Lady Redfield sniffled into her handkerchief. "It's not your skirt that pains me, Arabella. I had meant to wait to consult with my friends before telling you...oh, you'd better read it for yourself."

She handed Arabella the letter. She could hardly bear to watch Arabella's expression as she understood its contents. The poor girl would be in a heap of tears and lamentations in the coming seconds.

Lady Redfield found herself rather surprised by the lack of tears and lamentations.

Rather, Arabella set the letter down and said, "I see. I wondered what he was up to. He was attempting to stare me down at supper last evening and I could not work out what he was doing."

"But what *is* he doing? That is what I do not understand."

"I cannot be certain except, for his own reasons, he does not yet wish me out of his clutches. I would not be at all surprised if he does not still harbor hopes that he can pressure me into marrying that old crony of his. Yes, I suspect that is it. The fellow is from the north and he sends me somewhere in the environs of Newcastle. Well, he shall discover that he could send me to Shanghai to no avail."

Lady Redfield was rather buoyed by Lady Arabella's courage. Until she remembered one particularly salient fact. Lord Skeffington was her guardian. He had the power and she had no power.

"Oh dear, oh dear, oh dear..." she mumbled.

"Whatever is to happen," Arabella said resolutely, "it is only to happen for less than a year. I will be in my majority then and Skeffy will be out of luck."

"I cannot allow it, somehow I have to stop it, I really do,"

Lady Redfield said. "I have letters, they must go out with the footmen right away. All the ladies must be gathered to…well, to think of something."

Arabella nodded and did not express surprise at the letters' very short composition as she folded and sealed them. "I will take them out to Oscar this minute," she said. "Then I will change and give Flora this skirt and I will remain above stairs until you have need of me. I suspect you will wish to speak to the ladies alone and I further suspect they will fly to your side, but do call me if you need something."

Lady Redfield nodded gratefully.

Arabella stopped at a sideboard before leaving with the letters and poured Lady Redfield a large glass of sherry. She set it next to her, kissed her on the forehead and hurried from the room.

The dear, dear girl. She must not be taken away.

ARABELLA SHUT HER bedchamber door behind her.

She had kept her composure upon reading Skeffington's letter, though in truth she found herself badly shaken. What discomposed her the most was, wherever she would be sent, it would be without Mrs. Weston. Skeffy would hire some unpleasant person to act as her companion, she was sure of it.

What was he really doing? It might be that he planned on taking another run at her regarding that old man by separating her from everybody she held dear. He thought to weaken her defenses and thereby gain her consent to a distasteful marriage. The proposed match must convey some benefit to Skeffington, though Arabella could not know how. Gambling, most likely.

Further, there must be a reason she was not being sent back to Cornwall and her beloved animals. There must be a reason why she was to go somewhere remote in the north.

Perhaps the reason was only punishment. Perhaps he saw

that he had nothing to gain and wished to punish her for it.

But why now? Why let her come to Lady Redfield at all?

Perhaps he wished her to know what she was missing. That might very well be it, Skeffy was a very tall man in stature, but he was a very small man at heart.

Fortunately, she did not come entirely unarmed. She'd brought the papers she had taken from the Cornwall house. She could threaten him with what she knew about him.

It would be dangerous to do so, she knew. One did not explode the life of a man like Skeffington without consequences.

He might even do a violence to her. People often did when they had nothing left to lose. She might be walking in the park or getting out of her carriage a month from now or a year from now and be set upon. She might always have to look over her shoulder.

Perhaps it would not be worth it. Perhaps she ought to just go where she was sent and bide her time with whatever unpleasant woman Skeffy hired. The clock was ticking, after all. It would only be eleven months and then she would be free of him.

She changed her skirt and handed it off to Flora, who looked more and more dubious about it ever being what it had been. Arabella sat by the window and laid out fruit and nuts for the squirrels and stroked Rusty's head as he lay in her lap.

Below her, she saw the duchess' carriage sitting outside of Lord Blackwood's door. She was at least glad the duchess had not come into the garden. The lady fortuitously missed Arabella's fall from the ladder, as she did not imagine the duchess would have approved of her going up it in the first place.

Though she could not see it, she heard Lord Blackwood's front doors crash open. The duchess, accompanied by Oscar, came hurrying to the house.

Arabella smiled. Oscar had not had to travel far to track down that particular of Lady Redfield's friends. The duchess would provide comfort through her practical and very no-nonsense advice until the other ladies could arrive.

Though, what advice was there to give?

If Skeffy were determined to send her away, then away she must go.

Arabella's heart sank. She would miss the season. She would miss the balls and parties. That, of course, was a shame. But what she would really miss…no, *who* she would really miss, was Lord Blackwood. That was her own private secret and it would stay that way.

They were just at the beginning of their acquaintance and she had hoped, very privately… Well, no matter what she had hoped. He had already decided on Lady Constance, whoever she be. Even if that were not to be, a man such as that would not stay single for long. Half the ladies in London must have private feelings about him. No, not half, nearly all of them must have. How could they fail to?

She would see him at dinner on the morrow, and how bitter-sweet that would be.

She petted the squirrel's head as he slept, the little rogue full of nuts and bits of pear. "What do you think, Rusty? Am I to end a spinster? Or am I to encounter some gentleman I like just as much as Peregrine? It does not seem likely, does it?

>>><<<

ALL THE LADIES had gathered in Lady Redfield's drawing room, Lady Mendleton being the last. She'd hurried in and said, "Sorry. The baby, you know."

Nobody chose to answer whether they did know or not, though they most certainly did.

Lady Redfield suspected they did not wish to hear anything further, at this particular moment, regarding how advanced Lady Mendleton's granddaughter was. At least, she must assume so, as Lady Easton was seated next to her and muttered, "I suppose the baby is driving its own phaeton by now."

"Now that we are all here, we must devise a plan," the duchess said. "Cecilia, do give Louisa Lord Skeffington's vile letter so that she may catch up to us."

"I do not see that we have any legal ground to stand on," Lady Featherstone said. "At least, I could not imagine what it would be."

"He is unfit to be a guardian," Lady Easton said. "His morals are decidedly low, if he has any at all."

"Yes, but to attempt to do something in that regard," Lady Heathway said, "it would take years to make its way through the courts and Lady Arabella comes into her majority next year."

"We must do something now, right away," Lady Redfield said.

The duchess surveyed her group of friends. She said, "Our only recourse is to put pressure on the scoundrel. I will speak to Queen Charlotte. Louisa, direct Jasper to do the same, he and Lady Langley are forever going in and out of the palace. Clara, ask Bertridge to speak to the regent. The regent respects your son's opinions, and even fears his judgment a little, I think, even if they are not intimates. I will direct the duke to get Skeffington blackballed at White's."

"But if he's blackballed," Lady Featherstone said, "then he has nothing to lose. Remember Mr. Jacobs? There were some unintended consequences after we shut him out of society."

Lady Redfield noticed both the duchess and Lady Heathway looking askance at Lady Featherstone, as they had been the authoresses of that unfortunate plan.

"Fine. I will ask the duke to only threaten Skeffington with blackballing, if he chooses to go forward with this ridiculous notion of his," the duchess said. "Now, Anne, speak to Lord Ryland. Perhaps Ryland can hint he knows more about Skeffington's affairs than he actually does. He's supposed to be the great detective, is he not? Put him to work at least pretending to be."

Lady Featherstone nodded and said, "Of course Lord Ryland will be eager to consult with me over the case."

"It's not a case," Lady Heathway said.

Lady Featherstone ignored this salvo and turned to the duchess. "When you say Ryland is to hint of knowing about affairs, you mean actual *affairs*."

"Yes, assignations. We all know what a villain he's been on that front. We will hit Skeffington from all sides and bring pressure to bear until he gives this thing up," the duchess said, her tone all confidence.

Lady Redfield was relieved. It felt as if it must work. It must somehow work.

Lady Mendleton rose. "I must return to the baby. I will speak to Jasper when he comes into the nursery before dinner to see the baby. He is very faithful about visiting the baby. He really cannot believe how much she grows and all the things she can do."

As Lady Redfield rang the bell for her butler, Lady Easton said, "She must be out of her cradle and playing lawn tennis by now."

Lady Mendleton nodded graciously and said, "You tease me, but you cannot dampen my spirits. She is very advanced."

Hemmings opened the door for Lady Mendleton and led her out and on her way to return to the advanced baby. The duchess leaned forward and said, "Cecilia, why on earth is your butler in a neckcloth? And why is it tied as if a madman assaulted it?"

"I am afraid I do not know," she answered.

"Does he wear one tomorrow evening? To serve dinner?"

"I am afraid I do not know that, either."

"Do you not think you should find it out?"

Lady Redfield fidgeted with her handkerchief. It was too many upsets in one day. She could not manage more than one upset at a time, and even then she had the urge to call for her carriage and be away.

The duchess sighed. "Leave it to me, I'll find it out."

CHAPTER NINE

ARABELLA HAD GOT some notion of the ladies' plans regarding Skeffington from Lady Redfield. She did not know if it would have the least effect on her guardian, but she was touched that they were all so in earnest in their efforts.

As she waited for the hammer to strike by way of Skeffington's next communication, she was determined to enjoy whatever little time she had left under Lady Redfield's roof.

She thought, if she put her mind to it, that she could experience this evening's dinner without thinking of her troubles at all.

Peregrine was to attend, though she really ought not to even think of him as Peregrine. He was Lord Blackwood, and it was naughty in the extreme to call him by his given name, even if it were only in her thoughts.

There were other gentlemen who would attend too. Other single gentlemen the ladies had deemed suitable. Of course, poor Mr. Vance was not on the list. The ladies all thought him pleasant enough, but they could not get round his grandfather being in trade. It was a shame, and seemed silly to Arabella's mind, as he really was so entertaining. He struck her as the sort of gentleman she would like to have had as a brother.

Lord Ryland was of course invited, and he was unmarried, suitably titled, and very handsome. His sole interests seemed to be murder and forgeries, though. Even if she could get past that, he did not hold up against Peregrine.

A certain Lord Lymington was set to attend and was the eldest son of the Duke of Hastings. This seemed to be his primary recommendation. Lady Redfield had been on the fence about him, as she was not sure if they would have enough in common to talk about. Lord Lymington liked to talk about horses. Exclusively. Arabella had yet to mount a horse. However, the duchess had swayed Lady Redfield with the idea that a gentleman hardly noticed that a lady did not speak much if he was allowed to talk on a favored subject.

There were a few others coming, too. Arabella would be introduced to them all, but what she really wished was to be seated next to Peregrine.

She doubted she would be though, as he was not deemed one of the "eligibles" that she was meant to consider. *He* was supposed to be holding out for the arrival of Lady Constance next season.

Arabella shook out her skirt and readied herself to go downstairs.

Lady Constance would do everybody a courtesy if she jumped off the nearest bridge.

HEMMINGS SURVEYED THE dining table. It was just as it had been in days of old when the baron had taken the head of the table. Oscar and William had done an excellent job measuring each place setting down to the millimeter and he'd made very few corrections. Every piece of silver glinted in the candlelight and every piece of crystal sparkled.

Though Lady Redfield had at first proposed a seating of forty, Hemmings had bargained her down to thirty-four. Forty persons could indeed be sat at the table, it had been done in the past, but they would be packed in shoulder to shoulder.

He gently patted his neckcloth as he recalled his conversation with the duchess that had occurred only the day before.

Yes, it seemed now that he wore a neckcloth, he was being sought out by such persons as a duchess.

She'd wished to know *why* he was wearing a neckcloth. He supposed Lady Redfield had put her up to it. He came at the thing with all confidence.

"Hemmings," the duchess said, "why are you dressed so? Is there a wedding or a funeral in the offing?"

"Your Grace," he said, bowing. "There are no such life-ending or life-affirming events on my calendar at this precise moment in my history."

"A simple no would suffice," the duchess said. "What is this, Hemmings? Why do you wear a cloth?"

Hemmings had clasped his arms behind his back and said, "It has recently come to my attention, through the edifying acquaintance of Mr. Sindu, that I am well-advised to rely on my own judgment exclusively."

"I see. And so this is your judgment?"

"Indeed, Your Grace. It is a Baldeston-Gordian-Waterfall."

"A what? Do you plan to dress so for the dinner on the morrow?"

Hemmings had nodded in the affirmative.

"Hemmings," the duchess said, "how are the guests who are not familiar with you to know that you are the butler? How will they distinguish you from the other guests?"

Hemmings had in fact thought that question through. "They will know it, Your Grace, because I have opened the door to them. They will know it by how high I carry my head. They will know it as they see me direct the footmen in the ballet known as dinner. They will know it by the rarified air of the butler that I carry with me."

The duchess had thrown up her hands and said, "Lord help us."

Once again, he had followed his own judgment and he had persevered. Nobody had gone so far as to say he could not proceed as he planned.

Mr. Sindu was to be congratulated.

THE DAY PREVIOUSLY, Peregrine had got a double dose of his mother. The duchess had arrived, unplanned as usual, and practically threatened one of his footmen to retrieve her son and place him in the drawing room. That visit had been admirably short, as one of Lady Redfield's footmen had arrived with a bizarre note that only said: *Help now. Emergency. Dire.*

The duchess had flown out of his house and into Lady Redfield's like a swift on migration. As for himself, he'd looked out the window to see if Lady Redfield's house was on fire.

Her house had not been on fire and while he could only speculate on what the lady's dire emergency had been, he'd begun to silently thank Lady Redfield for calling his mother away so expeditiously.

Then the duchess had come back. *That* visit had been a deal more lengthy and had delivered news of varying sorts.

The first, and by far the most important, was that Skeffington was threatening to send Lady Arabella to some remote place in the north. The duchess was of the opinion that he still held out hope that he could push Lady Arabella into a marriage that would benefit him in some way.

The scoundrel! The rogue!

Peregrine was determined to do something about it...but what?

He still had not figured that out. But whatever it was, he was determined to do it.

In the meantime, he would see Lady Arabella this very night. He would see how she was holding up against Skeffington's terrible plan. In fact, Peregrine had the idea to turn up early, before the other guests began streaming in, to see what she would say about it.

The second matter brought to his attention was not one he considered his problem, until the duchess spent a quarter hour convincing him that it was. While he might not know what to do about Lord Skeffington, he did know what to do about this particular problem.

He bounded down the corridor and found Mr. Sindu in his library. Or he should say, Peregrine's own library. He still was not certain how it came to be part of Mr. Sindu's dominion, other than it had been pointed out that Peregrine didn't read much.

"Mr. Sindu," he said.

"Peregrine."

"The duchess was in high dudgeon yesterday on account of you instructing Mr. Hemmings to don a bizarrely tied neckcloth and present himself as a lord in Lady Redfield's house."

Mr. Sindu laid down his book, or rather, *Peregrine's* book, and said, "I advised him of no such thing."

"Then why has he done it? Why does he think you said he ought to do it?"

Mr. Sindu laced his hands together and said, "What really goes on in another man's mind is a question for the ages. It can only be guessed at."

"Then…what is your guess?"

"My guess is that I pointed out to Mr. Hemmings that he ought to rely on his own judgment. His own judgment alone."

"Why should he do that?" Peregrine asked, entirely confounded. "He has to follow the rules of his house, just like every butler does."

"Every butler does not, I certainly do not."

"You don't?"

Mr. Sindu sighed. It was a long and quiet sigh and one Peregrine had heard before. It generally preceded hearing something he had not known and wished he'd never been told.

Mr. Sindu waved his hand around the room. "I am the master of my own library. What rule of the house is that?"

Peregrine had no answer. He wished he knew. He turned on his heel and marched from the room, calling over his shoulder, "Do not put any more ideas into Hemmings' head!"

He really had to get control of his butler.

A footman opened the door for him to leave the house. Mr. Sindu did not open doors and was, in any case, too busy reading books in the library he'd stolen out from under his lord's feet.

ARABELLA HAD DRESSED early, and come down early, all under the guise of being by Lady Redfield's side as she made the inevitable little adjustments preparing for her dinner. Arabella had not herself ever hosted a dinner and could not imagine what needed adjusting, but Flora had told her that her mistress fluttered between dining room and drawing room for a good three-quarters of an hour before guests arrived.

She did not think she would be much use to Lady Redfield and it was not the real reason she'd come down early anyway. Her nerves had been in such a high state she could not bear to stay in her room. There was so much happening at once!

Skeffington's letter hung over her head like the sword of Damocles, though she was determined not to think of it. She pushed it out, it drifted back in, and she resolutely pushed it back out again.

Rusty had reached that perilous state in his recovery that all animals invariably did. They felt they were fully healed, and they were very close to it, but not quite. At that moment in their cure they felt driven to sow some oats, feeling the return to health. That, unfortunately, could bring on a setback. Arabella had resorted to the usual remedy to keep him on the quiet side—food. A lot of food. Thankfully, he was sleeping off a very big dinner when Madame LaForte had arrived to her bedchamber.

The modiste had come with a lovely dress, far more elegant

than anything Arabella had ever worn at dinner in Cornwall. It was a fine muslin slip dyed a deep blue with a match-colored silk overdress. Three silk cords twisted together, and of the same color, ran down the edges of the overdress right to the floor. There were no further embellishments and the charm of it was in the cut and the subtle details.

Arabella had not had any idea that there was so much to consider in designing a dress until Madame LaForte had explained it to her. Many modistes, according to the madame, would observe her fair looks and dress her in pale blues and yellows. This was a mistake, apparently. Pale colors would be insipid and make her look like a fairy cake.

Then, there was the further problem of Arabella being rather petite in stature. The solid color of the whole ensemble and the braiding running vertically would elongate her. As a final note, Madame LaForte made her promise she would never even think of wearing a horizontal stripe. It would chop her up and she'd look no better than a well-dressed mushroom.

She must suppose Madame LaForte knew her business as she did feel rather taller in the dress.

Along with the dress she wore this evening had come a riding habit. Her first riding habit. How she had longed for such a garment!

The jacket was a delightful bottle green with intricate braiding down the front and at the cuffs. The skirt was wonderfully full and she delighted in examining its construction. It was so clever, with the one side longer and the small loop to go over her wrist to hold it up when she was not on a horse.

Of course, she could not help wondering what Peregrine would think of it. He had promised to begin her lessons. She was determined to be skilled at riding; she did not wish to look foolish in front of him.

That led her to wondering what he was doing just now. He was right next door—would he wait to walk over until he'd seen many of the carriages arrive?

Lady Redfield had been circling the drawing room, peering into corners, and running her gloved fingers along the window-sills. Having completed the tour, she sped past Arabella toward the dining room.

The knocker on the front doors sounded with three sharp raps.

Lady Redfield froze in her tracks in the hall and stared at the door. Who was there? Had someone misunderstood the time?

Hemmings stepped forward and Arabella noticed he wore a *very* elaborately done neckcloth. There were so many knots to it that she thought it must take some time to get on and off. She hadn't known that a butler wore such a thing for a dinner, but she would tuck away that piece of information for when she had her own household to manage.

Hemmings nodded at Lady Redfield. It was a determined and comforting nod, as if to say, *Carry on, my lady. I will handle this.*

Lady Redfield nodded back and continued on her journey, no doubt to circle the dining table and assure herself that all was as it should be, just as she'd already done three times.

Hemmings disappeared from her view and Arabella heard the door being opened.

"Lord Blackwood," Hemmings said.

Arabella's breath caught. Someone *had* come early. Peregrine had come early.

"I am before time, I know," Lord Blackwood said from the hall. "I hope Lady Redfield does not mind it, we are neighbors after all. I see you still take Mr. Sindu's advice, Hemmings."

"I trust his judgment *almost* as much as my own, which I trust implicitly."

"Yes, I heard about that."

"Lady Redfield is still engaged in preparations, but Lady Arabella is in the drawing room, my lord."

"Excellent, yes."

Lord Blackwood came into the room.

Arabella worked to collect her thoughts. So far, the only two thoughts clamoring for attention were that Peregrine had come early. And why had Peregrine come early?

"Lady Arabella," he said bowing. "I suppose I am being a nuisance arriving before I was expected."

"Not at all, Lord Blackwood. We are always happy to see you." Truer words, thought Arabella. It seemed she *was* always happy to see him.

"Excellent, yes. Well, I did hope to catch you in private conversation before there were too many people milling about."

"Oh, you did?" Arabella asked. Her thoughts were swirling and repetitive now—*why, why, why?*

Lord Blackwood approached and motioned for her to sit. He said, "My mother has told me what Skeffington wants to do. He wants to send you away. I think it's vile."

"Yes, of course it is vile. He is vile," Arabella said.

"He cannot be allowed to get away with it," Lord Blackwood said.

"If he insists, I do not have any recourse," Arabella said. "But he can only insist for eleven more months and then he has no further hold on me."

"Those eleven months, though," Lord Blackwood said, looking at his hands as if there were something interesting in them, "the duchess said she feared he would try again to force you into a marriage."

"I will never be forced into a marriage," Lady Arabella said resolutely. "He might drag me into the church, but he cannot make me say the words."

"That is just what I think," Lord Blackwood said, looking up. "Nobody can force a person into marriage, no matter how much they wish to. That must be the person's own decision. For their own reasons."

Now it was Arabella who looked away. In a fit of daring, she said, "You at least have no concerns on that front, as I understand things are quite settled regarding Lady Constance."

She stole a glance at Lord Blackwood to see if he would confirm it. He looked as if he were searching his mind for what to say, then he shrugged.

"I'll tell you a confidence, as long as you keep it to yourself."

Arabella nodded, a little terrified over what she was to hear. He looked so serious! Had he and Lady Constance eloped and were already married and it was a great secret?

Softly, he said, "I have allowed my mother to go on with the delusion that I am not married because I've been waiting for Lady Constance. In fact, I am not married because I do not wish it for another two years at least. I have no intention of ever marrying Connie, she is like a sister to me. Though, I have no idea what I will say to the duchess when she eventually turns up. The truth must come out then, I suppose."

Arabella was at once gratified and struck down. He was not in love with Lady Constance, which was rather glorious to discover. But then, he was not in the least bit in love with anybody and would not even think about marriage for two years. What else could tell her more plainly that she was not at all in his thoughts? It seemed she was to be as a sister, too.

She'd been foolish to allow her feelings so much latitude on the subject of Lord Blackwood.

But then, her natural optimism began to tiptoe back. If there were one other bright spot, it was that he would not be married when she gained her majority and returned to London. Who knew what could happen then? She might bloom in those eleven months, she might even grow taller, though Mrs. Weston was convinced her growing days had long ended.

Lady Redfield fluttered into the room, looking this way and that as if checking that the furniture had not been moved while she'd been gone.

Lord Blackwood rose and bowed. "Lady Redfield, my apologies for crushing in early. I felt both you and Lady Arabella could use some support after hearing the news my mother relayed to me regarding Lord Skeffington."

"Lord Blackwood," Lady Redfield said, looking rather surprised, "that is very kind. Very kind, indeed."

"I do not presume to meddle with your seating arrangements," he went on, "but might I suggest that I take one side of Lady Arabella at dinner. She must be terribly shaken by recent developments, and it would be well to be seated by someone she already knows. Easier on the conversation-making side of things, if you see what I mean."

Lady Redfield peered at Arabella. "Oh dear, shaken, I hadn't thought. Are you shaken, my dear?"

Arabella *was* a bit shaken, though not for reasons Lady Redfield could guess at. "I am afraid I do find myself so," she said.

"Well of course, you would be, goodness I always think I'm the only one ever shaken as I do get shaken so often. Lord Blackwood, it is an excellent notion. I had planned on Lord Lymington doing the honors, the duchess does favor him, but that is all changed. You will take Arabella in. I'll put Lord Ryland on her other side. Yes, that will do very well."

Hemmings had appeared at the doorway. "My lady," he said.

Lady Redfield spun around and clutched at her neck. "Did something happen, what's happened, what's gone wrong?" she said.

"All is well, my lady. I only wished to go over the final wines list."

"Oh goodness, yes," she said, hurrying from the room.

"That was very kind," Arabella said. "To offer to take me in."

"As it happens, it was kinder than you know," Lord Blackwood said, laughing. "Lymington is a confounded fellow. He is the worst storyteller in the world. He always forgets some detail or other and then starts all over again."

"I understand he always likes to talk about horses."

"Always. Ask him anything in the world and he will bring it back round to horses. He's a jolly enough fellow, though."

They were silent for a moment, seeming to have run out of things to say. Finally, Lord Blackwood said, "That is a lovely dress. It does something for your eyes."

Arabella felt her face go red. Of all the things she and Mrs. Weston had spoken of and practiced in Cornwall, how to accept a compliment delivered by a gentleman had not been one of them. They really should have discussed it, particularly since Arabella was well aware that she did not blush prettily, but rather looked as if she'd been set afire.

"Are you well, Lady Arabella?" Lord Blackwood asked. "You look a bit feverish."

"Oh quite well, thank you," Arabella said, willing the scarlet from her face. "The dress, well, Madame LaForte says it makes me look taller, as she finds me too short."

"Too short?" Lord Blackwood said with admirable outrage. "Madame LaForte is deranged. What is this obsession with tall women? I do not understand it. I find *statuesque* to be a rather unfortunate condition. What gentleman wants to look straight ahead into a lady's face when a lady's face looks so much more charming upturned?"

Arabella took all this to mean that *he* did not find her too short and she was highly gratified to know it.

She heard the door knocker in the distance, though it seemed very far away. She was much too engrossed in upturning her face in case it looked charming. Even if it was still red.

"Peregrine!"

CHAPTER TEN

T HE DISTINCTIVE VOICE of the duchess pulled Arabella from her reverie. She fairly leapt up from the sofa and curtsied. "Your Grace," she said.

"Lady Arabella, you do look charming this evening, rather flushed, though. Peregrine, what do you do here so early? I only come myself because I know Cecilia works herself into a frenzy whenever people are to come through her door."

"I thought reinforcements might be required, considering what you informed me of yesterday," Lord Blackwood said smoothly, kissing his mother on the cheek. "As I am only next door, I thought I'd come early."

"You are a good sort of son, Peregrine. Always so attentive to anything I am involved in. I often lament those poor mothers who are saddled with sons who only wish to get away from them. I cannot fathom how they cope with it."

"Your company is always edifying," Peregrine said with a twinkle in his eye.

"Yes, yes," the duchess said, as if it were a foregone conclusion that her company was edifying. "But see here, Hemmings has gone mad and Cecilia has done nothing about it. The neckcloth, you know."

Arabella did not in fact know but was beginning to get the idea that maybe it was not so usual for a butler to don such neckwear for a dinner. Now that she was thinking about it, he might have been wearing it the day before too.

"I spoke to Mr. Sindu about it," Peregrine said, "but he says he only told Hemmings to follow his own judgment."

"Yes, that's what Hemmings says too. I am inclined to follow *my* own judgment in this matter. We will put it about that there is a secret society of butlers who serve in elevated houses who regularly meet to discuss the craft of superior service and exchange tips. Hemmings has been named the director of it, which is a great honor. The neckcloth signals that he is their elected leader."

Arabella pressed her lips together to stop from laughing. It seemed a rather complicated and farfetched sort of story.

"Mother," Peregrine said. "The questions such a fabrication would raise are endless. Who was the leader of this mystery society before? Where was *that* fellow's deranged neckcloth?"

"The neckcloth is new," the duchess said in supreme confidence. "It used to be sleeve buttons."

"I really think it would be more straightforward to just say the butler has gone temporarily mad. People will understand, they've got their own mad butlers at home."

"Nonsense. Lady Heathway and I are entirely agreed on the story," the duchess said. "Now, I must inform Cecilia and stop her fluttering about."

With that, the duchess sailed from the room, her signature brocade swishing behind her.

Peregrine and Arabella looked at each other. Arabella said, "Do you really have your own mad butler at home?"

Lord Blackwood shrugged. "Well, he's taken over my library, and doesn't take coats or open doors, so one of us is mad."

Arabella found herself delighted with that idea. When she'd lived in Cornwall, she'd developed a picture of what a London lord would be like. She imagined him terribly stern and running his house with an iron fist. It seemed Lord Blackwood was far more indulgent than that. She liked the idea very much.

"We are set to begin your riding lessons on the morrow?"

Lord Blackwood asked.

"Yes, yes, indeed," Arabella said, thrilled that he had not forgotten about it. Her new riding habit had come and been fitted, and all she now required was a horse and instruction.

"Let us go at ten o'clock in the morning," Lord Blackwood said. "It will be cool for the horses and there will not be many in the park. I presume you'd rather not be observed in the beginning stages of learning."

"I *would* rather not be observed," Arabella said gratefully. He really was so considerate to think of it.

"Bonny Betsy will be at the ready," Lord Blackwood said.

Lady Redfield hurried in with the duchess trailing behind and counseling her to slow down.

"You have heard about the secret society of butlers?" Lady Redfield asked. "And the sleeve buttons? We must all tell the same story."

Arabella nodded, though she did not know how in the world she would say anything about it without laughing.

Peregrine bowed. "The mysterious society that we know nothing about other than the director of it once wore sleeve buttons and now wears a diabolically tied neckcloth."

"Yes, that's the one," Lady Redfield said. "I've told Hemmings all about it and he's quite agreeable."

Arabella supposed he would be. There could not be anything particularly *disagreeable* in being made the director of a mysterious society.

The sound of carriages arriving penetrated the drawing room, the door knocker sounded, and the dashingly dressed butler strode through the hall.

"Here we go," the duchess said.

HEMMINGS HAD NEVER had an experience like it and silently

thanked Mr. Sindu. He'd followed his own judgment and barreled forward in a neckcloth and what was to be the result of it?

He was named the director of a mysterious society of butlers.

That there was, in fact, no such society mattered little. He had risen in estimation, entirely through his own efforts.

Since he had begun following his own judgment, he'd made other improvements. He'd pointed out to Lady Redfield that at so many of their previous dinners, guests were often milling about in the drawing room with nothing to eat or drink for too long a time. This was invariably due to some important person who was late. Lord Ryland, in particular, was notorious for coming late, always seeming to be held up by news of some crime or other.

Hemmings was firmly convinced that this made the beginning of the dinner rather dull, as everybody was starving and secretly resentful of the latecomer.

Lady Redfield had nodded as he talked, and then he offered the solution. Prior to dinner, he and the footmen would go round with glasses of champagne on trays. It would grease the wheels and the party would be merry upon sitting down at table.

Lady Redfield had vacillated about the idea, but he had pressed on until she agreed they might try it. Or at least, she hadn't said they couldn't.

It was a brilliant idea, sure to be taken up in other houses.

As far as Cecil Hemmings was concerned, there *ought* to be a mysterious butler's society and he *ought* to be its director.

PEREGRINE HAD FULLY expected the first guests to come through the door would be Lady Redfield's coterie of matrons. After all, the duchess had already arrived and he well knew those old girls were as thick as thieves. If talking to each other were money, they would all be rich as Croesus.

He was mightily surprised to find it was Ryland coming in

first.

Ryland was late to everything. He'd even, on occasion, been late to his own ball.

Why should he be on time for dinner at Lady Redfield's house?

As Lord Ryland practically sped toward Lady Arabella, he supposed that was why.

"Lady Arabella," Lord Ryland said with a quick bow.

"Lord Ryland," Lady Arabella said.

"I wonder if I may have a private word about…recent developments."

"Come now, Ryland," Peregrine said, "We all know you favor the cloak and dagger, but there cannot be anything so secret at a dinner."

It was a nonsensical thing to say, as evidenced by Ryland's expression.

"Lord Ryland," Lady Arabella said, "if it is regarding Lord Skeffington's plans regarding me, Lord Blackwood knows all about it from the duchess."

"I see, very well," Lord Ryland said. "I've paid a visit to Skeffington and alerted him that the string of seductions he's committed over the years is known by me and will be known by the wider world if he persists in sending you away. Society already knows he is a rogue, but they do not know how much of a rogue."

"Oh, I quite agree on that point," Lady Arabella said. "I suspect he's got some terrible secrets in his closet. I am sure it was unpleasant to approach him on the matter and so I do thank you, Lord Ryland, for making the effort on my behalf."

Peregrine did not see why Ryland must be thanked. The fellow was only doing what a gentleman must do.

He paused his thoughts, uncomfortable in the knowledge that he himself had not yet determined what to do.

Of course, he would think of something.

"Only God knows if Skeffington cares enough about his reputation to be chastened by my threat," Lord Ryland said.

"I can only be gratified that you have tried it," Lady Arabella said.

This was too much. She'd already thanked him, which was more than was necessary. Now she was gratified, too?

"I say, Ryland," Peregrine said, "can you give us any hints regarding the mystery you will pose at your ball's supper? Any chance you can give us a running start on the thing?"

This was, of course, meant to get Ryland off the subject of how helpful he'd been to Lady Arabella, as he had been thanked twice already, and onto the subject the man liked most—crime.

As Ryland nattered on about not giving out any information ahead, but hinting at how intricate the solution would be, Peregrine surveyed the room.

More guests had arrived and the apparent confusion over Hemmings and his neckcloth—who he was and what he was— seemed to be verging on the operatic.

He'd just heard the duchess loudly say, "No, I don't know the name of the society, it is a very great secret."

Lady Bretherington said something further and the duchess answered, "Yes, it used to be sleeve buttons."

If that were not amusing enough, Hemmings had just appeared in the doorway carrying a tray of champagne glasses and had begun handing them out to surprised guests.

Peregrine assumed this was another of Hemmings' efforts to follow his own judgment. Surprising though it was, he could not be against that particular idea.

Lady Redfield hurried over to them and said, "Arabella, do come and be introduced to Lord Lymington."

She led Arabella away and Ryland moved off, seeming to find no more reason to stay. Peregrine watched Lady Featherstone catch sight of Ryland and start moving through the crowd after him like a trout fighting against the current. Only, this trout was clutching the emerald brooch she'd won at Ryland's last mystery evening.

Lymington was talking enthusiastically to Lady Arabella, and Peregrine could not know the particular story he was telling. Only that it would be about horses and it would go round and round until eventually petering out at the end—very like water circling down a drain. Lymington generally concluded one of his circuitous tales with something profound like, "Horses, you know."

Peregrine took a glass of champagne from Hemmings' tray and drank it down.

ARABELLA HAD SMILED until her face felt as if it would crack. Everything she'd been told about Lord Lymington had been correct. It had been a full ten minutes of talking to inform her that he once had a stallion who was adept at opening gates. Somehow, when she was certain he was nearly finished, he'd recall that he'd forgotten a salient fact, like the horse was bought at Newmarket, and then start all over again.

She had been vastly relieved when Lord Blackwood had come to collect her. More than relieved, really. How wonderful that she would sit next to him at dinner, rather than Lord Lymington. She really did not know how she would have managed it if Lord Blackwood had not stepped in and suggested the change.

And of course, Lord Ryland was very pleasant too. In his way.

The courses had begun to come out and Arabella heard various tidbits of conversation from around the table. Who had heard of this mysterious butler's society?

Had anybody been told what the sleeve buttons had looked like?

Had anybody ever noticed their own butler wearing unusual sleeve buttons?

How long had such a thing been going on and why the sudden change to a neckcloth?

Is the knot some kind of symbol? I've never seen such a thing.

"My mother has created a monster with that story she and Lady Heathway cooked up between them," Lord Blackwood said in a low voice.

"But why does Mr. Hemmings wear the neckcloth really, now that I understand it's not the done thing?" Arabella asked.

"Apparently, *my* butler told him to follow his own judgment. And that's his judgment."

"I see. Well, I do not suppose anybody could seriously be bothered by it."

"No," Lord Blackwood said. "It is just startling."

"He does look a bit dashing, though," Arabella said.

Lord Blackwood appeared to take exception to this. He said, "You know, dashing is not all it's made out to be, often. Oh, there are some gentlemen who appear dashing and go running off to accomplish errands and then expect to be thanked for it. I wonder about them. That is all I say."

Arabella had no idea what he was saying, nor why he was looking past her and at the back of Lord Ryland's head. She could think of no response at all.

"Did Skeffington ever tell you the name of the old fellow he was trying to push you to?" Lord Blackwood asked.

Arabella had not seen the change in topic coming, nor did she understand what it could signify. She said, "It was Rendiver. Lord Rendiver. Apparently, he is from the environs of York and he is a widower with a number of grown sons."

"Rendiver?" Lord Blackwood asked, the shock evident on his features. "Rendiver is not just a little old, he is *old* old. The last I saw the man was three years ago and even then he looked like he had one foot in the grave."

"I have been wondering," Arabella said, "what his part in this could be. Certainly, Skeffy has something to gain, though I know not what in particular. But what is this gentleman's part in it and why would he think I'd be amenable to throwing my life away in such a manner?"

Lord Blackwood looked thoughtful. "If a man has a hold upon another, it is usually a debt. As for Rendiver, certainly he thinks of your dowry, though why he might imagine you would agree to the noxious idea, I do not know. Perhaps he thought you would simply be guided by your guardian."

"Well if that is what he imagined, then he has quite the imagination," Arabella said.

Lady Redfield turned to the duke, signaling everybody else to turn to speak to their opposite dinner partner.

Arabella smiled at Lord Blackwood, and then turned to Lord Ryland.

"I understand from Lady Featherstone," Lord Ryland said, "that you have a great interest and rather vast experience with all sorts of woodland creatures."

"Yes, I suppose that is true," Arabella said. "When I lived in Cornwall, I cared for many injured animals."

"Interesting," Lord Ryland said. "I have not come across so very many wounded animals in my travels."

"I went looking for them," Arabella said.

"Ah, I see. I wonder then, if I might explain to you an unsolved and ongoing case involving a man who swears that a badger is stalking him with the intent of murdering him. The man has suffered financially on account of how many days he could not leave the house to do his work as the creature was circling his cottage and attempting to get in. He says it is vital to get rid of the thing before summer or his livelihood will be in shambles. No number of traps can trick the wily creature and he seems to always manage to avoid gunshots."

Arabella was surprised by the tale, as Lord Bushwick would never have behaved in such a bizarre manner.

"Goodness," she said, "how long has this been going on?"

"Two months, apparently," Lord Ryland said, "though it was only brought to my attention a fortnight ago. The very first day it happened, the man had just opened his door to find a badger running at him at full speed. He slammed the door shut, the badger crashed into it, and then the creature stayed at the door above an hour, clawing at it. That has since happened more than a few times. The man is scared out of his wits."

"And what does this poor man do for a living?"

"He is a beekeeper."

Upon hearing that the fellow was a beekeeper, the real case of things presented itself with all clarity in Arabella's mind.

She laughed and said, "The poor dear fellow. Here it is with spring just coming on, food sources for the badger will have been limited for the last few months. Your gentleman no doubt keeps an ample supply of his wares in his house, I presume. You see? The badger is only hungry and can smell the abundance of honey. He ought to feed it—apples from last season would do very well, but nuts or even bread in a pinch. Spring will advance and the badger will move off. Though, the gentleman ought to take steps to protect his beehives this summer. Badgers don't seem to mind stings at all, and they do so like honey."

"Yes, of course. I had not taken the man's occupation into consideration," Lord Ryland said. "Very clever, Lady Arabella."

Arabella nodded, but did not think there was much clever in it. Lord Bushwick and his friends had supplied the necessary information. She had once come upon a badger tearing apart a bee's nest, quite impervious to the swarm. She had been very lucky that the bees had not turned on her as she'd slowly backed away and left the scene of destruction. As well, Lord Bushwick himself had found a jar of honey in the pantry and laid waste to it.

Arabella felt a sudden clawing on her neck. She jumped as tiny pinpricks, very like bee stings, dug into her skin.

Then she was apprised of what had caused the sudden stinging.

Rusty had escaped her bedchamber. Now, he leapt on the table, sat on his hind legs, and nervously looked around, his eyes blinking rapidly. His bandaging was barely hanging on, as if he'd been working to get it off.

The shrieks accompanying his entrance grew louder. Lady

Redfield stared transfixed at the squirrel as Rusty made his way to a bowl of peas and sniffed at it. He picked up a pea between his tiny hands and ate it. Finding it satisfactory, he grabbed at another one.

Lord Ryland stood up. "Hemmings, fetch me a bag and I will clear the table of this rodent."

Arabella jumped up from her own chair. "No bag will be necessary, Lord Ryland. I will handle this."

She reached over to the bowl of peas and slowly pulled it toward her. Rusty followed, and the tableful of diners sunk into a horrified silence.

CHAPTER ELEVEN

WHEN RUSTY WAS in reach, she picked him up by the scruff of the neck, his four legs clawing at the air. Arabella swept up the bowl of peas too and walked quickly from the room.

As she climbed the stairs, she heard somebody say, "How could it have come from outdoors when it was wearing a bandage?"

Somebody else answered with, "Never mind the bandage, why is it going up the stairs rather than out the door?"

She jogged the rest of the way up and went into her room, kicking the door closed behind her.

"You really could not have been more naughty," she said, as Rusty looked at her with dark eyes. She set the bowl of peas on a table and plunked Rusty down next to it.

He seemed entirely oblivious to the havoc he'd caused, as he was wholly entranced by the peas.

Arabella deftly unwound what remained of his bandage. There was always a moment when it must be admitted that one of her patients was ready to return to the wild. Rusty's moment had come.

She opened the window, the sound of it causing his mother and brother to poke their heads out of their nest. She reached as far as she could and deposited a large handful of mildly crushed peas on the branch nearby them. Then, she carried Rusty to the window, placed him on the branch, and said, "Off you go."

Rusty scurried happily to the peas, his leg having no limp at all. His family came out to meet him there, and the recovery and reunification were complete.

"Now," she said to herself, closing the window, "I just must go back down and face everybody."

⇒⇒⇒×⇐⇐⇐

HEMMINGS WAS POSITIVELY staggered. It was meant to be *his* night. He was to introduce himself to the world as the butler wearing a neckcloth who was the esteemed director of a mysterious society.

It had started exceedingly well! By the time the guests entered the dining room, he had become known as the new director.

At table, many of the guests glanced at him when they thought they could do so unobserved.

Naturally, Cecil Hemmings observed everything.

They wondered about this society. They wondered how long it had been going on. They especially wondered if their own butlers had been admitted to it. Or if they hadn't, why not?

Lady Redfield had garnered some acclaim and renown as the lady whose butler was the actual director of the thing.

As well, the baron's sparkling wine served in the drawing room before dinner had been very well-received. He'd even overheard one lady say to another that the idea had likely come from the society.

Of course, it had been his idea alone, but he did not go so far as to disabuse her of her theory. Let the society take the credit, *he* knew the truth of it.

Cook's dinner had been received especially well, and Oscar and William acquitted themselves exceptionally.

It was the most perfect evening of his life until…

Until a squirrel had the audacity to mar his table.

And not just any squirrel. A squirrel that Lady Arabella was apparently already acquainted with.

Had it been living in the house? Right under his nose? Was that why the lady was always carrying up food in a napkin to her bedchamber? He'd thought she'd acted as a squirrel, but had she been actually feeding one?

Whatever the true circumstance, he would get to the bottom of it.

Lady Redfield had been entirely shaken. Lady Arabella, though, had seemed rather brazen about the whole thing. She'd returned to the dining room, having deposited the creature somewhere in the house, and laughingly said, "Squirrels *will* be squirrels."

The guests, being the well-bred people that they were, had all smiled as if they understood her and carried on with the dinner.

It was all exceedingly ghastly.

For now, he must do what he could to salvage the situation. The ladies had retired to the drawing room and the men sat over their port. Hemmings made certain the port flowed copiously. The ladies would have their coffee and tea tray. To further smooth matters, Hemmings had sent Oscar into the drawing room with another round of champagne.

Inebriation might be the only salve for this grievous wound.

PEREGRINE HAD CONSUMED his fair share of port after dinner. All the gentlemen had, as Hemmings never allowed a glass to go dry.

Naturally, much of the conversation had been taken up by two subjects—what did anybody know of this secret society the butlers had thrown together, and where had the squirrel come from?

He did not share what information he knew, which was more than anybody else did. There was no secret society, only a deranged duchess and her friend inventing the fabulist tale. As for the squirrel, he highly suspected his name was Rusty, and that he was Lady Arabella's project she had so recently written to Freddy about.

Ryland was often looked to, as he was meant to be the great solver of mysteries. He was far less concerned with the squirrel than he was with the butler's society. Peregrine was certain he was racked with frustration to think that there had been a secret society that had remained a secret from him.

Lymington, as was ever his habit, could not keep up with the conversation, as it had nothing to do with horses. He looked at turns lost and bored.

Peregrine's father, the duke, had been vastly entertained by all the goings on of the evening. He said it reminded him of the sort of eccentric parties his mother had thrown in the 1770s. He relayed the story of the duchess hosting a country party one summer that he'd watched unfold from the top of the stairs. It had been a hot night and all the doors and windows had been opened to let in the air. A goose wandered in through an open door and joined the illustrious company for dinner. Nobody had blinked an eye when it settled itself under the table. Though, various gentlemen had used the opportunity to goose their neighbor and blame it on the bird. Of those daring to try out the joke, King George was one, if the queen's shriek had been anything to go by.

Now, the men had repaired to the drawing room, and it had become a very merry party. Peregrine supposed it could not have been anything other than merry, seeing as Hemmings kept bringing in more champagne. As Lady Arabella very sensibly played the pianoforte rather than drank champagne, Peregrine had taken in the room.

If he was not mistaken, the duchess was a little tipsy. At least, he would assume so, as she'd just spilled an entire cup of tea on her dress. The duke was fast asleep in a chair. Ryland and Lymington were in a pointless argument over the cause of a thoroughbred's speed—was it the animal's lighter weight or larger lungs? Peregrine had heard them both make the same points over and over, like any drunken debate that was had in the wee hours at White's.

Lady Bretherington and Mrs. Roundly had cornered Hemmings and were attempting to wheedle information out of him about the secret society. Hemmings appeared flattered by it, clasping his hands in front of himself and nodding sagely.

Peregrine had actually heard him say, "Ladies, I would hardly be named the director if I could not keep the details of it secret." Peregrine wondered what those ladies would think when they woke on the morrow and realized they had cornered a butler and conducted an interrogation.

Peregrine, himself, had been watching it all unfold in a corner, taking glasses of champagne as they came round. When he was not being amused by some ridiculousness before him, he was deep in thought. He was determined to do something on Lady Arabella's behalf. For one, she was being treated abominably. For another, he would like it very much for Ryland to stop being thanked for doing something.

But what could he do? What did he have at his disposal? He did not have spies all over London like he suspected Ryland did.

As the party finally broke up, and there were various ladies leaning heavily on their gentleman's arms to get to their carriage in an upright state, it finally came to Peregrine.

He knew some things Ryland did not know. Ryland only knew that Skeffington planned to send his ward to some bleak northern outpost for no good reason at all. At least, he thought that was how much Ryland knew. Peregrine knew of Skeffington's desire to marry the lady off, and he more particularly knew who the gentleman in question was. He did not think even the duchess knew it was Rendiver. Who had even thought of Rendiver recently? The fellow hadn't been to Town in years.

That was his weapon. The knowledge that it was Rendiver.

He'd very determinedly weaved out of Lady Redfield's house and back into his own. He'd called for his carriage, despite Mr.

Sindu telling him he ought to go to bed.

What did that fellow know about chivalry?

When a gentleman set upon a course, the gentleman must forge ahead. The gentleman must not be turned from his purpose. The gentleman certainly did not pause to go to bed!

In any case, he was being very practical in calling for the carriage, rather than his horse. Nobody of any sense rode a horse after so many glasses of champagne, wine, and port.

Did Mr. Sindu consider that? Did he consider that Peregrine Hadleigh was a peer of the realm and must act honorably, even though it might be a great deal of trouble to him and he was very tired and would like to go to bed?

He thought not.

Mr. Sindu might have taken over his library, but he had not taken over his standards.

Linus had helped him into the carriage and he directed Bullford to take him to White's in no uncertain terms. Skeffington would be there. He was always there until dawn, gambling and drinking.

He would just take a short nap on the way.

ARABELLA HAD RETIRED after assuring herself that Lady Redfield was not too angry over Rusty's appearance at the dining table.

Good Lady Redfield, she was so kind! Of course, the matter had shaken her as it had not been at all what she had anticipated. She had been further shaken to understand that Rusty had been living in the house for quite some time. Arabella had soothed her with the idea that Rusty had since been returned to his family and would make no further appearances.

Overall, Lady Redfield had thought the dinner rather a success. The story the duchess and Lady Heathway had invented to account for Hemmings' neckcloth had played wonderfully well.

She also hinted that she thought both Lord Ryland and Lord Lymington had expressed no little interest in Arabella.

Arabella had admirably controlled her laughter over the idea of Lord Lymington. He would have not the slightest interest in her, unless she were to be found behind a stable door, suddenly transformed into a horse. As for Lord Ryland, even at dinner he was attempting to unravel mysteries. Murderous badger, indeed.

It did pain her just a moment that there was no mention of Lord Blackwood admiring her. Though, she felt that he did. At least, a little bit.

In any case, if there was any real success in the evening, it was to be laid at Hemmings' door. Not for his role in the invented secret society, but for his liberality with Lady Redfield's champagne. The party had got very merry under its ministrations and all thought of a squirrel on the table seemed to have been at least momentarily forgotten.

Arabella hoped it would stay forgotten, though she feared it would not. Lady Redfield herself might have other thoughts about it on the morrow, once the haze of champagne bubbles had left her.

She heard a carriage rumble to a stop outside. Arabella moved to the window and peered out.

It was Lord Blackwood's carriage. Goodness, where did he go so late in the night?

She cracked her window open, though she could not say why. She certainly was not going to call to him. She had not drunk so much champagne as to think *that* would be a good idea.

Lord Blackwood came down the steps, with his footman hurrying behind him.

He stopped, and he swayed. The footman took his arm with one hand and opened the carriage door with another.

Before he got in, Arabella heard him say, "Bullford! To White's. A scoundrel awaits!"

Bullford did not seem alarmed to hear it, as he only nodded. Arabella, though, was not so sure Lord Blackwood ought to be going out on the town in his current condition. Or setting off to see a scoundrel, whoever he may be. She hoped he was not planning on gambling. His ability to keep track of the cards would not be very expert just now.

Goodness, they were meant to meet at ten the next morning for her first riding lesson. She was not so certain Lord Blackwood would be in any shape to do so.

Arabella closed the window. There was nothing to do about it but wait to see what happened tomorrow morning at ten.

She would be ready, in any case.

LORD SKEFFINGTON SAT in his breakfast room with his coffee, brooding on his current situation. His head pounded and he felt the walls closing in—he was being pressed from all sides. Why on God's green earth did all these people think they had to interfere with his affairs? All over a chit of a girl who ought to be nothing to them.

The Duke of Stanbury had threatened to get him blackballed from White's. Lord Langley had pointedly told him he had the queen's ear and would discuss the matter with her majesty. Lord Gresham had threatened to get him blackballed from the Jockey Club, which would have severe repercussions on his purse, as he laid large bets there during the races. Lord Ryland had hinted darkly that he knew more about his liaisons than society would be willing to tolerate.

He was well aware that he was not particularly liked by any of those gentlemen, but he had not expected them to openly cross him over such a matter. He doubted they would have bothered, had they not been pressured into it by that ridiculous group of old women who liked to stir up trouble. They called themselves a society. He called them a rabble.

He was not certain what exactly Ryland knew about his liaisons, but he did not think he knew about the worst secret. The only secret that would entirely undo him. If he did, he would have said so. There had been only five people, including himself, who had ever known of that. Three were dead, and the fourth had no ability to pose any trouble.

As if all of that were not troublesome enough, he'd been accosted by Lord Blackwood the evening before at White's.

Blackwood somehow knew about Rendiver, which the others did not seem to. Blackwood claimed if he did not give up on his idea of sending Lady Arabella away, he would write to Rendiver and explain to him how revolted Lady Arabella had been upon being approached on the matter.

The drunken lout had then shouted, "Revolted, you hear me, revolted," three times. For himself, he'd finally left the club room after Blackwood had tripped over a chair, landed on the floor, and shouted, "Revolted," for the fourth time.

He did not think Blackwood understood the precise repercussions of such a letter. The fellow thought to shame Rendiver into backing off. He could not know that Rendiver had already been assured of Lady Arabella's agreement to the match.

It would be disastrous. Rendiver would call in his debt, he could not pay it, and then he really would be blackballed everywhere. He'd be one of those idiots who'd make a run to the continent and hope things would somehow sort themselves out, which they never would.

The door swung open and one of the footmen hurried in with a letter on a salver. "From the palace, my lord," the boy said breathlessly.

"What new circle of hell is this?" he said, snatching the letter from the tray.

He ripped it open and his heart sank even lower than it had been all morning.

Lord Skeffington—

A recent situation has been brought to my attention. It appears that you are guardian to a certain Lady Arabella Berestock. I was on very friendly terms with her departed father, and perhaps should have taken more of an interest in how the child got on over the years. Let me rectify that at once. The girl is currently being housed and chaperoned by Lady Redfield, a respectable lady. I see no reason why she should be ripped away from those who care for her and sent to live in some place that is foreign to her. Further, I am told that she is twenty. High time to get her married, in my opinion.

I do not favor the idea of sending her away. I do not find favor with it at all.

Charlotte, R

It was the final blow. The queen might not have said outright that he would pay if he continued with his plan. But it was plain enough, nonetheless. She could not truly give a fig what happened to the girl. No, Langley and his wife had talked her into taking a stand on the matter.

He must think of something to get round all these people, the queen included.

Over the next hour and three cups of coffee, he turned the problem round in his mind, looking at it from all angles.

It was impossible to send Lady Arabella away now. His idea that he could wear her down with privation would not succeed.

He must find a new approach.

Suddenly, an idea presented itself that was not particularly comfortable, but just might pull him out of this mess.

He would change the arrangement with Rendiver. Lady Arabella had experienced a sudden change of heart. She found her affections were elsewhere and, in fact, directed at his *own* person. In light of the trouble Rendiver had been put to thus far, he would vow to pay his debt and add two-thousand as soon as he was in possession of the lady's dowry.

Of course, Rendiver would agree to it. It would present the money he looked for, and would be so much less trouble than taking on a wife.

The only other piece of the puzzle was how to convince Lady Arabella.

He could not do it by force. No, he'd tried that and it had not worked. All he'd got for his trouble during the ill-omened trip to Cornwall was a coat in tatters and a lame horse. For all he knew of it, Lady Arabella just now housed *ten* badgers in Lady Redfield's house, ready to spring at him if she felt threatened.

He'd need to charm his way in.

Lord Skeffington drained the last of his coffee. He could do it, he was sure. She may not like him now, but he was a master at overcoming objections when it came to a lady's heart. Was he not known as the worst sort of blackguard for his ability to charm the skirts off any lady he set his sights on?

Unfortunately, he'd have to actually marry this one to get what he wanted. Of course, once married he would be in control. He could send her off to one of his estates where she could twiddle her thumbs forevermore. Nobody could tell him what to do with a wife.

Nobody ever had.

CHAPTER TWELVE

A RABELLA HAD BEEN up and rung for Flora by nine. She had suspected Flora would be free and Lady Redfield would remain abed this morning, and she'd been right.

According to Flora, Lady Redfield had just drunk a glass of bicarbonate of soda, taken a spoonful of laudanum, had vinegar rubbed on her temples, and had gone back to sleep. The maid had never seen her mistress in such a state as last evening. Arabella was to tell nobody, but Lady Redfield had fallen on the floor in her bedchamber and then laughed hysterically while Flora attempted to get her up. It had taken no end of time to get the lady into her nightdress and into bed. Though, once she was in it, she was asleep before Flora blew out the last candle.

Arabella had nodded gravely and suppressed the urge to laugh at the picture painted.

For herself, she was bursting with energy. Last evening, she had been very cautious with the wine and champagne and had only tea in the drawing room. Mrs. Weston had often laid out the dangers of drink, especially for a lady. She had allowed Arabella wine with dinner once she'd turned fifteen and had not pro-scribed the amount Arabella might take in, so that she might understand her limits. Arabella had made some mistakes in those early days and paid for them the following day. Not just in headache and stomach upset, but by hearing all the stupid things she'd said while under the influence of the wine. She'd caught on to the right amounts after not too many unpleasant episodes. It had been a valuable lesson—she never wished to wake and regret something she did or said.

In any case, there was enough to regret without wine being thrown into the mix, thanks to Rusty. This morning, the little devil had taken to running over to the window and peering in, and then racing off in a game with his brother. He had absolutely no remorse for breaking into Lady Redfield's dinner party.

Flora had helped her into her riding habit and she'd break-fasted, and now she waited in the drawing room. She was not entirely sure if Lord Blackwood would come. He might very well still be abed with his own bicarbonate of soda.

She heard the familiar clip-clopping of horses' hooves out of doors. Arabella leapt up and raced to the window.

There was Lady Redfield's carriage and there were two horses besides. One was a very grand stallion, who must certainly be Lord Blackwood's Alfie. And then behind, a charming mare. Bonny Betsy, it must be.

She raced to the door just as Hemmings came to find her.

"Yes, I see them, Mr. Hemmings," she said. "I shall go out to them."

"One moment, my lady," Hemmings said, lightly stroking his newly-starched and seemingly permanent neckcloth. "For propriety's sake, I have made arrangements. Lander will drive you to the park. A groom and Oscar will accompany you by riding outside the carriage. On no account is the carriage to be out of sight at any time. Lord Blackwood will know to take the old King's Road so that it may follow you. Lady Redfield would, naturally, have made the same arrangements. Had she not still been abed."

Arabella nodded at these directives, finding them as sensible as anything Mrs. Weston might have arranged. In truth, she was rather relieved that she was not to mount Bonny Betsy until they were in the park, as she did not like to imagine falling off and landing on cobblestones.

She donned her rather jaunty hat and hurried out the door.

Lord Blackwood was coming out of his own door and, surprisingly, did not look the worse for wear. In truth, he looked marvelous in his buckskins and close-tailored blue coat. It really complemented his coloring exceedingly well.

"Lady Arabella," he said, with a dashing bow. "Shall we proceed? I do not like to keep horses standing for too long."

"Yes, of course, Lord Blackwood," she said. Oscar held the door for her while Lander nodded his appreciation of not keeping horses standing about for no reason.

Arabella got in and sat back. The park was very nearby. She would have her first experience on a horse within the quarter hour.

THE HOUR THAT Arabella had just experienced had been thrilling. Lord Blackwood had shown himself a very thorough and patient instructor.

First, he'd advised getting to know Bonny Betsy by standing by her head, stroking her nose, and talking to her so the mare would become accustomed to her voice.

Then, he'd shown her how to mount, and had helped her do it. For someone so tall and lean, his arms had been remarkably strong. She would never have guessed at his strength. She would never have guessed how struck she'd be to have his strong hands touching her.

In truth, she'd been flustered by it, and afraid that her face had burst into unattractive flames. Lord Blackwood had not commented on it and only assumed she found herself nervous to be upon a horse. That turned out fortuitous, as he directed her to just sit calmly on the horse and get used to it until her nerves settled. They did finally settle, though Bonny Betsy had never been the cause of them.

He'd gone on to teach her how to use her left leg, or the crop on her right, and her reins to direct the horse on where she wished to go and how fast she wished to get there. For this lesson, *how fast* was strictly confined to a walk.

She did not mind at all going forward sedately, as it gave her time to get the feel of riding and it was also conducive to talking.

Lord Blackwood had pressed her for details regarding a certain squirrel who had made a surprise appearance on Lady Redfield's table and she had told him all about Rusty. He'd seemed very charmed with the story.

While he could not claim to have any deep feelings for a squirrel, he did lay claim to his affection for his horse and his dog.

"Alfie and Apollo are the two beings I love most in the world," he said.

Arabella had smiled and said, "It is not your parents?"

"Oh, them. Yes. Well, you know what I mean."

"Yes, I think I do," she'd answered.

They'd gone on to thoroughly discuss Hemmings' neckcloth, neither of them particularly opposed to it, though both of them wondering what sort of havoc the idea of a secret society would cause.

Now, they walked along a shady part of the road and Lord Blackwood said, "I was determined to see Lord Skeffington on your behalf, Lady Arabella, and I have."

Arabella was startled. She'd had no idea Lord Blackwood had any notion of approaching Skeffy.

"You have?" she asked.

"Indeed I have," he said. "I went to my club to find him last evening and of course he was there, he is always there late at night. I told him in no uncertain terms that he is to throw over the idea of sending you away. I was terribly firm and decisive about it."

Arabella suspected he *had* been rather firm and decisive, if his resolute expression now was anything to go by.

"What did he say to it, my lord?" she asked, fairly holding her breath for the answer.

"Oh, he'll give it up," Lord Blackwood said. "I am very convinced of it."

Arabella was beyond gratified. To think, Lord Blackwood had been setting off to his club to confront Skeffington when she'd seen him leave in his carriage the night before.

Certainly, that must hint at some regard? It seemed so. Would a gentleman go to such trouble for one he only viewed casually in a sisterly fashion? She could not be sure, but it did not seem likely.

And then, he was convinced he'd overcome her guardian!

All of Lady Redfield's friends had attempted to help, but it would be Lord Blackwood who was able to put a stop to the whole thing.

"Thank you so very much, Lord Blackwood. I can only be gratified that you made such an effort, when the difficulty is my own and not yours."

Lord Blackwood looked exceedingly pleased with the sentiment. "Lady Arabella, when a gentleman sees a wrong, that gentleman must make every effort to right it. No matter how late at night it must be done."

"That is very gallant," Arabella said.

Lord Blackwood seemed even more pleased to be named gallant. And why shouldn't he be? He must have been very tired last evening, at least he had certainly looked so when he'd set off. Another gentleman might have waited for morning, or more likely, done nothing at all.

They rode on in silence for some minutes, the only sounds the crunching of the carriage wheels that followed them, and the soft clip-clop of the horses.

As they were coming upon their original starting point, Arabella said, "Lord Ryland's ball is in two days' time. Do you attend it?"

Lord Blackwood did not seem over-enthusiastic to hear of it, which Arabella thought odd. She had assumed they were friends.

"Oh yes, I'll likely go," he said grudgingly. "Though, everybody does make such a fuss over it."

"I do not know about everybody," Arabella said, "but Lady

Featherstone is keenly looking forward to it."

Lord Blackwood smiled to himself. "That lady solved the mystery last season, the emerald brooch, you know. Nobody can fathom how she did it. She is a genial lady, but not exactly an incisive mind."

"Beginner's luck?"

Lord Blackwood erupted in laughter. "If only she were a beginner. Lady Featherstone has been working at it since Ryland began hosting such balls."

Arabella did not respond, though she could not fail to see the humor in it. Lady Featherstone was a darling, and so she wished her the same luck she'd had last season.

"You will attend it?" Lord Blackwood asked.

"Yes, Lady Redfield says that we will."

They had returned to where they had begun and Arabella was sorry for it. Bonny Betsy had been ever so kind and Lord Blackwood, well, he had been everything good.

LADY REDFIELD HAD not thought she would see her friends the day after her dinner. In truth, she would have preferred to stay abed all the day long. She really did not know how Hemmings' idea of serving a glass of champagne before dinner had ended up as also serving champagne after dinner. And so many glasses!

She could not say that the many glasses that had circulated had been unwanted, everybody seemed eager enough to take them, but what a head she had now.

Nevertheless, the duchess had arrived, then Lady Heathway, then Lady Featherstone, and finally Lady Easton. Only Lady Mendleton was missing, and she was no doubt at home with the very advanced baby.

"I thought you ought to be alerted at once," the duchess said. "Of course, Lady Heathway and I could not have foreseen how the story would grow wings. Everywhere I went today, it is all that's talked of."

"Lord Ryland told me he cannot fathom how such a thing has gone on under his nose for so long a time without him hearing anything about it. Did we say how long it had been in existence? I do not believe we did. In any case, he questioned his butler about it, but the man says he's never heard of the society."

"Well he wouldn't, would he?" Lady Easton said. "It doesn't exist."

"Yes, but Lady Clara now claims her butler is a part of it, and Lord Jeffreys said he'd been aware of it for quite some time," Lady Heathway said. "What are they thinking, laying claim to a society that does not exist?"

"Perhaps nobody wishes to be left out?" Lady Redfield ventured.

"It's a bit of a pickle," Lady Featherstone said. "Now Hemmings can never take that neckcloth off, lest people start looking around for the *new* director."

Lady Redfield sighed, as it seemed the neckcloth was permanent. Attempting to find the positive in it, she said, "At least all this talk about the neckcloth has overshadowed the idea that there was a squirrel on my dining room table last evening."

"Not entirely," Lady Heathway said. "The version that seems to be most accepted is that you have a pet squirrel and it is very fond of Arabella."

"Oh dear," Lady Redfield said. "I should not like Lord Skeffington to hear it. It would be one more arrow in his quiver about why Arabella should not stay with me."

As the ladies considered Lord Skeffington, the drawing room door opened and Hemmings entered, resplendent in his neckcloth.

"Lord Skeffington has come to call, my lady," he said in disapproving tones.

"What? Here?" Lady Redfield cried.

The lord himself walked round Hemmings and entered the

room. "Ladies," he said, "I hope I have not come at an inconvenient time."

"Lord Skeffington," Lady Redfield said. She felt fairly terrorized. Why had he come rather than send another letter? Did he come to forcibly remove Arabella from the house? She would like to ask him those questions, but all she could manage was saying his name.

"Lord Skeffington," the duchess said, "no doubt you thought to come here and find Lady Redfield alone and run over her with force. It will not do, her friends are with her and we will not depart. Furthermore, this idea of sending Lady Arabella to some remote location in the north is scandalous and will not be borne by polite society. Though, I wonder how much *polite* society has ever concerned you."

Lady Redfield had at first been gratified when the duchess had started talking. But then, she'd kept going. Lord Skeffington would go mad over her words against him.

She was rather surprised to see the lord smiling. And, it was not that awful smile she'd experienced in his drawing room, the smile that was not really a smile. He was looking downright friendly. What was the meaning of it?

"Ladies," he said smoothly, "I have no wish for anyone to depart the room as what I have come to say can be known publicly. First, Lady Redfield, rest assured that I have reversed my decision and will not remove Lady Arabella from your competent care."

Lady Redfield was staggered. Who was this gentleman? He looked like Lord Skeffington, but he did not talk like Lord Skeffington.

Could it be that all of the pressure her friends had exerted on him had produced this miraculous turnaround? All she had hoped for was a grudging defeat. Now, he looked positively happy. It was exceedingly strange.

"Second," Lord Skeffington continued, "I believe I owe you an explanation for my actions thus far. You see, I have been blind to my own inclinations. I suppose gentlemen are prone to such things, at least Miss Austen would have you believe it. I have acted in a contrary fashion because the truth of it is…I wish to marry Lady Arabella. I know she does not favor me at this particular moment and I thought perhaps if she were away from London for a time I might place myself back in her good graces."

The ladies stared at Lord Skeffington. Lady Heathway said, "You are not serious?"

"Indeed, I am."

"But Lord Skeffington," Lady Featherstone said, "if I am to examine the facts, as I am wont to do thanks to Lord Ryland's training, is it not true that you attempted to force Lady Arabella into a marriage with some older gentleman from the environs of Yorkshire?"

"That was years ago," Lord Skeffington said. "Before I realized that I loved her. In any case, *forced* is a strong word. If I had forced her, it would have come to pass. I mentioned it, and the idea was rejected. That is all."

"Lord Skeffington," Lady Easton said with a sniff, "does it not concern you at all that your newly discovered *love*, as you call it, will go quite unrequited? Lady Arabella will never have you."

"I admit that I have a steep hill to climb," Lord Skeffington said. "I am up to the challenge, however. Now, of course, I will begin to call on the lady. You will not mind it, as I am her guardian."

Lady Redfield hardly knew how to respond. She would very much like to bar the door against him, but how could she? He could decide to remove Arabella at any time.

"This is a foolish enterprise, Lord Skeffington," the duchess said.

Lord Skeffington smiled and said, "Are we not all fools for love?"

The drawing room door opened and Arabella came through it, looking wonderful in her riding habit, her cheeks pink and eyes bright from her recent exercise. She took in the scene and those bright eyes narrowed.

She said, "What do you do here, Skeffy? Still intent on closeting me away for the next eleven months? I had understood that Lord Blackwood disabused you of that idea."

Lord Skeffington bowed, though Arabella did not return the courtesy.

"I have no intention of closeting you away, Lady Arabella. Though, Lord Blackwood's opinions have nothing to do with it. I have discovered my true heart and realized I wished to send you away so that you would not engage yourself to another before I had time to press my suit."

Arabella's face darkened to an alarming shade of red, very like a ripe tomato on the verge of bursting its skin. "Your suit? Have you lost your wits? You could not maroon me on a deserted island in the south seas to convince me to entertain your *suit*. My feelings for you do not materially differ from those of the badger that escorted you out of Cornwall the last time you stepped foot there."

Arabella turned on her heel and marched out of the room, slamming the door behind her.

Lady Redfield was both admiring and taken aback by Arabella's forthright expressions. Where had she ever learned the courage to speak to a man like Skeffington in such a dismissive manner? It was rather inspiring.

A door slamming overhead alerted the party that Lady Arabella had reached her bedchamber.

She glanced at Lord Skeffington to see if he would finally lose his temper over the many insults that had been hurled in his direction in her drawing room.

He only smiled in a rather diffident manner. "As I mentioned, it will be a steep hill," he said. "But over time, Lady Arabella will come to understand that she has transformed me. Oh, I know, I have had the reputation of being a bit of a rake, but that is all over."

"A *bit* of a rake is going rather easy on yourself," Lady Easton said. "I have heard from my nephew that you have an actress living in your house."

"A nonsensical rumor," Lord Skeffington said. "Now, I will take my leave, as all that can be accomplished today has been done. You know my intentions, I will call again on the morrow."

Lord Skeffington made a sweeping bow and departed the room.

After the door had closed, Lady Redfield murmured, "What now?"

"Remain calm, Cecilia," the duchess advised. "As Clara so presciently pointed out, Lady Arabella will not have him. He will buzz round here like a fly and you cannot keep him out any better than you could an actual fly at an open window. However, this particular fly will come away with nothing for his trouble."

Remain calm. Yes, that was what she ought to do. Maintaining calm would be so much easier if people were not forever doing something to disrupt it!

"I will write Louisa about these recent developments," Lady Easton said, "as she will not be aware of any of it, I do not think. She's likely not left the house since last evening."

"Of course she wouldn't have," the duchess said. "The VAB consumes her every waking hour."

"The VAB?" Lady Featherstone said, appearing puzzled and trying to work it out.

"The very advanced baby," the duchess said.

Lady Heathway snorted, which was very unlike Lady Heathway. "The VAB," she said, "that is amusing. I shall write Grace the joke, she will be exceedingly entertained."

"Has anybody actually seen this baby?" Lady Easton asked.

"I have," Lady Featherstone said.

"What does it do?" Lady Heathway said.

"It lies there," Lady Featherstone said. "Sometimes awake, sometimes asleep. At least, that's what it was doing two days ago."

"About as advanced as I thought," the duchess said.

ARABELLA HAD STORMED up the stairs and slammed her bedchamber door behind her.

How could one day be both marvelous and disastrous? Her time in the park on Bonny Betsy, accompanied by Lord Blackwood, had been positively glorious.

She knew how to ride now. At least, if the speed was a walk. That was exceedingly gratifying. But the real happiness had come from Lord Blackwood. He had been so kind, so patient in his instruction. He had such a natural affinity for animals. When she had considered what a London gentleman would be like, she had not thought whether he would have as keen an interest in animals as she did.

Of course, there had been the bearing rein situation in the beginning, but once he'd realized it was cruel, he had rectified the situation at once. She'd really been very moved to hear him speak of his feelings for both Alfie and his rascally dog Apollo.

Then, she discovered that Lord Blackwood had been to see Skeffy and laid him out over his very stupid idea of sending her away. There was something thrilling in the idea that Lord Blackwood could at once be gentle with his animals and daringly strong against a blackguard. Daringly strong on *her* behalf.

They had made plans to ride on the day after the morrow too. Was that not something? He might just as easily have made the appointments weekly, but he'd insisted on continuing on with it right away, lest she forget what she'd learned over the course of passing days. She must have one day to recover, in case she had strained a leg while engaging in a new activity, and then it must be right back on the horse.

She had been almost floating when she'd entered the house. She'd let herself in as neither Hemmings nor the footmen had been about. She knew well enough that she would find all the ladies in the drawing room. Carriages were lined up at the curb and she'd seen the duchess' coat of arms. Where one went, they all went.

Arabella had been determined to face them and see if any one of them was condemning of Rusty making his appearance on the dining table, or whether they were rather sanguine about it, as Lady Redfield had been the night before.

The last thing she had expected was to find Skeffington in there with them.

No, that was not the very last thing. The very last thing was the idea that he would court her.

She supposed she should not be so surprised. It had to do with money, with her dowry. He was pinched, and he thought to rectify the matter with her twenty-thousand. She had always suspected that he had something to gain when he attempted to push her into a marriage with old Lord Rendiver. They had cooked up some deal between them. Perhaps Rendiver would pay over a portion of her dowry to him. Now, seeing that would not happen, he thought he might as well take her on himself.

How dare he claim Lord Blackwood had nothing to do with his reversed decision? Lord Blackwood had very obviously gone in fierce and overcome him. That was likely the beginnings of this ridiculous idea. Skeffington had seen he could not win against Lord Blackwood in the matter and so had decided to change course.

She wondered how Lord Blackwood would take the news that Skeffington planned on attempting to court her.

Attempt was surely the operative word. How did he propose to get anywhere with it when she despised him so? How did he *dare* attempt it, considering what she knew about him?

Well, Lady Redfield could not bar him from the house as he was still her legal guardian, but he would find no friendliness inside its doors. Not from her, he would not. He would find a very cool reception, when he could find her at all. She would make herself scarce as much as possible. There was even that stand of trees at the back of the garden. She could absent herself there with a book in the afternoons.

She would tell Hemmings where she was so that he would not raise an alarm at her absence. Arabella felt Hemmings would welcome the chance to frustrate Skeffington. Anything that upset his mistress did not find favor with the butler, and Skeffington certainly did that.

There was a soft knock on the door and Lady Redfield came into the room.

CHAPTER THIRTEEN

"MY DEAR," LADY Redfield said, crossing the room and taking Arabella's hands, "you are not to distress yourself. The duchess says he will be like a fly at an open window. He will get in, but he will be of no more consequence than that."

Dear Lady Redfield. She had really become a very good friend to her. Almost as much as Mrs. Weston had always been.

"I believe the duchess is right," Arabella said. "He will only be an annoyance, as I think I made clear to him."

"Goodness, very clear," Lady Redfield said. "I would have been positively quaking at your age." The lady paused, then she said, "Though, I do my fair share of quaking *now*, so I suppose it is only differing temperaments."

"I think your temperament is lovely, and I could not have ended up with a more perfect person to steer me through a season."

Lady Redfield became exceedingly flustered by her words and sat on the edge of the bed. "Heavens, well that is very kind, very kind indeed."

"It is only the truth," Arabella said. "Now, what do you propose I wear to Lord Ryland's mystery ball, or mystery supper, or whatever it is?"

"Ah, let me think," Lady Redfield said, recovering herself, "what is your view on the violet silk?"

"I view it an excellent suggestion. Come, now that is settled, we will go downstairs, and I will ask Mr. Hemmings to bring us tea. We will forget Skeffy was ever here."

"Oh, yes, let's do," Lady Redfield said.

THOUGH IT WAS not his usual time for walking, Hemmings had spotted Mr. Sindu setting off toward the square. Such were his feelings after listening by the door upon Lord Skeffington's arrival, that he felt a walk would do him good.

He was not usually in the habit of listening at doorways, but the lord was of such a terrible reputation that he felt he must stand by were the fellow to become violent or make threats.

Eavesdropping, he discovered, was not for the faint of heart. When he'd heard the front doors opening, he'd had to jump into a closet meant for brooms and dustpans to avoid being spotted.

It had been Lady Arabella and he'd had no way to stop her and warn her before she went in to see Lady Redfield. What was he to do? Jump back out of the closet and claim he'd been checking the brooms?

Lady Arabella had gone in, and shortly thereafter had given Lord Skeffington the what-for. Apparently, she was the owner of a badger who held a very low opinion of the gentleman. He only hoped the badger was not somewhere in the house, as that squirrel had been.

The girl then came storming out of the room and bounding up the stairs as he pretended to organize letters on the hall table.

The whole thing had been nerve-wracking and ended with the idea that Lord Skeffington was to be a regular visitor, though nobody wished him to come!

Now, he sped up his walking until he was, by all appearances, jogging. He finally caught up to his friend.

"Mr. Sindu," he said, breathing heavily.

"Mr. Hemmings, you are out of breath," Mr. Sindu said.

"I walked very quickly to catch up to you, I will not prevaricate on that point," Hemmings said, drawing in deep breaths.

"I am honored that my company is sought, Mr. Hemmings."

Hemmings, now beginning to recover himself, said, "Indeed it is sought! My neckcloth is due to your wise advice and it has become a set thing."

"Ah yes, the society of which you are a director," Mr. Sindu said, smiling. "Peregrine told me all about it."

"There is that," Hemmings said. He paused and said, "Do you think it wrong to allow Lady Redfield's friends to believe such a thing? Ought I to make it clear that I wear a neckcloth because *I* decided to wear it?"

"Let them think what they will," Mr. Sindu said. "A fool may be ill-equipped when it comes to developing sound opinions, but nevertheless, they are responsible for whatever harebrained ideas they choose to adopt."

Hemmings nodded in full agreement, though up until now he had not considered the lords and ladies of the *ton* to be fools prone to harebrained ideas.

"Is that all that troubles you, Mr. Hemmings?" Mr. Sindu said.

Mr. Sindu was really remarkable. He had some sort of intuition about the state of those around him and it made him very wise.

"You are very incisive, sir," he said. Hemmings poured out the story of Lord Skeffington's visit, leaving out the part when he'd stepped into the broom closet.

"So you see, he's determined to court Lady Arabella, but the lady herself wants nothing to do with him. Lady Redfield is very distressed."

"Why should Lady Redfield be distressed?" Mr. Sindu asked. "He will come and he will go and nothing will result from it. Has Lady Redfield not already decided who Lady Arabella should marry?"

"No, at least, I do not believe she has. Should she? I rather think she was leaving that to Lady Arabella."

Mr. Sindu laughed rich and deep. "Leave it to the young lady? What a novel idea. I certainly would not allow Peregrine to go forward in such a fashion."

"You would not?" Hemmings asked, fascinated.

"Never. I know perfectly well who he will marry."

"Does *he* know?" Hemmings asked breathlessly.

"Not yet," Mr. Sindu said. "I will keep my thoughts to myself for now, but when it is time, I will tell you all about it, Mr. Hemmings."

Hemmings was at once gratified that he should be trusted with such information and stunned that it was Mr. Sindu who would decide who Lord Blackwood was to marry. It seemed impossible.

And yet, what was impossible for Mr. Sindu?

PEREGRINE WAS EXCEEDINGLY satisfied with his morning. He had woken with a pounding head such as he'd rarely experienced. It had felt as if he should not rise, but rather stay abed and sleep through it. But he could not, he had too much to say to Lady Arabella.

Mr. Sindu, who he was beginning to notice did next to nothing except reading for his own pleasure and ensuring that the footmen accomplished everything that needed doing, had at least deigned to treat his rather poor condition. He'd sent up a bicarbonate of soda, and a cup of willow bark tea with a drop of laudanum.

Within the hour, he began to feel better. Not quite his usual self, but no longer wishing to close the curtains and crawl under his sheets.

Speedily enough, he'd been dressed and out the door and followed Lady Arabella's carriage to the park. What an adorable little figure she made in her riding habit! Then, they got on with the project very smoothly with not the least problems.

Was Lady Arabella a natural on a horse, or was he a natural instructor, or was it both? He supposed it mattered little, as they had experienced an excellent excursion, whatever the cause.

Bonny Betsy had been a little lady all the way through, not giving a moment's trouble. Once he was certain that Lady Arabella had settled in her seat and was in no danger of falling off, he'd sprung on her the news that he'd seen Skeffington on her behalf.

Peregrine had always maintained a distantly cordial attitude with the man, so that was thrown over. He supposed he'd have to cut Skeffington when he saw him next. Certainly, he would no longer attend any of the betting events the man so often arranged.

He did not mind it! What were horse races and cock fights and boxing matches to the amount of gratitude he'd been the recipient of as they walked their horses through the park?

Lady Arabella had merely been thankful and gratified by Lord Ryland's efforts. For his own efforts, though, the lady had been thankful, gratified, *and* of the opinion that he had been gallant.

He supposed he had been, rather.

Mr. Sindu came into the drawing room and sat down. Another habit Peregrine was certain he ought not allow to go on, though he had no idea how to turn back the clock on it. He probably should have said something straightaway, but he hadn't.

Mr. Sindu had been a childhood friend. Back then, when he had first come and was working on the home farm, they had run off regularly to fish at the river or explore the woods. He had been "Amandeep" then and full of wonderfully bad ideas.

When he'd been made a footman, or rather, bullied his way into the job, he'd often come to Peregrine's room when he was dismissed from duty. They'd play cards or range their armies of soldiers across the floor and plan out battle strategies. They'd had their first brandy together, after Amandeep emptied the dregs left in all the glasses from his parent's dinner after the men had left the table.

One day, he decided that nobody was to call him Amandeep anymore. He was at an age, he said, where he would demand more respect. He was Sindu.

Of course, the duke's butler dismissed the idea.

They should have all seen where it was going when Amandeep had pretended at deafness until Rumsford had given up and changed to calling him Sindu.

A few years later, when Peregrine was of an age to set off on a grand tour, Sindu had announced he would accompany him as a manservant. Peregrine was amenable, as he'd thought Sindu would act as his valet. He did not, though he was perfectly happy to supervise the valet they hired in Italy. As far as Peregrine could gather, now that he was looking back at it, Sindu's primary duties had been cautioning him on this or that idea and dragging him out of gambling establishments. At the end of the trip, Sindu had announced he would be Peregrine's butler. And that from that day on he would only be known as *Mr.* Sindu.

"Peregrine," Mr. Sindu said, "are you aware that Lord Skeffington has been to see Lady Redfield?"

Peregrine leapt from his chair. "The villain! Did Skeffington really think to cross me and take Lady Arabella away when I told him not to do it?"

"Sit down, if you please," Mr. Sindu said. "He has since left and he has gone alone."

"So," Peregrine said, realizing that Skeffington had not dared to take Lady Arabella away, "my words struck home. I told him he better not dare remove the lady from the premises and he hasn't."

"Very courageous," Mr. Sindu said.

Peregrine narrowed his eyes. There were times when he could not work out if Mr. Sindu was complimenting him or mocking him.

"Lord Skeffington has suddenly reversed any number of

opinions," Mr. Sindu went on. "He will not remove the lady from her current circumstances, and he intends to court her, which I believe is a new idea."

Peregrine was struck dumb. Skeffington? To court Lady Arabella? It was nonsensical. It was outrageous. It was…revolting.

"No," he muttered.

"Yes," Mr. Sindu said implacably.

"She'll never accept him," Peregrine said. "Never."

"I find that a very probable prediction," Mr. Sindu said. "Nevertheless, he will be about the place often as he goes forward with this ill-advised idea."

"Will he?" Peregrine said, not very successful in keeping the outrage out of his tone.

"Undoubtedly," Mr. Sindu said. "It would be pleasant for Lady Arabella, I believe, if some other person was also often about the place."

"You mean me," Peregrine said.

"Very insightful," Mr. Sindu said.

Peregrine ignored that comment, as he was certain he was being mocked.

"Perhaps I will," he said.

Mr. Sindu rose and said, "I will retire to my library now. You are having a roast chicken for your dinner, and it will be served at eight o'clock. I suggest you retire early so that you are not in need of bicarbonate of soda in the morning."

⇻⟨⟨⟨

THE DAY FOLLOWING his unpleasant meeting at Lady Redfield's house, Lord Skeffington had not the slightest wish to attend Ryland's ridiculous ball and mystery supper. For one, it was laughable to watch lords and ladies who could not light a drawing room fire on their own attempt to unravel a murder. For another, it made him slightly uncomfortable to know that there were people like Ryland in the world. People who were not satisfied to believe what they were told and would instead be forever peering under rocks to uncover what they might. And for a third, it galled him to accept Ryland's hospitality after his recent visit and "warning" regarding Lady Arabella.

He had almost thought Ryland might rescind the invitation, but he had not. Ryland had likely assumed that he would bow out of his own accord.

Which he would have, had not Lady Redfield planned to take Lady Arabella. She was going and so must he. When he'd told those matrons that he had a steep hill to climb in regard to her affections, that had been putting a good face on it. It would be more like clawing his way up the Swiss Alps.

When she'd mentioned her feelings being no more genial than that wretched badger in Cornwall, he'd wished to slap her. More concerning, though, had been her crediting Blackwood with anything. Of all the people those ladies had set upon him, including the Queen of England, why had she placed all her faith in the effectiveness of Blackwood?

It spoke of some interest or admiration she had for the fellow. Did Blackwood hold an admiration for her too? That would be an extremely knotty problem. Blackwood would be a duke someday, a fact that irked him no end. The whole world would look favorably upon a match between Blackwood and Lady Arabella. He must be certain that wasn't in the works.

He strode into Ryland's house, determined to make some arrangements to his advantage. First, he would get himself on Lady Arabella's card for dinner, second, he would talk to Ryland about placing his friend Crackleton at his table. It would pay to have Lady Arabella be exposed to those who admired Lord Skeffington. With any luck, he could solve the mystery too, and give Lady Arabella whatever stupid prize Ryland had thought up this time.

As ARABELLA HAD been dressing for Lord Ryland's ball, she could not help but to glance out her window. She could not help but to notice that Lord Blackwood's horse Alfie was standing outside his house, a groom holding his reins.

She'd wished that Flora would hurry with her buttons so that she and Lady Redfield might set off. If they left soon, they might leave at the same time as Lord Blackwood.

"This is some dress," Flora said, working her way up the buttons.

Flora was right, it was some dress. Madame LaForte had claimed it a triumph of proportions. It was a serenely soft silk in the darkest shade of violet. Its only adornment was on the capped sleeves—they had the slightest puff at the seam and were embroidered in like-colored thread with a profusion of violets. This, the modiste said, widened her shoulders, which in turn created the illusion of her waist being even smaller than it was. That, combined with the straight fall of the skirt, gave her height and symmetry.

Arabella had learned quite a lot from Madame LaForte, not the least of which was she should not dress herself in pastels and she should avoid an overfull skirt, lest she look like a short fairy cake.

Flora had taken so long with the buttons and then had fussed with her hair rather endlessly that Arabella had given up all hope that they might casually encounter Lord Blackwood on the street.

However, when they finally departed, his horse was still there waiting for him. Then he had come bounding out of the house just as they were getting into the carriage.

He'd very gallantly proposed escorting them to Ryland's house and of course Lady Redfield had acquiesced.

Arabella wondered if she did not flatter herself in speculating that Lord Blackwood might have specially waited for them. It was a lovely idea, anyway.

She had opened her carriage window and Lord Blackwood had ridden alongside her. What had come next, she could not have dreamed of.

"Lady Redfield," Lord Blackwood had said, leaning down over Alfie's neck to see her, "I fear Lord Skeffington will make himself troublesome this evening. He shall wish to get on Lady Arabella's card, particularly for supper."

Lady Redfield had been shaken by the idea. "Oh dear, I should not wish Arabella to have to...but then what could we...oh, perhaps we should not go!"

"No, no, not at all, Lady Redfield," Lord Blackwood assured her. "We must just outfox him, that is all. When we arrive, hand over Lady Arabella's card to me. I will see it filled before Skeffington gets anywhere near it."

"That is exceedingly clever, Lord Blackwood," Arabella said. In fact, it was rather thrilling. What lengths he was going to! And, perhaps, of those gentlemen who would pencil in their names, he might be one of them? What Lord Blackwood was doing entirely unnecessary, as she would simply refuse Skeffy if he attempted a run at her. However, she would not for the world tell him that.

Lady Redfield had been instantly relieved that a solution had been so easily found.

Now, they'd arrived and been greeted by Lord Ryland, dashing as he ever was, despite his penchant for murders and forgeries. Arabella was handed her card, which was just as quickly handed over to Lord Blackwood. He hurried off into the crowd in the ballroom.

"Lord Blackwood really is so enterprising, is he not?" Lady Redfield said, cheerful now that all potential difficulties had been whisked away.

"Very enterprising," Arabella said.

"The duchess does always say that he is such a devoted son that her concerns are his concerns. I cannot claim to hold such sway over my own boys. Their concerns are mainly horses and cards."

Arabella did not answer, though she did think the duchess rather overestimated Lord Blackwood's devotion. After all, he'd already told her that he loved his horse and his dog above all others. She presumed the duchess would be mortified to know it.

As they made their way to the ballroom, Lady Featherstone came sailing toward them. The lady was resplendent in a green brocade, her emerald brooch taking pride of place on her heaving bosom.

"I am glad I have found you," she said breathlessly. "This shall be a night of glory, I am certain of it. Lord Ryland has dropped the hint to all interested parties that this year's mystery is to include the actions of something other than man. I am certain there will be some sort of animal. You see?"

Arabella did not see, and she was certain that Lady Redfield did not see either, if her wrinkled brow were anything to go by.

"You, Arabella! You are my lucky charm. You have such a knowledge of animals that it is sure to be an advantage. I insisted to Lord Ryland that I must be at your table and he has agreed. Is that not delightful?"

It *was* rather delightful. Lady Featherstone, in general, was a delight and nobody could be more enthusiastic regarding Lord Ryland's mysteries than she.

"This is advantageous indeed," Lady Redfield said. "I had begun to wonder if we might be unlucky enough to end with Lord Skeffington at Arabella's table."

"Two birds, one stone, Cecilia," Lady Featherstone said, softly stroking her emerald brooch. "Now, I must be off. I am going to hint very heavily to Sir Richard that he ought to take me into supper. You know how much he loves his dogs, that must come as an advantage too. We shall be towering mountain of animal facts between us."

Lady Featherstone hurried off, just as the duchess came up behind Lady Redfield. "Gracious," she said, "on these nights,

Anne is like a chicken ahead of a fox, wings flapping wildly and never quite getting off the ground."

"Though, she did win last year," Lady Redfield said.

"Yes, that is still mystifying. In any case, I very much doubt lightning strikes twice. We must all be prepared for her morose feelings on the morrow. I suggest complimenting the brooch, that always cheers her up."

"Are the rest of our friends here?" Lady Redfield asked.

"All except Lady Mendleton. The VAB, you know. She claims she could not be comfortable here, considering a murder, when a defenseless baby lies alone in her nursery. You would think they hadn't any servants to keep an eye on that baby."

The duchess sailed off. Arabella said softly, "What is a VAB?"

"It's the very advanced baby," Lady Redfield said, clearly suppressing an urge to laugh.

Arabella did the same. It would not be kind to mock Lady Mendleton's abject adoration of her granddaughter. It was rather sweet, after all. Though the duchess may have had her fill of the subject.

CHAPTER FOURTEEN

ARABELLA AND LADY Redfield proceeded into Lord Ryland's ballroom. It was clear enough by the crowd that Lord Ryland's ball, followed by a mystery at supper, was one of the events of the season.

Mr. Vance spotted her and made his way over. "Lady Arabella, Lady Redfield," he said. "Lady Redfield, I understand you are to be congratulated on your butler's recent ascension to director of this mysterious society I keep hearing about."

"Oh, yes, well, thank you, though I do not suppose I had anything to do with it," Lady Redfield said.

Arabella suppressed the urge to giggle. Rather, she said, "What does your own butler say of it, Mr. Vance? Is he a member?"

"I am afraid he has been entirely left out of it," Mr. Vance admitted. "I suspect the house of a grandson of a tradesman is not elevated enough for the likes of the society. My poor butler has never even heard of it."

Arabella could only approve of Mr. Vance's good sense in foregoing to lay claim to any knowledge of something that did not in fact exist. She had come to understand that there were more than a few in society who had taken an entirely different route, even going so far as to claim their butler a member. Lady Jacobson had even said her butler was a past director, as evidenced by his sleeve buttons.

Mr. Vance looked at her hands and said, "You have not yet retrieved your card, Lady Arabella? May I go fetch it for you?"

This, now, was rather awkward to explain. Arabella thought it might be best to relay the case if it, with no explanation at all.

"Lord Blackwood currently has possession of my card," she said simply.

That there ought to have been some explanation was clear, as Mr. Vance did seem confused to hear it. However, being a practical sort of fellow, he turned and searched the room.

Arabella did too, and followed his gaze as it settled upon Lord Blackwood, his head rising above the crowd of gentlemen just now surrounding him.

"Ah," Mr. Vance said. He made a quick bow and was just about to move off in the direction, when Lord Skeffington approached.

"Lady Redfield, Lady Arabella," Lord Skeffington said, bowing to the ladies. Rather dismissively, he said, "Vance."

"Skeffington," Mr. Vance said, no less dismissively.

Arabella was rather impressed by it. Mr. Vance might be only the grandson of a gunmaker, but he was not cowed by Skeffy.

"I'll be off, ladies," Mr. Vance said cheerfully. "Lord Blackwood must hear from me forthwith."

Lord Skeffington's eyes followed him, watching as he made his way to the crowd surrounding Lord Blackwood.

"What on earth is Blackwood doing?" Lord Skeffington asked. "He does not have the effrontery to take bets in the middle of a ballroom?"

Arabella did not answer, feeling rather loath to tell Skeffy anything. Lady Redfield appeared frozen and entirely unable to speak.

"Lady Arabella, if I may? Your card?"

It was just then that Lord Skeffington seemed to realize that she did not, in fact, have a card in her hand.

"Where is it?" he asked bluntly.

"Lord Blackwood offered to manage it for me," Arabella said.

"A very kind offer, was it not? After all, I am new to Town and there may be those who have less than honorable intentions toward me. Lord Blackwood will weed them out."

Arabella watched Lord Skeffington carefully. As he took in her words and understood their meaning, he got a look she had seen before. It was one of controlled rage.

"Ridiculous," he muttered, and stormed off toward Lord Blackwood.

"It's all rather frightening," Lady Redfield said quietly.

Arabella took her hand and squeezed it. "Do not allow him to frighten you. It is his only talent and if you strip him of it, he is nothing."

Though she said it, she was not quite sure of it. She thought Skeffington might be a dangerous man, if pushed to an extreme. However, she would not like Lady Redfield to have nightmares about it.

In any case, Lord Blackwood was very gallantly, and daringly, on their side. What could be better than that?

Arabella watched Skeffington push his way past other gentlemen and say something to Lord Blackwood. Lord Blackwood shook his head.

He had refused Skeffington! He had refused to allow him to put his name down, just as he said he would.

He really was marvelous.

⇥⟫⟫✕⟪⟪⇤

PEREGRINE HAD BEEN ready to depart for Ryland's ball a full half-hour before Lady Redfield's carriage was pulled up to her house.

He'd thought about setting off, though his inclination was to wait for them. He'd said he might set off, and then Mr. Sindu had said, "That seems unwise, when Lady Redfield must be readying herself to depart and the lady and her charge would be gratified to have an escort."

As much as he did not like the constant stream of advice coming from his butler, sometimes it was convenient to pretend he was only taking a suggestion and not that he'd had the same idea.

He had waited and then, as they'd trotted through the streets, he'd sprung his plan to keep Skeffington well away from Lady Arabella. They had seemed gratified about that too.

Once word had gone round Ryland's ballroom that he was in possession of the lady's card, that he was the keeper of the chance, gentlemen had surged in his direction.

It was rather disconcerting, how many of them surrounded him. He knew, of course, that Lady Arabella was beautiful, particularly this evening in that heart-stopper of a dress. But somehow, he'd not taken other gentlemen into consideration.

He'd only been thinking of himself and Skeffington.

Since he was the arbiter of who would get on the card and who would not, he wisely chose those who would pose no difficulty for anybody. Sir Richard was a safe bet. The fellow was already in his early forties and even if he was not, he was exasperating about his beloved spaniels.

Then there was Lymington. If Lady Arabella was not tired of hearing of the incredible spaniels, then she could hear about Lymington's incredible horses.

A few others were fairly callow youths who would attempt bon mots and compliments that would be ill-formed and awkwardly delivered. They were still at the practicing stage and clumsily trying things out. They would make anybody cringe.

The only gentleman of any real substance to make his way onto the card was Vance. Peregrine might have put him off, but then he'd spied Skeffington marching over. He'd given Vance the last spot.

Skeffington had been furious, but he had, in the end, been outfoxed.

Somewhere in the deepest reaches of Peregrine's mind, he realized he was perhaps going to undue lengths on Lady

Arabella's behalf.

After all, he must be careful to avoid leading the lady to any ideas. He was not yet ready to consider such things.

He did not think.

But was that as set in stone as he had imagined? What if he were wrong? What if he waited two more seasons and the lady had since married and then nobody turned up that he liked as well as her? Rendridge's sisters, according to him, were a high-strung duo—always laughing or crying. What if all the ladies not yet out were like that?

He perhaps ought to consider that risk, as so far, nobody had turned up that he liked as well as Lady Arabella. Perhaps nobody ever would.

Well, he would put those questions aside for the moment. Just now, he was returning to Lady Arabella's side, triumphant with her card. He could not help feeling just a little bit like a knight of old returning from a quest.

"My dear Lord Blackwood," Lady Redfield said, "I was almost in terror when I saw Lord Skeffington approach. I got the distinct idea he was angry that you'd had possession of Arabella's card."

Peregrine nodded as he handed Lady Arabella the card back. "He had a bee in his bonnet, as my mother would say. But there was nothing he could do about it. He called it an absurd machination. I replied that it had been an effective one."

Lady Arabella seemed inordinately pleased to hear of the exchange. He added, "Then I simply stared him down until he went away."

Peregrine could not say positively that he'd stared Skeffington down, but he *had* looked him in the eye, and the man *had* left.

Lady Arabella examined her card to see the results of his efforts.

She flushed, no, not just flushed, her face deepened in color to very red. He would have asked her if she were developing a fever, but he had been acquainted with her sufficiently that he knew it was only her coloring. He got rather red like that himself on occasion, due to his own coloring.

Lady Redfield peered over at the card. "You take Arabella into supper, well, that is very considerate Lord Blackwood. Really very considerate. Now, who are some of these other gentlemen? I feel I do not know them."

"They are no danger at all, Lady Redfield," Peregrine said. "I have made sure of that."

"It's very comforting, Lord Blackwood," Lady Redfield said. "It really is very comforting."

Peregrine bowed. As yet, Lady Arabella had said nothing about what she found on her card. He hoped she was not disappointed to find his name down for supper. No, of course she could not be. Could she?

He could not linger to find out, though.

He bowed and said, "I'd best make the rounds and add my name to a sufficient number of cards, else Ryland will be put out."

He sauntered off into the crowd.

⬥⟫⟫⟫⟪⟪⟪⬥

ARABELLA HAD NOT known what she might expect when Peregrine, Lord Blackwood, had returned with her card. She'd had hopes that he would put his own name down, though she had not gone so far as to hope for supper.

But that was what he did! He put his name down for supper. That, combined with the idea that they should be seated with Lady Featherstone, made the upcoming mystery a positive delight.

And then, he'd so forcefully driven off Skeffington. She felt very protected by Lord Blackwood. Admired by him, even.

Other than Mr. Vance, she had not known the other gentlemen on her card. However, she did now.

Lord Blackwood had claimed that none of them would pose a danger, and nothing truer could be said about it.

Mr. Hankin was just out of Oxford, where he'd gone simply for the love of learning. He had formed an idea that anybody in his vicinity must wish to know what he'd learned. He recited an astounding amount of facts about ancient Greece as if he were dancing with his proctor.

Lord Mackleson seemed intent on turning himself into a rake, though he was currently so far from that objective as to make Arabella wonder if any number of years would help him to it. His convoluted turns of his phrase had made her *own* objective suppressing any laughter that came bubbling up. Her eyes' brilliance shamed the stars in the night sky indeed. Her eyes were a rather uninspired light blue, but this apparently was of no consequence.

Mr. Restorin did not have nearly as much to say for himself, in comparison to Mr. Hankin and Lord Mackleson. Rather, he perspired to such a degree that little droplets ran down the side of his face. Her gloves began to feel damp, and she could not imagine how much water poured from his hands to seep through his gloves and into her own.

Mr. Vance had been a great relief after that series of trying encounters. He was so cheerful and so clever. He was of the opinion that the secret society of butlers did not, in fact, exist. He could not say why such a story had begun to go round but he wondered if Lady Redfield's butler had made the whole thing up to explain and defend his new mode of dress.

Arabella thought he did not know how close to the truth he was. All he hadn't guessed was that it had been the duchess and Lady Heathway who had conspired together to cook up the story.

She thought it rather liberal of him to say that if Hemmings *had* made the whole thing up, it was rather inventive. The fellow must be devilishly determined to wear what he liked and Mr. Vance supposed he ought to be allowed to get on with it. In any case, he said, the *ton* were rather like zoo animals waiting for their next meal. If they did not have something to chew over, they began pacing their cage and clawing at each other.

As entertaining as he had been, Arabella could not help but be distracted. She could not help but to look forward to what was to come.

Now would come Lord Blackwood.

She had kept a discreet eye on him throughout the evening. There he was, escorting this or that lady through a dance. Always graceful, usually smiling.

He was so popular! Every woman must wish to place her hand in his and be led forward. How could they not?

They must pine for him, all the while thinking that his heart lay with Lady Constance. Arabella knew that it did not, but it did not belong to anybody else either.

At least, that was what he wished.

Perhaps he would not get precisely what he wished? It was not terribly unusual for a young gentleman to change his mind. At least, Mrs. Weston had assured her it was not, generally highlighting the idea with some tragic story of disappointed hopes.

Would her own hopes be disappointed? Most likely.

And yet, she still could not stop herself wishing to be near him. She just could not. She might be disappointed in the end but having hopes this moment was thrilling.

"Lady Arabella," he said, joining her and leading her to their place.

As they waited for the musicians to start up, Lord Blackwood said, "I presume you have enjoyed yourself thus far? I feel I must take the credit or discredit, seeing as I arranged your partners."

"I did wonder about that, Lord Blackwood," she said teasingly. "Mr. Vance was very amusing, as he always is. However…"

Arabella really did not think she need say more about it.

Lord Blackwood said, "Well, now, perhaps the others are…not quite seasoned. But you were quite safe, which was the point."

Arabella shivered just the littlest bit. He had her safety in the forefront of his mind. She might forgive any sort of Greek lecture, or bizarre compliment, or even dripping hands for that.

The music began and he led her expertly through the changes. There was such an elegance about him. He towered over her, as did many men. And yet, he did not make it seem awkward, as it sometimes was.

Most of the gentlemen preceding him may not have been quite seasoned, but Lord Blackwood was every inch the polished gentleman.

"I understand from my mother," he said, "that we will have the rare honor of being seated with Lord Ryland's keenest competitor."

"Indeed," Arabella answered. "Lady Redfield says Lady Featherstone will be very downhearted if she does not prevail again this year. Though, she also says that nobody imagines it likely that she will come out victorious."

"Then we ought to do everything we can to help her to it," Lord Blackwood said. "She is a pleasant lady and there cannot be anybody else who cares so much about it."

Arabella thought that was very kind. Very kind, indeed. It was a marvelous idea.

"She will have every effort from me," Arabella said. "Though, I am afraid I have no practice solving mysteries and further afraid she has put great stock in the idea that I have experience with different sorts of animals."

"I believe we are rowing in the same direction," Lord Blackwood said. "Though I suppose I have had practice attempting to solve a mystery, as I have attended these nights in the past, I am always flummoxed by what the solution turns out to be."

"I think you are being modest, Lord Blackwood."

"No really, it is the truth."

It was very charming, how modest he was.

"We will just have to do our best," Arabella said.

"Yes, we will. We will prop up Lady Featherstone from all sides. If she fails, if *we* fail, which I am afraid is a likely outcome, we will console the lady. The duchess says complimenting her emerald brooch usually does the trick."

The dance went on, both resolved to do their very best for Lady Featherstone.

If Arabella were to examine her thoughts closely, the most interesting thing about the upcoming supper was not helping Lady Featherstone. It would be working with Lord Blackstone, exchanging ideas, following clues, their heads together.

Lady Redfield said that there were many who would make a cursory attempt at the mystery, and then give it up and talk amongst themselves until the thing was solved. She was often one of those persons as she generally could not make heads or tails out of the circumstances.

The last one had hinged on a trick of the voice. Who had been thought to be speaking had not, and somebody else had, or some such thing. Lady Redfield said she ought to know more about it, since Lady Featherstone had often gone into great detail on how she worked it out.

The dance was over far faster than the previous dances had been. It was not that it had been actually shorter, it had just seemed so.

Arabella could dance with Lord Blackwood all the night long, if such a thing were permitted.

Now, it was time for supper. It was time to encounter a mystery and somehow keep Lady Featherstone's spirits afloat.

⟫⟫⟫⟪⟪⟪

LORD SKEFFINGTON HAD found himself blocked from all sides. First, he could not get himself on Lady Arabella's card. She'd not even had her card. What was this, handing over a card to a gentleman to manage? Of course, its sole purpose had been to keep him off it. Of that, he was certain.

But, was it not scandalous? Why had Lady Redfield agreed to it?

Was there an engagement in the works?

If there was, he'd need to do something about it before it was announced. What, he could not say, but something to break it off.

His second plan, which had also not met with success, was to talk Ryland into placing him at Lady Arabella's table.

He knew Ryland did not care for him, but such a request from another gentleman should have been easily granted.

Ryland had refused, explaining to him that he'd already promised Lady Featherstone that *she* would be seated with Lady Arabella so unless he was planning to escort that lady there was nothing he could do. Why in God's name was Lady Feather-head getting in his way? Did she somehow imagine that Lady Arabella would help her win another emerald brooch? Perhaps she wished to wear two, one on each bosom, to look a greater ninny than she usually did.

Or perhaps the duchess had put her up to it. That duchess, always swimming in brocade no matter the weather, and insisting on getting her own way. Yes, that was probably it.

He would really rather be gone home to his actress, who would return from the theater and, noting he was not yet at home, would drink his brandy and rifle his drawers for money while pouting prettily and wearing very little on. He would be happy to leave Lady Cressely in the lurch. He'd put his name down for her supper, she being one of the only single ladies who might agree to it. She was nearing thirty and her desperation would not allow her to be put off by a man like himself, with a reputation as a rake.

The evening would be dull, indeed. A ridiculous story would be folded up under their plates and, as they were meant to be solving it, Ryland's uninspired supper would come round. It would be the same as it ever was—roasted chicken, roasted beef, broiled fish, and a selection of vegetables with odd sauces. Ryland's cook seemed determined to make his mark with bizarre combinations. Last year had seen leeks in a browned butter sauce. It had been revolting and if his own cook had tried such an outrage, he'd be packing up before the night was over.

Skeffington forced a smile as Lady Cressely came tripping up to him, all titters and desperate cheerfulness.

What a night.

CHAPTER FIFTEEN

A FOOTMAN LED them to their table, where Arabella found Lady Featherstone already seated.

"I am at sixes and sevens just thinking about it," Lady Featherstone said, staring down at her plate. "It is very hard to stop myself from having a peek at the mystery, but I *will* control the urge."

Her dinner partner, Sir Richard, nodded sympathetically. "I note the same with my spaniels whenever they see something interesting to eat on a table. Once, when there was a plate of sliced ham sitting there, I saw a teardrop roll down Edgar's face. He stayed away, though; he places my feelings above his own."

Arabella had already heard quite a lot about Sir Richard's remarkable spaniels, though she could not be certain whether Lady Featherstone would favor being compared to them. As for herself, she would have wished to have checked poor Edgar for an eye infection, rather than assume he wept over ham slices.

Lady Featherstone said, "My Tulip is just the same," she said. "She cannot bear to see me unhappy. She whimpers at the least sign that I am affected."

"There is something special about spaniels, is there not?" Sir Richard said. "They feel things more deeply than other dogs— you can see it in their eyes."

"Indeed, I have often thought so," Lady Featherstone averred.

Arabella glanced at Lord Blackwood, who appeared delighted with the exchange. She suppressed a smile. Lady Featherstone's and Sir Richard's dogs seemed no less astounding than the very advanced baby.

Perhaps they were the very advanced dogs. Or as the duchess would call them, the VADs.

The dining room had filled, and Lord Ryland dinged his glass.

"My friends," he said, "I am always gratified to see so many regulars to this little experiment, year after year. For those of you who are new to my strange little supper, you will find this year's mystery folded under your plate. The prize for solving it is very special, very special indeed. Use your minds and carry on!"

Lord Ryland had hardly finished speaking before Lady Featherstone lifted her plate and grabbed at the paper, knocking over a wine glass in the process.

Sir Richard attempted to hand over a handkerchief to blot the spill, but Lady Featherstone waved him off. "Never mind that, Sir Richard! Read! Read as if your very life depends upon it!"

It was clear to Arabella that Sir Richard had not perceived the seriousness of purpose that Lady Featherstone had brought to their little table. He looked a little frightened as he pulled out his own sheet of paper.

Arabella and Lord Blackwood did too, lest Lady Featherstone scold them for dawdling. As the soup course came round, and Lady Featherstone scolded the poor footman for imagining she wished for soup at such a moment, Arabella read the enclosed description with interest.

Mr. John Kramer, age thirty-two, was found dead in the cabin of his canal boat on August 22nd, 1811, while moored on the Severn near Tewkesbury. The hatch and windows were closed, the body was covered in tiny pinpricks to the skin, forty-eight of them containing bee stingers. A third of the pinpricks were almost colorless and the rest were dark purple. Aside from the markings, the skin was smooth in appearance and not yet bloated. There were up to three hundred dead bees found inside the cabin with him.

Mr. Kramer and his partner, Mr. Markham, were engaged in the transport of goods, some from neighboring towns and some imported, on their way to Tewkesbury, Evesham, and Stratford. The load Mr. Kramer had been transporting at the time of his death included twenty-five pounds of lemon grass, twenty-eight bolts of common cotton cloth, five pounds of tea, and an assortment of various household items. The goods were packed into every available space, including the small cabin Mr. Kramer and his wife used for sleeping.

Based on the condition of the body, the coroner believes Mr. Kramer was dead for less than twenty-four hours before he was discovered. Cause of death was initially deemed misadventure, by an overwhelming number of bee stings. Even the inside of Mr. Kramer's throat was found to house several dead bees.

There were no bees still living in the cabin when the magistrate arrived some hours later.

Mr. Kramer was discovered by his wife, Mrs. Peggy Kramer, when she returned from an August 19th trip to see her ailing mother in Winchester. Upon opening the cabin door, Mrs. Kramer was set upon by bees. They were many but lethargic and she swatted away most but she was forced to quickly close the hatch and exit the area. The lady was stung multiple times on the face and hands and reported what she had discovered to the local magistrate, presenting with multiple red welts on her person.

The canal boat concern, initially known as Jonquil Goods, became Kramer and Markham in 1804, after being passed down from Mrs. Kramer's father, a long-time canal man. Peggy Kramer, née Miss Jonquil, had grown up on the boat, was an experienced operator, and well-known along the Severn and the Avon. The boat had been in disrepair and the partner was brought in to inject needed capital for repair and expansion.

Mr. Aldous Markham, age 28, was the partner brought in and resides in Tewkesbury. Mr. Markham owns a farm on the outskirts of town where he produces dairy milk, cream, butter, cheese, and honey. When questioned by the magistrate, Mr.

Markham averred that he was in Manchester on business at the time, and that on his return, he was informed by a farmhand that one of his hives had been damaged. His servants have all sworn that he was away, though Mr. Markham has not been able to provide evidence of it, as the inn where he purported to stay subsequently burned to the ground and the man he was to meet regarding some business arrangement did not turn up for their meeting. It has since been learned that the man died in a factory accident.

The only person who can be confirmed to have been nearby the canal boat during the timeframe of death was farmer Kenneth Pearson, age 52. Mr. Pearson freely admits having several times warned Mr. Kramer to move his canal boat away from his fields. Mr. Kramer had made the habit of stopping there overnight and its presence was disturbing to his cows. Witnesses say Mr. Pearson was voluble in the local tavern regarding his displeasure and had sworn he "would sink that boat, one of these days." Mr. Pearson has admitted to unmooring the boat twice, while its owners slept on it.

It initially seemed as if Mr. Kramer had experienced an unlucky encounter with a swarm of bees, but it was later found to be murder.

Was it Mrs. Kramer, wishing to rid herself of her husband? If so, how did she do it? Was Mr. Markham really in Manchester at the time? Or perhaps he wished to become sole proprietor of the concern and used his own bees to do the job? Did farmer Pearson finally come to a breaking point with this intruder upon his peace? Perhaps the farmer spied the swarm going into the cabin and shut the hatch, preventing Mr. Kramer's escape.

Who was responsible for this very terrible end to a man's life and how did they do it?

The only clue I can give you is—timing is everything.

Lady Featherstone had applied her lorgnette and nodded knowingly as she read along. "Well, of course, it must be the partner. Nobody can confirm that he was ever in Manchester at all. And then, the man had bees. Who else could it be?"

Arabella did indeed think it rather coincidental that Mr. Markham was a beekeeper. Though, she was not as convinced by the lack of corroboration for the Manchester trip. After all, how could Mr. Markham have known that the inn he claimed to stay in would burn and the man he planned to meet would die? If he had never gone and was hoping for an alibi, those circumstances seemed a deal too lucky to be true.

"Of course, my mind does also go to the farmer," Lady Featherstone said. "It's clear enough that he does so love his cows. What might a person do to protect a beloved creature?"

"I must agree on that point, my lady," Sir Richard said. "Why, if someone attempted to hurt my spaniels, well…"

"It is just so, Sir Richard," Lady Featherstone said enthusiastically. "If some villain attempted harm to my Tulip, I'd lay my life down to protect her. Or perhaps my butler or one of the footmen would lay *their* lives down. Somebody would lay their life down!"

Arabella was beyond amused. She said, "Lord Blackwood, what do you make of the farmer?"

"Well, I think I agree with Lady Featherstone's assessment of the farmer's feelings. When I think of somebody hurting Alfie or Apollo, I do not know what I should do about it, but it would be very terrible. That person would be my enemy forevermore."

Arabella believed the line of thought that was developing at table could be directly attributed to them all being highly sympathetic to animals. She was not so certain it was right, though. All that was known was that the farmer liked to spout off in the tavern and had unmoored the boat twice. Did that really speak of a dangerous fellow, or just a foolish one? And where on earth did he get the bees? Certainly, if he maintained a hive, it would have been noted.

The only clue they'd been given was that the solution hinged on timing. But what timing?

The soup had been cleared and now a fish course was coming round. As interesting as the mystery was, it really was very awkward to eat as they went along.

Lady Featherstone appeared to have no intention of trying, as she'd moved her plate to the side and laid out her sheet of paper, peering over it as if she looked down a well to see if it held water.

Lord Blackwood leaned over to Arabella and said softly, "I cannot make heads or tails of this story, though my bet is on the wife."

"Why ever would you think it?" Arabella asked.

"Because to kill a person by locking them in with three hundred bees takes a certain sort of fury. The sort of fury that money or irritation alone cannot engender. If the partner wished to knock him off, I imagine he'd think of a more discreet way to do it than use his own bees. The farmer must be ruled out entirely. There are loud-mouthed gentlemen all over England, nearly always to be found in taverns, spouting off about something. I doubt that farmer had actually even unmoored the boat previously, but just bragged that he did."

Though Lord Blackwood had not particularly analyzed the clues, how interesting that he'd analyzed the players. It was not a direction she would have thought of.

"If you are correct," Arabella said, "then we must be able to explain *how* she did it."

"Ah, there's the rub," Lord Blackwood said.

"Oh, I see how it was," Lady Featherstone said to the table. "The farmer went to the partner's house while he was in Manchester, though I am still not convinced he *was* in Manchester, and then steals a hive. He takes it back to his farm and he waits for nightfall, when both the bees and his victim are sleeping. Then, he creeps along with it, opens the hatch, drops the hive, and slams the hatch shut. He probably sat on the hatch while the poor fellow banged on it and cried for help."

That was rather a gruesome picture, though only existing in Lady Featherstone's rather robust imagination. "But Lady Featherstone," Arabella said, "there was no hive found inside the cabin, just bees."

"Goodness, you're right," Lady Featherstone said, tapping her lorgnette on the table. "Wait, perhaps they were in league—the farmer and the partner! The partner brings over the bees and shakes them into the cabin and takes the empty hive back to his farm!"

"But then," Lord Blackwood said, "what does he need the farmer for?"

Lady Featherstone wrinkled her brow. "To keep the cows calm? So they don't stampede and knock down all the fences?"

Arabella smiled, though she thought Lady Featherstone did not perhaps have a great deal of experience with cows. She was also beginning to think that the lady's triumph at the last mystery supper had been just as amazing and improbable as her friends had claimed.

Still, they must help her if they could. Arabella bent her head once more over the clues.

Lord Blackwood said, "Look at this—the wife travels to tend to her sick mother and only stays one day. What was wrong with the woman? A sniffly nose that cleared up in hours?"

That *was* an inconsistency. Certainly, traveling that distance must indicate a certain seriousness that would not be resolved in a day. The mother certainly had not died, or that would have been noted and the daughter would have stayed on to make arrangements. It was very odd.

But what if the wife had never traveled at all and had remained in the neighborhood? Her never having gone to Winchester was just as likely as Mr. Markham never having gone to Manchester. But then, why bees? How had she managed the bees?

Lord Blackwood said, "Lady Arabella, you've spent so much of your time traipsing around the countryside, you must have seen bee stings galore."

"I do not know if I would categorize it as galore, but certainly Mrs. Weston and I have encountered enough stings, and Freddy is particularly bad—they seem to love him and then he swats at them."

"What I find unusual," Lord Blackwood said, "is that there are so many different reactions to the stings. Holes where the stinger remains, tiny white dots, purple dots, and the wife's raised welts. Is that the case? That there are so many different types of reactions? I've only seen welts on myself."

Arabella peered once more to a description of the body. The purple dots. She had never seen such a thing. And then, the description that other than the markings, the skin was smooth, with no welts at all, despite being stung so many times.

An idea came to her. "Lord Blackwood, all along I have been imagining the horror of shutting that cabin hatch and holding it closed while a man dies in agony."

"As have I," he said, "that's why I'm convinced it was the wife. The fellow threw his weight around once too often and that was that."

"But, I do not think that is what occurred," Arabella said, "I believe that Mr. Kramer was dead before the bees were introduced to the cabin. I believe the bees are meant to throw suspicion to the partner. The purple dots, they are not from the bees, they are from poison. The lack of any welts was because he was stung *after* death. You see, the wife poisons the husband, throws suspicion on the partner, and the boat is hers again."

"If that is the case, she must have been really, really angry."

"I suppose she was, or very greedy. She poisons him, she takes a hive from the partner and carefully brings the bees to the boat. I just don't know how she got the bees in there without the hive."

"It's the partner, I am sure of it," Lady Featherstone said to Sir Richard. "He goes to Manchester, burns down the inn, murders his associate and hurries back to Tewkesbury with nobody being able to say how many days he was away. Certainly, that must be it."

"Goodness," Arabella said quietly to Lord Blackwood. "How did I not notice this before. Lemon grass. She lured them in with lemon grass. I know this works, as the farmers in Cornwall use it when they wish to lure bees to a new hive."

"Ah, I see," Lord Blackwood said, "the bait was conveniently already there for her, as she well knew. She must have planned it for some time. She needed to have the lemon grass onboard, the partner away, and the boat docked in the vicinity of Mr. Markham's farm. The poor old farmer would have been the next in line to be accused if Mr. Markham found a way to wiggle out of it. After all, she could not have known that his alibi from Manchester would fall apart so completely."

"Just so," Arabella said.

Lord Blackwood wrote down what they had deduced, then he said, "That's all well and good, but..." Lord Blackwood said, glancing meaningfully at Lady Featherstone.

"Oh, yes, indeed," Arabella said. In a louder voice, she said, "Lady Featherstone, I believe you've put it all together for us."

"Have I?" Lady Featherstone asked.

"I believe so. You mentioned the purple dots probably not being stings, so of course that must be due to poison, and then you said how much bees like the smell of lemon grass and you noted that the partner could not be so lucky as to have all trace of his trip removed as an alibi, and you noted how odd that the wife only spends one day in Winchester, *and,* of course, how the victim's skin showed no welts."

"I said all that?" Lady Featherstone asked, brows wrinkling. "I suppose I may have, my mind has been racing full speed with facts, suppositions, and theories."

"We have been taking in all of your insights," Lord Blackwood said gallantly. "I hope you do not mind that I had put myself forward as your scribe?"

With that, Lord Blackwood handed Lady Featherstone his own paper, on which he had laid out the series of events that pointed to the wife, and how she'd managed it.

Lady Featherstone looked mightily confused as she took the paper. She held up her lorgnette and examined Lord Blackwood's solution.

As she read, she murmured, "Yes, I might have said that...well, I suppose I did instinctively know that all the pinpricks were not from the bees...certainly, he must have been dead when the bees were introduced...what had Lord Ryland said, timing would be everything...naturally, when you put it all together, of course it was the wife."

She laid the paper down. With a heavy sigh, she said, "Lord Blackwood. I may have said much of this, but you have put it all together. You must go and claim your prize."

"Me? I haven't done anything but write down all *your* conclusions," Lord Blackwood said. "Now, mind you, your ideas were coming at me so fast it was a challenge to keep up. I only hope I have done your keen mind the proper justice."

Lady Featherstone was entirely flustered. "My ideas, well, they do sometimes come on so fast I can hardly keep track of them...as for my keen mind, it's all in the training, you know..."

"Well done, Lady Featherstone," Arabella said.

"Yes, exceedingly well done," Sir Richard said. "Your mind moved so fast on the thing that I was entirely lost and befuddled."

Lady Featherstone's brow cleared and she leapt up from her seat with such energy that she very much resembled a rabbit popping out of its den.

"Heavens above, I've done it," she cried. "I've done it again!"

CHAPTER SIXTEEN

L ADY FEATHERSTONE TURNED on her heel and headed straight for Lord Ryland, waving her solution to the mystery over her head. Or somebody's solution, anyway. More than a few of the guests noted Lady Featherstone's direction and the hum of the room grew louder as conversations were had about it. There was not a person in London who did not know of last year's unlikely win and the prize of the emerald brooch.

"Goodness," Arabella said softly, "I hope we are right in our guesses."

"We must be," Lord Blackwood said. "It was a positively diabolical plot and one only a woman could dream up."

"I should be very offended by your opinion of women, Lord Blackwood."

"Don't be. Men are rather simple creatures. My father is a duke and half the time he has no idea where he is going or why. The duchess tells him what he ought to wear and that she's called the carriage for eight, and he's dressed and ready to go at eight. If my father ever decided to murder the duchess, he'd no doubt go to her for advice about it as a matter of habit. On the other hand, if it were *she* set on getting rid of the duke, she'd likely execute a month's long plan to make him believe he was going insane and then have him committed, thereby remaining a duchess rather than a dowager. I suppose it is well that they are fond of one another."

Arabella found this example rather alarming. And perhaps true. The duke did seem to take his sole direction from the duchess and, considering the story of the butler's mysterious society, she could well imagine the duchess creating something equally inventive and elaborate if she ever settled on murder.

Arabella watched Lady Featherstone hand Lord Ryland the paper with a look of triumph. The lord appeared mightily surprised, but he took it nevertheless and scanned it. He slowly nodded in the affirmative.

Lady Featherstone clutched at her brooch, wavered slightly, and was caught by two footmen before she hit the floor. A vinaigrette was waved vigorously under her nose and she recovered herself, though she remained sitting in the chair that had been hastily fetched for her.

Lord Ryland dinged his glass and the room fell to silence. "Charming ladies and esteemed gentlemen, the mystery is solved. Lady Featherstone has prevailed for a second year in a row, once more showing her incisive mind and nimble thinking.

"The murderer was the victim's wife, Mrs. Kramer, and it was almost a perfect crime. Mrs. Kramer killed her husband with arsenic and she knew she had to cover that up. How better than make it seem as if he'd been stung to death. She stole a small hive from Mr. Markham and after her husband was dead, she sets the hive in the cabin. The bees smell the lemon grass and come out of the hive to investigate, she removes the hive and shuts the hatch.

"Of course, the bees now trapped in the boat's cabin become exceedingly agitated and sting Mr. Kramer repeatedly. As he is already dead, his body does not produce welts or any other reaction. Those bees still living die quickly without water. Mrs. Kramer, if you will recall, *did* have welts from stings, though she wasn't stung when she claimed she'd found the body, she was stung the day before when she'd put the bees in the boat. She'd hoped to get rid of her husband via murder, and her husband's partner by framing him for the crime, or if not him, then the farmer. In the end, she would be the sole proprietor of the boat, just as she liked it.

"When Mrs. Kramer realized her plan was unraveling and suspicions were upon her, she took the boat and headed it straight over the nearby weir. It having rained substantially in the days prior, what happencd next was a foregone conclusion. The boat itself can still be seen further down the weir, capsized and caught on branches and debris. Mrs. Kramer herself is presumed drowned.

"Now that you know the who and the how, you'll want to know the prize for unraveling this difficult mystery. In some hands, this prize may have little meaning, but I know Lady Featherstone and every other member of my criminal society will appreciate its true value."

Lord Ryland nodded to the footmen at the doors and then one of them came into the room carrying a long rectangular white velvet pillow. Laid upon it was a walking stick. It did not appear expensive and had no embellishments. It did appear well-used, however.

"Lady Featherstone," Lord Ryland said, "I now present you with the walking stick of Monsieur Eugène François Vidocq."

"Vidocq!" Lady Featherstone cried. She began to fan herself, then she gave her fan to a nearby footman so that he might take over the duty.

"This walking stick has traveled with Vidocq through many of his adventures," Lord Ryland said to Lady Featherstone, "and may it now travel with you through your own adventures."

Lord Ryland turned to the crowd and said, "For those of you unacquainted with Monsieur Vidocq, he has been a deserter, an adventurer, a womanizer, a thief, an escape artist, and now has founded the Sûreté in Paris to investigate criminal activity. There will be few people in the world who understand the criminal mind like Vidocq. By the by, Lady Featherstone, the top may be twisted off and you will find a very sharp blade in the handle, should you ever have need of one."

Arabella thought Lord Ryland's guests might not care so much about Monsieur Vidocq, but it seemed that many had a soft spot for Lady Featherstone.

The crowd erupted in *bravas,* and *well-dones,* and *cleverly-solveds.*

Lady Featherstone rose majestically and took possession of the walking stick. She bowed to the crowd and walked sedately with it back to the table.

"We've done it," Lord Blackwood said.

"Yes, we have," Arabella said.

There was something wonderful in the idea that they'd worked together, both seeing some aspect of the case that the other did not. All with the goal in mind of helping Lady Featherstone to victory.

Arabella was so pleased that they'd been successful at it and would not mind spending every evening in such pursuits. Though, perhaps not always attempting to work out a murder. They might work to solve all sorts of mysteries, like who took the last fairy cake. That would be pleasant and without the grim reflections of a murder plot.

How many times had Lord Blackwood brushed her hand as they examined their papers or scribbled a note or clue? Really, it seemed he had almost done it intentionally some of the times. She hoped so, anyway. Mrs. Weston had explained to her that this was a common thing among gentlemen and was a testing of the waters. Did the lady recoil from the touch and appear outraged? Or did she simply pretend she had not noticed?

Arabella had pretended not to notice.

As pleased as Arabella was for Lady Featherstone's victory, she suspected the duchess and Lady Heathway would be dumbfounded, at the very least. Perhaps even irritated. Lady Featherstone was just now advancing through the crowd, nodding condescendingly as if she were Queen Charlotte herself. The clacking of her new walking stick was loud on the marble floor and Arabella supposed it would be a sound that would often accompany her going forward.

Lady Featherstone was a delight.

Everything was a delight just now. After the evening had

ended, Peregrine, Lord Blackwood rather, had escorted their carriage back to Grosvenor Square and he had made arrangements with Lady Redfield to continue the riding lessons on the morrow.

Delightful.

»»»«««

LORD SKEFFINGTON PACED his library as Nellie trailed behind him, pulling at his sleeve. Her makeup was still on from the stage and it looked garish away from the footlights.

He turned and grabbed her arm roughly. "For God's sake, go wash your face and stop complaining over things that cannot change to suit you."

Tears erupted in Nellie's eyes, as they always did. She was quite a skilled actress, after all.

"Aldy," she said plaintively, "it really is too hard of you to stay away so much and then you are so distracted when you are home and now you say I have to go live in an apartment somewhere?"

"Yes, that's what I said. I can't very well have you here while I'm pretending to be reformed and pressing a suit with a lady."

"A suit! With a lady?"

"Yet again, that is what I said. I intend on marrying her at her earliest convenience and then sending her to the countryside. It will have little effect on you."

"Little effect?" Nellie said, her voice rising in pitch. "Little effect?"

Nellie picked up an inkwell and threw it at his head. It hit the wall behind him and splattered ink all over the wall and floor. She grabbed at a paperweight and hurled it.

She did not hit him that time either, as she had rather terrible aim and he was well-accustomed to avoiding her missiles. The paperweight did, however, make contact with the window and sail through it.

He crossed the room, picked her up, threw her into the hall, shut the door and locked it. She would pound on it and carry on, but eventually she would run out of strength and go away.

He needed to think without Nellie hanging on his arm and whining about her life. She really was getting to be more trouble than she was worth. Perhaps he would rent her an apartment, pay the first month, and then bar the door against her. She would send letters, she would rail at his butler on the doorstep, and she would finally go away. Let somebody else put up with her temper.

Ryland's mystery supper had been tiresome in the extreme. Why was he to care whether some boatman got killed by a hundred bees or a thousand bees?

The evening was, however, very instructive. He'd kept a close eye on Lady Arabella's table. First, Blackwood had commandeered her card, then he'd taken her into supper. Throughout the evening, Lady Arabella and Blackwood had their heads together like a pair of conspirators.

His worst fear was looking more and more likely. Blackwood took a particular interest in Lady Arabella, and it seemed she returned the interest.

For himself, it would be difficult enough to woo the lady from the place of disadvantage where he just now stood. But if Blackwood was to propose, it was all up.

He could not attempt to pose as the more eligible suitor, not when Blackwood was to be a duke and he himself perhaps had a reputation that was not exactly unsullied.

He could not win that way. He could only hope to win if he were the *only* suitor.

Somehow, Blackwood must be got out of the way. Somehow, Lady Arabella must be convinced that Blackwood was no good. If that were to happen, she would question her own judgment. Certainly, that would lead her to question her judgment of himself.

How to accomplish it, though? That was the question that would keep him awake. He must figure out how.

A niggling little idea began to form in the back of his mind.

He so rarely paid attention to a gentleman's ramblings when at cards. But had not Blackwood told of a good joke? Had he not been attempting to outdo his friend Rendridge, who claimed to weave and dodge whenever his father brought up the subject of marriage? Had not Blackwood explained that his mother, the duchess, did not pressure him to marry because she was convinced he pined for a certain Lady Constance Melberry, to be out either next season or the following? Had he not explained that he and Lady Constance were like brother and sister and neither of them would ever countenance a romance between them?

Yes, he had. So, while his friends knew the real circumstance, Lady Arabella would not.

He would just have to inform her of it, and then urge her to go to the duchess for confirmation. Let Blackwood come off as a blackguard who wooed where he did not intend to settle and then he would see what she made of the fellow.

That just might be enough to knock Blackwood out of the running.

There were others to worry about, of course. Particularly Ryland and Vance. Ryland had shown some admiration for the lady, so that was a concern. Vance certainly had regard for the lady too, but Vance was easy enough to dismiss, his family having been so recently emerged from trade.

It would be his purview as guardian to turn away any man who tried for her hand, and he would.

The problem was, he could only exert that power for eleven months.

Blackwood was the real danger, he thought.

The way the two had been heads together and laughing and, if he had not been mistaken, touching hands…they might be happy enough to wait eleven months.

Nellie shouted through the door, "I'll not stay around to be treated like this! I'll be off!"

Skeffington knew well enough it was an empty threat. He also knew that Nellie would indeed be off, though she did not yet know it.

PEREGRINE WAS PLEASANTLY surprised by how enjoyable Ryland's mystery supper had been. He'd always found the mysteries rather tedious and never paid much attention to them, but this time had been different.

Lady Arabella had been such an interesting and intelligent partner at the game. She'd been *so* interesting, in fact, that he'd dared what he had not yet had the urge to dare near any lady of quality—he'd brushed her hand. Several times.

She'd pretended she hadn't noticed, which he had been led to believe meant the lady *had* noticed but hadn't minded.

And then, their efforts had been a success and Lady Featherstone had claimed her prize. Of course, the duchess would be incensed over that clacking walking stick the lady had use of now, but that was hardly his problem.

As the evening ended, it seemed only rational to escort Lady Arabella and Lady Redfield home again. After all, what were neighbors for? Then of course, arrangements needed to be made to continue the riding lessons. He had made a commitment to his mother about that.

He poured himself a brandy and sat in the drawing room. He would have sat in his library, that being the usual place for a gentleman to sip brandy and review the day, had not his butler commandeered it.

Mr. Sindu had not bothered to greet him at the door, he'd left that up to the footmen. Now, he sauntered in, poured himself a brandy, and sat down.

"Well?" Mr. Sindu asked.

"It was very good, surprisingly good, actually," Peregrine said. "Lady Arabella and I were able to assist Lady Featherstone to her second victory in as many years. The old girl was delighted."

"I see," Mr. Sindu said. "You escorted Lady Arabella to supper."

"Well I had to, didn't I?" Peregrine said. "There are many dangers to a young lady with a large fortune. Many indeed. I managed her card, which I do not believe has been done before. Oh, maybe a father has done it, but she hasn't got one. It was a master stroke, I thought, then of course, I took her into supper also. As that can be quite dangerous."

"Yes, food and drink can be lethal. At least, Socrates thought so."

"You know what I mean," Peregrine said. "It is not the imbibing, it is the time spent in close quarters."

Mr. Sindu nodded, as of course he had known what was meant.

"Lord Skeffington, in particular, needed to be held at arm's length, and he was. Right from when Lady Arabella set off from the house to getting home again, he never had a chance to approach."

"It is a job well done, Peregrine."

Peregrine glanced at Mr. Sindu suspiciously, as often one of his compliments was not a compliment at all.

It seemed his butler was in earnest though, as he slowly nodded and looked deep in thought. As if he had decided something, Mr. Sindu stared at the glass of brandy in his hand and said, "So, when do you propose to Lady Arabella?"

Peregrine leapt up, spilling his brandy down his shirtfront. "What?" he cried.

Mr. Sindu regarded him. "I see it is not the right time to inquire. I will ask again another day."

"There is really no need to ask again—"

Mr. Sindu set his brandy on a table and made to depart. Over his shoulder, he said, "You might consider Lady Tredwell's masque ball, since you will wear masks. You both go as red as beets over the slightest provocation. It is not altogether attractive."

With that, his butler disappeared into the great hall.

What was the man thinking? What was he saying? How had Mr. Sindu got it into his head that he and Lady Arabella...that they would...that he would...

Peregrine paused. He was not so entirely lacking in self-awareness that he did not realize that he'd grown very fond of Lady Arabella.

Perhaps more than fond.

She was such an adorable creature! Certainly, there was no other lady like her. What fun they'd had, mulling over the various personalities of the animals in their sphere. His conversations with her were not at all like his conversations with other ladies.

He'd thought his conversations at this dinner or that ball with this lady or that had been exceedingly adequate and usual. He supposed they had been, but it occurred to him now that they'd also been rather dull.

With Lady Arabella, he had not spoken of the latest play, or even more tedious, the latest gossip. No, they'd talked of real things. She thought deeply and felt deeply about who was around her, right down to a naughty squirrel.

He had already examined the idea that waiting two years to consider marriage might not end up exactly as he'd originally thought. For some years he'd imagined that if he just refrained from looking around until he was ready, the perfect lady would be nowhere nearby. That lady would come into view when he *was* ready, and he *did* look about himself.

What if fate had sent her early, though? What if she were like a passing ship, never to come this way again? What if he stood on a distant shore and watched her sail by, only realizing too late that she was not just *a* ship, she was *the* ship. What if he eventually discovered that there would be no other ship?

Peregrine poured himself another brandy. A very large brandy. Certainly, he must need it if he'd begun to think of Lady Arabella as a ship.

CHAPTER SEVENTEEN

L ADY REDFIELD SAT by the window watching Arabella skip charmingly down the front steps in her riding habit. Lord Blackwood was on his horse, and a groom held Bonny Betsy while Arabella was helped into the carriage. They were on their way to the park and the whole scene spoke of delightful youthful vigor.

Lord Blackwood really was so kind! He had been so attentive last evening, ensuring that neither Lord Skeffington nor any other undesirable person come close to Arabella. He'd even put himself out so far as to take her into supper.

Now, he would carry on with her riding lessons. Just now, the lord watched her approvingly as Arabella swept up her skirts and climbed into the carriage.

What a charming young gentleman. Lady Redfield had, from time to time, wondered if the duchess had not overestimated his worth. Silently, of course. She sometimes shocked herself with the ideas she had and would never dare say them aloud. So when she had wondered if the duchess made too much of her son, she speedily followed up that thought with the idea that all mamas were prone to it. She certainly viewed her own offspring as superior. Except for those times when they did or said or looked or smelled somewhat less superior.

However, now that she had got more fully acquainted with Lord Blackwood, she really could not claim that the duchess had exaggerated. Lord Blackwood really had showed himself to be exceptional.

A very small and niggling idea began to itch at the back of Lady Redfield's mind. It was the sort of thing she would prefer to ignore, as it was likely to be unpleasant.

Nevertheless, it would swim to the surface of her consciousness.

Was Lord Blackwood so exceedingly considerate of everybody? Or every young lady he encountered? Or…was something growing between him and Arabella?

The idea made her heart pound and she had the urge to dive under a sofa.

It was not that he would not be eminently suitable. Goodness, what a match it would be!

No, it was not that. It was the duchess. The duchess had very firm ideas about a match between Lord Blackwood and the still at home Lady Constance Melberry.

The duchess did not like her plans overthrown. She would be unhappy. She was so frightening when she was unhappy. She was sometimes frightening when she was happy, but always frightening when she was unhappy.

As if she had managed to conjure her from thin air, the duchess' carriage pulled up to the front of the house.

Lady Redfield sat motionless with her hands folded in her lap. Now that the idea that Lord Blackwood might have an interest in Arabella had occurred to her, it seemed as if it must occur to everybody. It must be written bold in the air in front of everybody's eyes. Particularly in front of the duchess' eyes.

Was that why the duchess was striding toward her stairs and looking very determined?

When Lady Redfield was in a near-panic, she had the urge to run and yet no will to do so. She was prey to a predator, keeping still and hoping not to be noticed.

The door to the drawing room swung open and Hemmings said, "My lady, the Duchess of Stanbury."

Lady Redfield would have clutched at her heart, had she been able to make her hand move.

"Well?" the duchess said, charging into the room. "What on earth will we do about it?"

She knew!

Lady Redfield stared at the duchess in abject terror.

The duchess sat herself down and said, "Really, Cecilia, we must put a stop to it. The emerald brooch was quite enough, but that walking stick is the absolute limit! Anne click-clacked all over Lord Ryland's dining room with that thing last night. Did you know there is an actual blade in it? She pulled it out three times to show people! What is she planning? Will she begin chasing desperate criminals through the rookeries? Are we to be accompanied by that weapon forevermore? Far be it for me to attempt to rein in another person's eccentricities, *except* when it involves me. People were amused, which does not reflect well on us or on our society."

The duchess' diatribe had given Lady Redfield time to think. She would usually be frightened of such vitriol, but as it was not on the subject of Lord Blackwood and Lady Arabella, she found she could hold up well against it. Perhaps it had only been her imagination that there was something between them. Surely it was.

She had got herself into a state over nothing.

As for Anne's new walking stick, she really did not see what they *could* do about it.

"Well?" the duchess asked. "Have you any ideas at all?"

"Ideas, hmm," Lady Redfield said. "I am not certain it is an idea, but when I wished something the baron did to go away, I simply pretended not to see it."

The duchess glanced around at the drawing room filled with the baron's treasures from India and frowned. "You may be better at that than I. I do not see how you ignore the riot of color surrounding you, nor how any of us ignore that walking stick."

"I suppose anything can be ignored if one really tries," Lady

Redfield said, thinking back to the most challenging things she had ever ignored. "When the baron went through a...an unfortunate period of life, he dyed his hair black and I pretended not to see it. Not even when the weather grew hot and black rivulets ran down his neck and onto his neckcloth. Around that same time, he began wearing a corset, and then eventually even..."

"Even what?"

"Padding on the front of his thighs," Lady Redfield said softly, the memory still a haunting one. One moment there had been her comfortable baron and the next a stranger walking the halls. A stranger with black hair and bulging thighs and a red face on account of a corset tied too tight. It had been terrifying and she'd locked her bedchamber door at night until he gave it up.

"And you said nothing? Nothing to dyed hair and padded thighs *and* a cinched in waist?"

"Nothing."

"And it all went away?"

"Eventually."

"I give you credit for patience, Cecilia. If the duke ever descends the stairs in such a state, I shall send him right back up them. Well, we are to ignore the walking stick, then. With any luck, it will accidentally fall into a fire one of these days."

Lady Redfield nodded, though she secretly thought Anne ought to be careful with her stick when nearby the duchess. She would not be surprised to see the duchess casually kick the stick into a conveniently located fire.

"By the by," the duchess went on, "I passed Peregrine and Lady Arabella on their way to the park for some riding lessons. It is a wonderful thing about my son—he does not have to be nagged and reminded. He agreed to conduct the lessons and he carries on with it no matter the trouble to himself. He has a fine sense of gentlemanly responsibility. Then, of course, he would move heaven and earth to please his mama."

Lady Redfield hoped that love for a mother or a sense of

responsibility was all it was. Or if it was something more than that, the duchess would not lose her temper over it.

Hemmings opened the door once more and, as Oscar brought in a tea tray, he said, "My lady, Lord Skeffington has arrived."

"So soon?" Lady Redfield whispered.

Lord Skeffington, as appeared to be his habit, did not wait to be led in but skirted round Hemmings and came into the room.

"Lady Redfield, Your Grace," he said, bowing. He rose and scanned the room, obviously looking for Arabella.

"She is not here," the duchess said with her usual forthright manner.

"Yes, I see," Lord Skeffington said. "As her guardian, I do inquire..."

"She's gone out shopping," the duchess said. "She's got the carriage, Lady Redfield's maid, two grooms and a reliable coachman. She's quite safe."

"Anything in particular she shops for?" Lord Skeffington asked.

He really was a dreadful fellow. Lady Redfield could see perfectly well that he intended on setting off after Arabella. She must be grateful that the duchess had been here and ready to manage his inquiries. She very well knew she could not think on her feet as fast as the duchess.

"It seems Lady Arabella is keen to locate a book about squirrels," the duchess said, "so I expect she'll try Lackington and Allen."

Lord Skeffington bowed once more and took his leave. Hemmings showed him out.

"That was very clever, Theodosia," Lady Redfield said.

The duchess nodded in agreement, seeming not the least surprised that a person had noted she was clever. She said, "Amusing too. Imagine poor Mr. Lackington's expression upon realizing that Lord Skeffington darkens his doorway. Wherever Skeffington spends his hours, I am quite certain he's never set foot in a bookshop."

ARABELLA WAS ALL high spirits. Lord Blackwood had advanced her lessons to trotting, which had gone exceedingly well. Dear Bonny Betsy was so responsive to everything that was asked of her that it was no trouble at all to master the new gait.

Then of course, Lord Blackwood was such a fine teacher! He was so attentive and good humored. He was knowledgeable, and yet explained everything so very simply.

He was exceedingly insightful too and understood his horses' temperaments. Alfie longed to be approved of and would work hard for a master who was generous with approbation. Betsy, on the other hand, was less excitable and relied upon routine. She would expect an apple when she returned to her stall, she would get one, and she would be entirely satisfied with the excursion.

Arabella thought most gentlemen would not take the time to understand the temperament of their animals, but they should! All species had overarching temperaments and habits, the mouse would never be a fighter, but within that broad range there was a panoply of differences. Mr. Prickles' love of biscuits and preference for underneath a table in the drawing room as living accommodation were solely his own and no other hedgehog's. Sir Slippery had so far preferred a bathtub rather than a river. Was that at all sensible? No, of course not, but it was only Sir Slippery's uniqueness showing itself.

She and Lord Blackwood had discussed these matters thoroughly and gone on through the park very jolly, occasionally passing by or speaking to someone they were both acquainted with, or sometimes it was an acquaintance of Lord Blackwood and he would make the introduction.

It was not the fashionable hour, and so most they encountered were serious about their horses and had taken them out for much-needed exercise in the cool of the morning.

It was edifying to note who cared for their horseflesh more than its ability to make a fine appearance in a crowd.

Mr. Vance had been out on his stallion, cantering through the park. A few other gentlemen who favored horseracing and hoped their own might win a race were out too.

The only other lady they encountered was Lady Langley, accompanied by her husband. They were on a mad gallop, laughing and waving to Lord Blackwood as they passed him.

As Arabella knew Lady Langley to be the mother of the very advanced baby, she assumed Lady Mendleton was just now pacing the nursery and looking for further signs of advancement.

Two hours had flown by and they had circled the park. They were both cognizant that there did not seem much more they could do for this lesson. Especially considering Lander was beginning to look grim at the reins of Lady Redfield's carriage and Flora was determinedly staring out the coach window with one eyebrow raised.

As the groom helped Arabella from Bonny Betsy, Lord Blackwood said, "I suppose I shall go home and then in the afternoon, I will walk about my garden. I always find it a pleasant time of day for the garden."

"As do I," Arabella said. "I should not be surprised if I do the very same. And then, just before dinner, Flora will walk with me in the square."

"Interesting. I often walk in the square before dinner as well."

"Perhaps I will see you there. Or in the garden."

"I shouldn't doubt it. Do you and Lady Redfield go out this evening?"

"No, we do not. It is to be a quiet evening in with just the two of us."

"Ah, lucky to have two to dine, I always think. I also do not have particular plans, but dining alone…well, I could always go to my club, I suppose."

"But I am certain Lady Redfield would be delighted to have

you. If of course, you would wish it."

"Never mind what I would wish, Lady Arabella. I cannot depend upon good company where I have not been invited by the lady of the house."

"Oh, I shall tell her. I am sure she will send over an invitation."

"Of course, I cannot speculate, but were that the case..."

"I am sure that will be the case."

By this time, Arabella was inside the carriage and leaning out the window. Lander, who had been quietly sighing, began to put more breath and sound into it.

Lord Blackwood tipped his hat and cantered off.

Arabella sat back. It had seemed, when she'd woken at dawn, that only the morning held possibilities. Now, it was to be all the day long. She would go to the garden, she would walk in the square, and with any luck at all Lady Redfield would invite Lord Blackwood for dinner.

It would be one long, endless possibility.

"What with ridin' round here, walkin' you in the garden, and then walkin' you through the square, I hardly know how I'll have time for Lady Redfield," Flora said.

"You needn't walk in the garden, Flora. You may sit, which will be a more comfortable attitude if you are to be my scribe. Freddy quite depends upon my regular letters."

"Does he?"

"And I must write Mrs. Weston, too."

"Of course," Flora said resignedly.

"Just think, until now I had nobody to write to and no news to send. Now, I have two people to write to."

"And yet *I* do the writing..." Flora muttered.

IT WAS A fine day and Hemmings had made arrangements to walk with Mr. Sindu through the square at one in the afternoon. For himself, it was an ideal time of day to slip away. He'd assumed the same for Mr. Sindu, though that gentleman had since corrected the assumption. Mr. Sindu never *slipped away*, he simply left through the front doors whenever he wished. A well-regulated household, he said, ought to be able to carry on without the constant presence of its leader.

As they strolled through the greenery, Mr. Sindu said, "Mr. Hemmings, I have had something on my mind. Something that I have examined from every angle. I prefer to closely examine a course of action before proceeding, you understand."

"Yes, of course, quite right," Hemmings said. "If I do not overstep, might I inquire into the nature of the dilemma?"

"It is simply this—I am not at all satisfied with the view from my bedchamber. I find I am also not satisfied with the room's size, or its lack of a dressing room, or its general appointments. The carpet shall be, in a year or two, approaching shabby."

Hemmings at first could not imagine what sort of substandard room had been issued to Mr. Sindu. Had he been put on the south side of the attics for the warm months?

But then, Mr. Sindu had lamented the lack of a dressing room. He'd never heard of a butler's quarters that came with a dressing room. He'd never heard of a butler needing a dressing room.

"A dressing room, Mr. Sindu?" Hemmings asked.

"Yes, of course, where else is my valet to organize my wardrobe?"

"Your valet, sir?" Hemmings asked, nearly staggering on the path.

"Indeed," Mr. Sindu said, "I hired him yesterday. He is even now pressing and brushing my clothes and making up an inventory."

"But…how?"

"Mr. Hemmings, who hires servants for a house? The butler. That's how. The butler determines the needs of the household and hires accordingly. Which I have done."

"What will Lord Blackwood say?"

"About my valet? Who knows. I suspect it will be little enough, as all of Peregrine's attention will be on the idea that I've moved myself into a guest bedchamber. You see, Mr. Hemmings, in that way I will attain a suitable view, the right size room, and a commodious dressing room."

Hemmings could hardly take in what he was hearing. He clutched at the railing that ran along the path. Mr. Sindu was proposing to move himself into the lord's floor of the house!

It was a line that could never be crossed. It was a line that was no less firm than if it were a heavy iron door bolted shut. It was the great divide between the *ton* and the rest of the world. It was the chasm that separated master and servant.

The great and bold Mr. Sindu intended on crashing through that iron door and leaping over the chasm.

"But Mr. Sindu," Hemmings said, beginning to become very concerned for the future of his friend, "will not Lord Blackwood dismiss you for the impertinence?"

Mr. Sindu smiled. "It is interesting that you chose the word *impertinence*, Mr. Hemmings. That is one of the favored words in their arsenal, you see, along with insolence, impudence, brazenness and so on. These are the arrows they fire to convince those like us that we have done wrong whenever we assume the mantle of our own worth and manliness. They must do this, you see, to hide the truth of it all. There is nothing special about them and they know it. A long-ago king controlled an army and doled out rewards by way of land and titles, that is all that has ever happened. Their blood is no more rarified than any other and their minds are often less than average, as they have had so little to cross them and force them to think."

"You have hired a valet and intend on taking over one of the bedchambers on the main living floor," Hemmings said in a breathy voice. "Mr. Sindu, you are turning *yourself* into a lord!"

"No, Mr. Hemmings," Mr. Sindu said, "I have no wish to be a

lord. I turn myself into nothing. I simply become more of what I am—Mr. Amandeep Sindu."

"But certainly Lord Blackwood will—"

"Do not concern yourself with Peregrine," Mr. Sindu said. "I have issued him instructions for his future happiness and if he is not an idiot he will follow them. He has far more important things to accomplish than wondering where I am sleeping."

Of course Hemmings remembered that Mr. Sindu had taken it upon himself to select a wife for Lord Blackwood, as extraordinary as that seemed. Is that what he referred to now? Hemmings had not quite believed that Mr. Sindu could take such a liberty.

"Do you refer to your selection of his wife, Mr. Sindu?"

"Yes, of course. Lady Arabella will do very well, if only Peregrine will get on with it."

"Lady Arabella?" Hemmings asked. "But Mr. Sindu, I am afraid that the duchess is set on a person named Lady Constance Melberry. I have heard her spoken of several times."

Mr. Sindu seemed not at all affected by this news and laughed heartily. "Lady Constance? Dear me, no. The poor duchess, she does imagine she is rather a mastermind, does she not? The truth though, is somewhat less interesting. The lady is a genius at taking her feelings and turning them into ideas that masquerade as facts in her mind. That is where her confidence comes from, you see? Everything she wishes to be true seems to be true—a very comfortable way of going on but not to be relied upon."

Hemmings walked unsteadily down the path, the shrubbery brushing his legs as he made the occasional swerve. Every time he walked with Mr. Sindu, another veil fell from his eyes.

He had, until these last few months, carried on with very ordered thinking. Very English thinking, if he were not mistaken. Everybody had a place and it was right that it was so. The chimney sweep need not wonder what a lord did all day, a lord need not wonder what troubles a dairy maid might encounter. Everybody had been placed in their proper spot by God's hand.

Now here was Mr. Sindu, a veritable Robespierre ready to

overthrow the established order.

Hemmings did not know what to think of it. He was all for boldly going forward with a fine cloth tied jauntily round his neck, and he had been delighted to assume the directorship of a mysterious society of butlers that did not exist, but these other ideas…

He supposed all he could do was watch how things progressed in Lord Blackwood's house. It was a dangerous course Mr. Sindu had set for himself. It was an exciting one though too. It was as if Mr. Sindu were some brave explorer, resolutely setting sail and never fearing going over the edge of the world.

"Do not appear so fretful, Mr. Hemmings," Mr. Sindu said. "I will manage Peregrine, as I always have."

CHAPTER EIGHTEEN

ARABELLA HAD NOT felt she had so much to do in one day in her life. She had ridden with Lord Blackwood in the park, then come home to speedily change from her riding habit to a day dress, and then race downstairs to explain to Lady Redfield that she must invite the lord to dine.

Lady Redfield had not seemed as enthusiastic over the idea as she would have thought.

"Dear Arabella," she'd said, "it would seem too much, I am certain. Lord Blackwood took you into supper last evening, and then to the park this morning and you propose having him to dine when we are not even hosting a dinner?"

"Yes, of course that is all true," Arabella said. "But he finds himself in a very uncomfortable circumstance. If he is not to come here, he must dine alone with nobody to talk to."

Lady Redfield had wrinkled her brow and said, "Why does he not go to his club?"

"Oh dear, the club," Arabella said. "There was some reason he could not go there, though I do not remember the details. Please, dear Lady Redfield, we must not sit here happily having conversation over dinner while allowing Lord Blackwood to dine entirely alone. It seems very cruel."

Fortunately, one thing Lady Redfield would never, ever was cruel. She relented and wrote the note, sending it next door with Oscar.

That done, Arabella skipped out into the back garden with Flora unenthusiastically trailing behind with her writing instruments.

Arabella had paused, listening for any sound of Lord Blackwood or Apollo in the garden next door.

So far, nobody had entered Lord Blackwood's garden. That was a shame, but she would not fritter away her time. He might still come and in the meantime, she had plenty to accomplish.

"All right, Flora," she said, "we'll start with Mrs. Weston's letter."

Flora had laid out her writing things and poised her pen.

My dear Mrs. Weston, I hope and pray that your visit to your sister is going marvelously well and that your brother-in-law and his brother, the bishop, are proving just as genial as you have always known your sister to be. It comforts me to think of you off having a very jolly time.

I, myself, have had some jolly times since we parted. I have taken riding lessons from Lord Blackwood and today we worked up to a trot. At our next lesson we will attempt a canter and I have all confidence in Lord Blackwood's good instruction and Bonny Betsy's patience to keep me seated.

Last evening, we attended Lord Ryland's mystery dinner and Lord Blackwood and I sat with Lady Featherstone and a genial gentleman named Sir Richard. Lady Featherstone prevailed in solving the mystery once more, though I like to think that Lord Blackwood and I had some little hand in it. Anyway, she won a wooden cane that belonged to some French fellow, it has a hidden blade, and she seems delighted with it.

If there has been anything to mar this time in London, it is Skeffy, which will be no surprise as he generally mars everything he touches. First, he threatened to send me away. That did not work at all, as the ladies gathered round their forces and set upon him. Lady Redfield says that even the queen wrote him a note expressing displeasure with the idea. (Can you imagine the queen concerning herself with me?) But it was Lord Black-

stone who delivered the final blow and made Skeffy reverse course.

Now though, he claims he will court me.

"He doesn't!" Flora interjected.

"Oh yes, he does, Flora," Arabella assured her. "He is precisely that vile. Now do write the following, as I know precisely what Mrs. Weston's feelings will be."

I need not be there with you to see the revulsion on your features, as they mirror my own. He shall get nowhere with the idea but will insist on making a pest of himself. I have told him as much, but he pays no heed.

He attempted to get on my card last evening, but he was outfoxed as I did not have my card! Lord Blackwood had it and managed it for me. Lord Blackwood thought up the idea and I thought it was very clever and also very kind.

Lady Redfield said the Skeffy turned up here today, but I was already gone off to the park with Lord Blackwood and he did not find me. That is how it shall be between Skeffy and I— he shall look and I shall hide.

Lady Redfield and I do not go out this evening but have a quiet dinner at home. Lord Blackwood comes to us, as he is our neighbor and has found himself at loose ends.

My most dear Mrs. Weston, you are to know that you are in my thoughts always.

All my love, Arabella.

Flora laid aside the paper. "Harrumph," she said. "There was more news of Lord Blackwood than anything else and no mention of the squirrel, I see."

"Thank you for reminding me, Flora. Please add a postscript as follows:"

I had the honor of healing the leg of a young squirrel named Rusty these past weeks. He only made himself inconvenient to Lady Redfield's guests one time and was otherwise very well behaved. He is back with his family now. Also, Freddy writes that Sir Slippery will use the fountain on fine days only but at least that is progress. Mr. Prickles remains exclusively interested in eating biscuits and dragging soft things under his table to further pad up his burrow so that is, of course, not progress.

⋙⋘

PEREGRINE HAD ENTERED the garden and would have made himself known, had not Lady Arabella been dictating another letter. Her missives were too charming to interrupt.

Though, this one to Mrs. Weston had been different than the missives composed for the mysterious Freddy regarding how he got on with his hedgehog and otter. He had been mentioned quite a few times and in glowing terms!

Of course, he could not reveal his presence in the middle of it, and certainly not when the maid chose to point out how often he'd been mentioned and certainly not while his face might be a deeper shade of red than was ideal.

But then, the maid had begun pressing to go inside with all sorts of nonsensical ideas about the heat and the sun being no good for such a fair lady.

Lady Arabella had pointed out that she wore a hat. But then as the debate wore on, she'd begun to falter.

Peregrine had run to the back door, opened it, and then slammed it shut, as if he were just now coming out.

"What a charming day to be out in a garden," he said loudly.

"Oh, hello Lord Blackwood," Lady Arabella called back.

"Lady Arabella," he said. "I have asked my gardener to leave me a ladder so I might check the soundness of the top of the wall. If the stones become loose there, it compromises the entire structure."

"Goodness, does it?" Lady Arabella asked.

Peregrine was certain he'd heard the maid mutter, "Stuff and nonsense."

Louder, the maid said, "Lady Arabella, I am certain that if Lady Redfield wishes the top of her walls checked, she will not wish it done by you."

"Oh, but she has been so kind," Lady Arabella said. "Any little courtesy I might provide…"

Peregrine had been climbing on his side and now Lady Arabella appeared on her side.

"Hello," he said.

"Hello."

They both stared at the top of the wall, seeming to look for those loose stones that could bring the whole thing down.

Peregrine ran his hand over the top of the stones and Lady Arabella did the same.

"Hmmm," Lady Arabella said, "is this one loose? I cannot quite tell."

Peregrine ran his hand to where he might find her own. He lightly brushed over it. She slowly pulled back. Very slowly though.

Her hand had been ungloved, as was his own. It was something, to touch her skin. He had a great urge to leap over the wall and take her in his arms.

"What do you think?" Lady Arabella said, determinedly peering at the stone in question.

Peregrine marshalled his thoughts back to the completely invented reason for checking the top of the wall. He said, "I do not believe it has come loose, but rather that it is on the *verge* of coming loose. You were very clever to spot it."

Lady Arabella blushed prettily. Well, not prettily exactly. More like a sudden flame engulfing her features. It might not be the usual sort of blush, but Peregrine was beginning to find it very charming, nonetheless.

"Well, I don't know how clever it was," Lady Arabella said.

The maid muttered, "Heaven help us."

The sound of an opening door behind him pulled Peregrine's attention from the maid's utter disdain of him.

He had just time to look behind him and see Apollo racing in his direction.

Knowing he was just moments from being knocked off his ladder by his highly affectionate and over-enthusiastic dog, Peregrine gripped the rails.

"Apollo!" Lady Arabella called. "Stop this instant!"

Miraculously, the dog did attempt it. Apollo had gained such speed that he was not altogether successful and ended up rolling a somersault on the ground and stopping against the ladder with a thump.

Lady Arabella stood on tiptoes and peered over the wall at his dog. Apollo struggled to his feet.

"Excellent work, my darling," Lady Arabella said to him. "Now do be a dear and come up and say hello."

Apollo was all accommodation to the request and launched himself on his hindquarters, his front paws resting on the top of the wall. He drooled and panted and looked for all the world as if nothing happier had ever occurred.

Lady Arabella patted his head and said, "I find your manners much improved. Oh, I know, you do still struggle. That is perfectly natural at your age and you are not to feel bad about it."

Judging by Apollo's expression, he did not feel the least bit bad about it. He generally did not feel bad about anything and was probably not inclined to start now.

The dog was so enthusiastic and delighted to have joined their party at the top of the wall that both Peregrine and Lady Arabella were entirely engaged with him.

Peregrine did hear the maid down on the grass fussing away and saying, "Goodness, now, Lady Arabella, do come down. You really must come down," but neither of them paid her any heed.

That was, until a second, less welcome voice, intruded.

"Lady Arabella," the deep voice said.

Peregrine looked past Lady Arabella's shoulder to see Lord Skeffington standing there, arms folded and looking in a fury.

Lady Arabella herself did not look as perturbed as Peregrine felt. She glanced behind her and said, "Skeffy, what on earth do you do here?"

"I have come here to inform you that I will join you for dinner. I have just seen Lady Redfield and arranged it."

"Do not be tedious," Lady Arabella said. "You know perfectly well that poor Lady Redfield does not wish it. In any case, we have already arranged for Lord Blackwood to attend us and there is no extra place. Cook will not have planned for enough, so I suppose it must be for another time."

"It will not be for another time and if there is not enough room, Blackwood can bow out."

"He certainly will not," Lady Arabella said resolutely.

"I certainly will not," Peregrine said, "I have already accepted, it would be bad form, you know."

"I care nothing for form," Skeffington said. "Lady Arabella, I will attend you at eight o'clock. I must hope you have deigned to descend your ladder by then."

With that, Lord Skeffington turned on his heel and marched back into the house.

As Peregrine watched him go, he could not help noticing Lady Redfield at a window, wringing her hands.

"Pay him no attention," Lady Arabella said. "Eat before you come, though, as I think there really will not be enough."

Peregrine nodded. "I ought to take Apollo in now, lest he overheat himself."

"Very good thought," Lady Arabella said. "I, myself, will rest, and then Flora and I will take our constitutional through the square at seven."

"Ah yes, I planned to go at the same time."

"Yes."

ARABELLA HAD GONE inside to find Lady Redfield. For a moment, she'd thought to ask how Skeffington had managed to worm his way into dinner, but just as quickly she knew how—Lady Redfield could not hold up against such a person. Skeffington had bullied his way in, she was certain of it.

She found the lady fretting in the drawing room.

"Oh dear, oh dear," Lady Redfield said, attempting the teapot with a shaking hand.

Arabella laid a hand over hers and said, "I'll do that, Lady Redfield."

She poured two cups as Lady Redfield said, "I could not stop him you know. I cannot forget that he could take you away at any time. Even with all the pressure we've brought to bear upon him regarding that ghastly idea, he could still do it if he liked. And now, oh dear, he's to dine with us."

Arabella handed Lady Redfield her cup and said, "You must calm yourself, there is no reason for alarm. Skeffington can only eat your dinner, he cannot eat *you*."

"You are so brave in the face of all this, Arabella. Goodness, if it were me at your age undergoing these trials, I should be crouched in a closet somewhere. How proud your father and mother would be to see you carry on so steadily."

"I do always hope they are proud, though I cannot take credit here. Whatever courage and good sense I've picked up must be laid at Mrs. Weston's door. She has been very insistent that I face my problems head on. Chin up and eyes straight ahead, is what she's always told me. So, that is what I try to do."

"Chin up and eyes straight ahead," Lady Redfield murmured. "Yes, that is very good. It sounds like something Lady Heathway might say. I ought to try it, I really ought."

Arabella picked up Lady Redfield's hand and kissed it. "You do not give yourself enough credit by half, you know. You lead a household and from what I have heard, you have raised a passel of fine boys. I am sure the baron is delighted with how you've carried on. Now, I will soon go out for my constitutional with Flora through the square, then I will change for dinner. We will get through the evening well enough—I have told Lord Black-wood to eat something before he comes as we really have taken Cook unawares."

"Lord Blackwood still comes?" Lady Redfield asked in some surprise.

"Of course he does, why ever should he sit home alone on account of Skeffington making himself a nuisance?"

"Oh dear," Lady Redfield whispered. "Chin up and eyes straight ahead, I suppose."

PEREGRINE WAS AT once buoyed up and on edge.

How delightful had been that little excursion to the garden. To hear of himself written about in such glowing terms. And then, to meet at the top of the wall, and brush hands.

But then Skeffington's arrival had been like cold water thrown over them.

What was the man thinking, pushing in like that?

No matter, the rogue had attempted to push him out, but he had not succeeded. He would go to the dinner and keep an eye on Skeffington. If the man got out of line, he would call him to task. He would not allow that creature to bully two innocent ladies.

First, though, he must have a shave and change clothes and prepare to escort Lady Arabella through the square before dinner.

He bounded up the stairs and then suddenly stopped. A man he had never seen before was coming down them.

"Who the devil are you?" he asked.

The man bowed and said, "Roberts, my lord."

"What are you doing here?"

"I have been recently hired as Mr. Sindu's valet."

"His valet?" Peregrine asked, incredulous.

"Indeed, my lord."

Peregrine turned on his heel to go back down the stairs. "I'll have a word with my butler about this. I presume he's in the library. A valet! This is really going too far!"

"My lord, he is not in the library just now. I left him in his bedchamber."

Peregrine froze, except for his eyes as they slowly traveled up the staircase. "His bedchamber?"

"Yes."

"And which one would that be?"

"The third door on the right, my lord."

Peregrine jogged up the stairs, hardly knowing what he was walking into. Why must his butler always push things? He was never satisfied. First the library, and now a bedchamber on his own floor?

At the rate they were going, it would only be a matter of weeks before *Lord* Sindu was ordering *Mr.* Blackwood about the place.

Of all the pointless things he'd learned in school, nothing practical had ever been offered. It would have been nice if somebody had explained what to do when your butler was taking over your own house.

He threw open the door to the bedchamber that the newly-hired Roberts had directed him to and found his butler sitting in a comfortable chair by the window, feet up on an ottoman, and reading the newspaper. He was dressed in a fine silk banyan of dark green which looked a little familiar, as if he'd had the same himself once but had not seen it for a while.

"Sindu!"

"It is *Mr.* Sindu, if you please."

"Oh, is it? Are you certain it is not Maharajah Sindu or King Sindu or Emperor Sindu?"

"I am certain, as I hope you are, too."

"This is outrageous," Peregrine said, looking around and recognizing various things from other parts of the house. A vase the duchess had just given him for his new accommodations sat on a chest of drawers, filled with fresh flowers from the garden.

"Peregrine," Mr. Sindu said, in that tone that made it seem as if Peregrine might be only eleven, "the view from my old room was hideous, the room itself too small, the ventilation substandard, and there was nowhere to put my valet."

"As I assume I pay that valet's wages, he is *my* valet."

"I suppose he could serve us both, but Turnbury would be entirely put out."

"This cannot go on. Every time I turn around you have taken something. First the library, and now a room on the family's floor? And then, it is taking a rather large liberty to hire a valet with my money. It will not do!"

"You find it all exceedingly impertinent, insolent, impudent, and brazen, I am sure. However, as the only family that resides on this floor is you, I really do not see the inconvenience of it. Further, were you to acquire a family, for which I have high hopes, I will move forthwith. I understand that both you and Lord Skeffington dine at Lady Redfield's this evening. The beginnings of your family reside in that house by way of Lady Arabella. It does not take the mind of a maharajah to divine what to do about it."

"Stop hinting that I should propose to Lady Arabella!"

"I have never hinted, I have only said."

"*If* I decide to propose to Lady Arabella or anybody else, *I* will decide when and where."

"Of course."

"Now see here, Mr. Sindu, I have overlooked many things...many, many things, on account of us having known each other since we were children. But that courtesy can only go so far."

Mr. Sindu calmly laid down his paper and carefully folded it. "Peregrine," he said, "you have nobody so invested in your future happiness more than Amandeep Sindu. I think you know this. The duchess confuses your place in society with your heart and your happiness, she sees them as one and the same. I do not. The duke believes the duchess right in all things. I do not. As for where I sleep or who dresses me or where I read my books—"

"*My* books!"

"Very well, where I read Peregrine's books and that he cannot be bothered to read himself, these are all unimportant details in comparison to the service I have rendered you in the past and will render you in future."

The man was really impossible. Of course, Peregrine was well aware that Mr. Sindu looked out for him. He was certainly aware that his butler had saved him from ruinous bets, ill-advised liaisons, scurrilous acquaintances, hawk-eyed matrons with unmarried daughters, unfortunate brawls, and no end of fraudsters wishing to part him from his money when they'd traveled the continent.

But how was he to explain to other people that his butler had a commodious room no less in size than his own, had hired a valet, and had ejected him from his own library?

"Nobody must know of this," he said, pointing at his butler. "You understand me? Nobody must know."

Chapter Nineteen

ARABELLA DID NOT usually change for her walk with Flora, as she would just have to change again for dinner.

She did change today, though, as she had a very pretty walking dress that she thought would suit.

As the clock chimed seven, she strolled out the doors with Flora, though the maid looked as if she'd rather stroll right to her own room instead.

Lord Blackwood was just coming out too, and Arabella was gratified that he'd paid such close attention to the time.

"Lady Arabella," he said, striding toward her.

"Lord Blackwood."

"Might I accompany you on your walk?"

"Yes, of course."

And so they strolled down the paths through the shrubberies.

"Skeffington has a bold nerve, pushing in where he is not wanted," Lord Blackwood said, "but he shall find the two ladies he imposes upon not without protection. I will not stand for any bullying."

Arabella was very moved by his speech. She did not really think she needed protection from Skeffy, as she had been managing him for years, but it was lovely to think that Lord Blackwood was so set on doing it.

"Of course, Lady Redfield and I must be very gratified to know it," she said.

"Well, I do not ask for any sort of gratification. It is only doing what is right."

They walked in silence for some minutes, only accompanied by Flora's quiet sighs.

"How does Freddy get on with the menagerie?"

"Oh, wonderfully well. He really does have the touch with all sorts of animals. Of course, Sir Slippery and Mr. Prickles are presenting a challenge right now, but he'll overcome their objections to going back to the wild one of these days."

"Ah, very good news."

"Yes, I suppose it is. Though I worry about that situation. Sooner or later, Skeffy will throw Freddy out. Skeffington's always wished to rent the place and, now that he can, I do not see what would hold him back from it."

"That rogue is outrageous. Everything he does is either wrong or causes a problem."

"Agreed," Arabella said, "though that will not help Freddy or Mr. Prickles, or Sir Slippery or Mrs. Murder and her kittens, or the Nightlys or Mrs. Twitch-nose and her extended family. They shall all be thrown to the road. Or worse."

"We must beat him at his own game, then."

"How?"

"Let's see, what's required is a new place for Freddy. He shan't need a big place, I dare say. Some sort of farmhouse would do, I imagine."

"A farmhouse would do very well," Arabella said. "But neither myself nor Mrs. Weston have the means to set him up. I can't touch anything I have until I reach my majority."

"Yes, I see. Though I do not suppose that any question of money should sink the scheme. Money can always be found."

"Can it? I have not ever had that experience."

"Oh certainly. In fact, I've often considered buying a small place in Cornwall nearby a river that I might use as a fishing lodge. Is there a river nearby? I imagine so, as you've got an otter."

Goodness, yes," Arabella said. "We can see it right out the windows and it is only a quarter mile away."

"Naturally, if I did set up a fishing lodge, I'd need a caretaker of some sort. I suppose Freddy would be up to the task. I'll send my solicitor down and see what can be done."

"That is too kind, Lord Blackwood!" Arabella exclaimed.

"Nonsense," he said, his face flaming. "It is only what is right."

As Arabella noted his very red face, she knew her own must be equally red.

How extraordinary that he would extend such a courtesy. Did he really wish to have a fishing lodge in Cornwall, or did he only say so? Whichever it was, such an effort must indicate some regard for her.

Certainly it must.

"We'd best turn now," Flora said, "else you'll be coming in late to change."

Arabella was surprised that so much time had passed so quickly. Still, there was a dinner to come, even if they must be burdened by the tedious Lord Skeffington.

Perhaps Skeffy would get sick, or be accosted on the road, or shot by an enemy, of which he surely had many. There might be no end of reasons he would not come.

If he did come, though, Arabella was determined to pay him the least amount of attention possible.

Her attention would be wholly engaged elsewhere.

As they parted at Lady Redfield's doorstep, she said, "Do not forget to eat something ahead of time, lest you starve this evening."

HEMMINGS COULD NOT help but look upon the evening's arrangements as irregular. The schedule had been that Lady

Redfield and Lady Arabella were to stay at home and dine in. A simple enough thing.

Then had come the addition of Lord Blackwood.

Then had come the addition of Lord Skeffington.

Was it a dinner party or was it not?

Mrs. Beltrain, never of particularly even-keeled nerves to begin, had fairly lost her mind in the kitchens. There was not enough on hand!

She'd already threatened to quit twice. Exasperated, Hemmings had warned her that if she tried it a third time, he would accept her resignation and cook the dinner himself. That idea, coupled with the knowledge that Lady Redfield no longer overruled him on such matters, had stopped her tirade.

It had not stopped her weeping, though. He'd left her searching the larder for whatever she could throw together on such short notice while shouting at the kitchen maid to fetch her a spare handkerchief.

As if randomly adding people to dine was not irregular enough, Lady Redfield had sent for him and delivered some very bizarre instructions.

"Hemmings," she said, "this evening will be at best awkward, or at worst...I really do not know what. I think our best chance of avoiding any unpleasantness is to not allow the thing to drag on. This is not a party, it is only two extra people stopping by for dinner."

"What is a *stopping by*?"

"I am sure I do not know, I just cannot think what else to call it. In any case, we will dispense with courses, well, not the soup I suppose, but once soup is out of the way, bring everything else at once. That should speed things along."

"As for the *everything else*, my lady," Hemmings said, "I am not at all clear on what that will be. As you know, our weekly grocer's and butcher's orders will not come until the morrow. We had arranged a small chicken and some vegetables, along with a modest salad and a cheese plate, as with only two ladies…and that left just enough for the servants' dinner and then breakfast on the morrow."

"Oh dear, I suppose Mrs. Beltrain finds herself at sixes and sevens."

Hemmings did not answer that comment, though he felt the cook was closer to tens and elevens if her weeping and shouting was anything to go by.

"You must tell her she is not to upset herself," Lady Redfield said. "She may serve whatever can be had, I do not care how haphazard the whole thing is. Please do ensure there is enough for the servants, I had far rather have Lord Skeffington go hungry than one of my own household."

Hemmings was rather fortified by that. Whatever irregularities were to be experienced this night, the staff took precedence over all else. He thought Mr. Sindu would very much approve of the notion.

"Now, about the wine," Lady Redfield said, "I do not wish either gentleman to overindulge. Or to indulge much at all. You are always so good about noticing signals and glances, do not be so good at it tonight. As for port, do not leave the bottle on the table! Pour them small glasses and then depart the room with it. That will stop them lingering. And good heavens, no champagne in the drawing room tonight! No champagne anywhere, in fact."

Poor Lady Redfield had begun to wring her hands and Hemmings well knew the cause. It was not on account of Lord Blackwood, who he knew to be the son of the duchess and a pleasant gentleman who allowed his butler all sorts of original things.

No, it was Lord Skeffington. *He* was the troublemaker.

Well, a butler may not be able to speak out against his mistress's guests, but a butler might well be in a position to make a person's visit decidedly uncomfortable.

He would speak to Oscar and William. Lord Skeffington would receive only the barest of courtesies. The very barest.

LORD SKEFFINGTON HAD imagined that if he had an entire evening to work at it, he might begin to sway Lady Arabella's opinion of him.

He was certain it could be done, if only Blackwood had stayed away.

Not only had Blackwood *not* stayed away, but the devil had the nerve to turn up early. As he'd had the same idea himself, they were both just now sitting in the drawing room waiting for the ladies to descend.

They sat at opposite ends of the room, Blackwood scowling like a bishop dining with a courtesan.

From what he'd seen today, and looked upon now, there could be no doubt that the man had a strong interest in Lady Arabella.

It must be stopped. She must be convinced to think less of the fellow.

The butler opened the doors to the drawing room and Lady Redfield entered, followed by Lady Arabella.

She was looking rather lovely in a dark green silk with a like-colored netting. She might be found quite palatable, if only she never spoke.

"Lord Blackwood, Lord Skeffington, welcome," Lady Redfield said in her usual flutter.

He had no idea how Baron Redfield had ever cohabitated with such a creature. She seemed always on the verge of flying away like a sparrow.

Though, by the looks of the drawing room and its rather bizarre furnishings, perhaps the baron had not been anything sensible himself. They might as well be in Bombay.

Blackwood had practically flown to the ladies' sides before he'd even had time to rise.

"You are very kind, Lady Redfield, to accommodate me when

I am at such loose ends, and on short notice too," Lord Black-wood said.

Lord Skeffington said, "Lady Redfield, Lady Arabella," and executed a short bow.

Lady Redfield acknowledged him. Lady Arabella looked through him as if he were an ephemeral mist.

To Lord Blackwood, Lady Redfield said, "We are happy to accommodate, as well as we can of course. I am afraid we serve nothing very elaborate this evening."

The butler cleared his throat and said, "Dinner is served, my lady."

"Oh excellent, yes, well, no need to tarry I shouldn't think," Lady Redfield said nervously.

Before receiving any direction from his hostess at all, Black-wood put his arm out for Lady Arabella, leaving him to take in Lady Redfield.

Relations between them seemed very...familiar. Too familiar. And what was the rush into the dining room for? One might almost imagine that Lady Redfield was set on getting them through it and out of the house as fast as possible.

He took Lady Redfield's arm, setting his teeth. If Blackwood thought he was to have extensive private conversation with Lady Arabella, he would be very disappointed.

Lady Redfield's dining room was just as strange as her draw-ing room. For one, the intricately carved table of Indian origin did not even fit the proportions of the room, which could have easily held fifty. One might squeeze thirty round that piece of furniture, but only if everybody were prepared to bump elbows.

"Do take the bottom, Lord Blackwood," Lady Redfield said. "My husband was so very fond of you as a boy, he'd be pleased to have you hold his place."

Lord Skeffington pressed his lips together. Apparently, no courtesy was too great for Blackwood.

He had barely had time to lift his napkin before soup was before him. The butler came with the wine and he stared incredulously as the fellow poured him a quarter of a glass and very determinedly avoided his eye.

Blackwood managed to get half a glass, though no more than that.

It was abundantly clear that Lady Redfield did not mean for anybody to be comfortable this evening. Not even herself, apparently. She was making her way through her soup as if she were in a race to the finish.

He tasted it and he could not think why she went after it with such enthusiasm. Clearly, it had been watered down.

"Tell me, Lord Blackwood," Lady Arabella said, "what is the history of your favored horse? He is a magnificent creature, but I have yet to hear of his lineage."

Blackwood seemed delighted to be asked, as was very typical of a gentleman. Skeffington himself could not be bothered to wax on delirious about his horseflesh but as so many men were, it seemed a usual feminine gambit.

"Ah," Lord Blackwood said, "He was sired by Selim, thereby his line going all the way back to the Byerley Turk. His proper name is Alfred the Saxon, though I call him Alfie."

Skeffington attempted to keep his expression neutral, though the amount of disdain he felt for a gentleman inventing a pet name for a horse was extreme.

"He has such fine sensibilities," Blackwood went on, "it is as if he can hear my thoughts."

Ah. Now his magical horse was a fortune teller.

"Oh yes," Lady Arabella said, "I am convinced that if an animal cares for you, it will pay close attention to you and learn to divine your meanings."

Skeffington had heard enough of these fantastical imaginings.

He said, "Lady Redfield, do you plan on attending Lady Tredwell's masque?"

The lady had finished her soup and the butler and footmen began clearing the course, though nobody else had finished. His bowl was practically swiped away from him.

"Oh, the masque," Lady Redfield said, "perhaps, well, what I mean is, no firm decision has been made. We are still...up in the air about it."

"Why?" Skeffington asked bluntly.

"Um, this or that, here or there, schedules, you know."

Of course, he did not know. One received an invitation and either accepted or declined. It was not a writing of the Magna Carta.

The servants brought in the next course and considering what a conglomeration of bits and bobs it was, Skeffington guessed it to be the only other course coming.

There was an exceedingly small roast chicken that he could have easily finished off on his own, an equally uninspired salad, a small bowl of peas, another of roasted potatoes, rolls, butter, two apple tarts, and a cheese board.

He should have eaten before he arrived.

He glanced at Lady Redfield to see if she were ashamed of such a paltry spread. As she fanned herself and put on a forced smile, he supposed she was.

Though he'd thought he'd managed to change the subject from Blackwood's prescient horse, somehow the two of them were right back to animals.

Lady Arabella said, "I have always considered it an honor to be a part of the healing of one of God's creatures. Even when they do not seem to appreciate it very much. At least, outwardly. There are some, like badgers for example, who struggle with trusting a person and instead fall back on their natural defensive instincts. Of course, for a badger, those instincts will always drive them to attack. Lord Bushwick became rather renowned for it before he finally set off into the wild."

Skeffington gritted his teeth. Lord Bushwick was no doubt the creature who had shredded his coat the last time he visited Cornwall. If that were not aggravating enough, he could well guess that Lady Arabella purposefully mentioned it to throw a barb at him.

"Lord Bushwick?" Lord Blackwood said. "He is one I had not heard tell of."

"He returned to his natural surroundings over a year ago. Truthfully, while I will never regret nursing him, Mrs. Weston and I did agree that a badger regaining his strength is a badger who should be out of doors. I do not think we would try the same again."

"All creatures have their own temperaments, I suppose," Lord Blackwood said.

"Yes, but then their own personality within the temperament range, making each a unique individual."

"Of course that must be right," Lord Blackwood said. "I have a whole stable full of horses, and yet they are all of different personalities.

The conversation could not be more banal. The food on his plate would not feed a child. Lady Arabella wished to taunt him.

He was getting nowhere.

But he had to get somewhere. He had no other option.

Somehow, he must break apart this burgeoning felicity between the two lunatics who thought animals were no less than people dressed in furs.

Somehow, he must marry Lady Arabella. Though, she'd be far better suited for a job in the Royal Menagerie.

ARABELLA HAD FOUND the dinner more entertaining than she would have expected, considering Skeffy was at table.

For one, the dinner itself had verged on the ridiculous. It would have been very suitable for her and Lady Redfield to consume, but adding two gentlemen into the mix had made it seem absurd.

Poor Mrs. Beltrain, she had clearly been forced to water down the soup. Arabella guessed that she'd ransacked the larder and came up with a few more blocks of cheese and some rolls for her troubles. The grocer's and butcher's weekly deliveries would all come on the morrow and Mrs. Beltrain was unlikely to be wasteful, so the cupboards had been bare indeed.

Perhaps most amusing was the appearance of two dessert tarts, though there were four people at table.

Naturally, these had been pushed onto the ladies, and Arabella had happily complied. She would not have liked to see Skeffington have one, as she was certain he was starving over his meager plate. Nobody had told him to eat beforehand, as she had told Lord Blackwood.

Despite Skeffington being at table, or perhaps because of it, she and Lord Blackwood had a really engaging conversation regarding animals of all types.

Skeffington very clearly did not have an affinity for them. Why would he, he did not seem to have an affinity toward anything living, beast or man.

He had obviously found the discussion very tedious, which had encouraged her to carry on with it.

She thought he would go mad when she brought up Lord Bushwick. His lips had transformed into a thin line and she could see he gripped his fork until his knuckles went white. Arrow launched and target hit.

Now, she and Lady Redfield were in the drawing room, having left the gentlemen to their port.

Lady Redfield paced back and forth and said, "They shan't be in there long, I told Hemmings to pour small glasses and take the port bottle with him."

"Very clever, Lady Redfield," Arabella said.

She was vastly approving of the strategy, as she really did not think it a good idea to leave the two men alone and assisted with port for too long a time. Not when Lord Blackwood had such stern ideas about keeping Skeffy in his place.

"Did you want tea, my dear?" Lady Redfield asked. "I rather hope not, as I was thinking of saying we'd run out."

Laughter bubbled up inside of Arabella. For all Lady Redfield's viewing herself as frightened and ineffectual, she could be rather ingenious.

"And then," Lady Redfield continued, "I asked Hemmings to bring you a tonic so I could claim you had a headache. You need not drink it, of course."

"But it will speed them on their way," Arabella said.

"Just so," Lady Redfield said. "The quicker we get Lord Skeffington out of the house, the better, to my mind."

Arabella nodded. "I will lounge on the sofa, appearing suitably enervated. And, after the meager dinner Skeffy has just had, one hopes he has a headache of his own and that once he leaves he will not think to come back."

"Oh dear, that dinner really was dreadful, was it not?"

"It was wonderfully dreadful. Though I am sure Lord Blackwood did not mind, as he knew to eat ahead of time."

CHAPTER TWENTY

PEREGRINE COULD NOT make out Hemmings on this particular night. Rather than just setting the glasses and placing the port on the table, he'd poured out two paltry glasses and then rushed from the room with the bottle, cradling it like a newborn babe.

He supposed he should not mind it, he had no interest whatsoever in conversing with Skeffington.

He drained his port and waited for Skeffington to do the same so they could join the ladies in the drawing room.

Rather than drink his port, Skeffington only stared at it. He said, "As you are fully aware that I am Lady Arabella's guardian, you will not take it remiss if I inquire into your dealings with the lady."

Dealings with the lady? Dealings was what Skeffington had with his long line of actresses. Peregrine had no *dealings* with Lady Arabella.

"She is my neighbor, and Lady Redfield is a great friend of my mother's. Of which both facts you are perfectly aware."

"That is not all though, is it?" Skeffington said. "There seems to be a certain…familiarity between you."

Peregrine crumpled his napkin in his hand. "If you imply that there is anything at all untoward—"

"I implied nothing," Skeffington said sharply. "I said there seems to be a certain familiarity. If you are courting the lady, you are to know that I will not approve it. She is too young, if not in age, then in mental capacity."

If Peregrine had been within reach of a bottle of port, he surely would have poured himself another, very substantial, glass. Instead, he said, "Skeffington, we all know you are attempting to court the lady yourself and we all know she'll not have you. As for who I choose to pursue, if anybody, that is my business and not yours. Further, your reign of terror ends in eleven months and, if half of society including the queen have anything to say about it, you'll finish out your duties quietly."

Peregrine watched Skeffington's fingers grow white around the rim of his glass. He finally did drain his port then. He rose and said, "I'll finish off my duties as I see fit. As I am still her guardian, I am warning you off. I do not wish you to approach the lady."

With that, he turned and headed for the door.

Peregrine leapt up and followed him. "I'll not be warned off," he called after him.

As he followed Skeffington into the drawing room, Peregrine mastered his composure. He must do, for the ladies' sakes. He was certain Lady Arabella would play the pianoforte. With any luck, he could push Skeffington into playing piquet with Lady Redfield. He knew from the duchess that she was particularly dreadful at cards.

The sight that greeted him was not what he'd expected.

Lady Arabella seemed to have wilted on the sofa. She leaned back while Lady Redfield laid a compress on her head.

"That tonic you've taken will do you good, my dear," Lady Redfield said.

She turned to the gentlemen entering the room and said, "Poor Arabella has come down with a headache. Also, we are out of tea."

Peregrine could hardly control his laughter. Nobody in England ever ran out of tea. No household would ever allow the tea stores to dwindle in such a manner. The servants would stage a revolt without tea.

As for Lady Arabella's unfortunate condition, when Skeffington briefly looked away, she winked.

"Well, we'd best be off," Peregrine said. "We have already overtired the ladies. Lady Redfield, I do thank you for having me on short notice. Lady Arabella, I pray the dawn sees you free of headache."

He bowed. Then he very determinedly waited for Skeffington to take his leave.

It was obvious enough that the man saw through Lady Redfield's ruses, but there was not much he could do about it.

He delivered a rather irritated-seeming bow and said, "Lady Redfield, do allow me to send a tin of tea to you on the morrow. I should not like to think of my ward experiencing any privation in this house."

Hemmings showed them out and Peregrine nearly guffawed on the steps. Skeffington's horse was already there, waiting to carry him away.

He left the man fuming and jogged into his own house.

LADY REDFIELD HAD felt her nerves growing more taut by the hour. The dinner the evening before, if one could call it a dinner, had given her a headache. It was all well and good to pretend that Arabella had a headache to get the gentlemen out of the house, but she'd actually developed one.

Dear Flora had soothed it through various ministrations, perhaps the most effective being a dose of laudanum and soft-spoken encouragements before she got in her bed. This morning, her maid had applied a cold cloth to her head and she really began to relax and feel better. After all, nothing terrible had happened at the dinner. All was well.

But then the duchess had sent a note, calling all of the Society of Sponsoring Ladies to Lady Redfield's house for a conference of some importance.

Why?

The dread that carried a possible answer swirled round her stomach. The duchess had somehow seen that there might be something developing between Lord Blackwood and Arabella. Lady Redfield had been waiting for the blow, like a noblewoman faced with a French guillotine.

The duchess would come to demand she put a stop to it.

Lady Redfield fiddled with the handle of her fan. She felt like a child waiting to be scolded for doing wrong.

But what could she have done to stop it? What could she do now? Ought it not be the duchess who should take it up with her son?

If there was anything to take up. After all, nothing had been actually said.

Whatever was to be laid at her door, whatever accusations hurled, she would not wish for Arabella to overhear any of it. She'd sent the girl out to the garden to collect flowers for various arrangements around the house.

Lady Redfield leaned back against the sofa and glanced out the window. The duchess had a habit of arriving early. She must be prepared.

And there was a carriage, just now coming to a stop.

As the arms on the door came into view, relief washed over her. It was not the duchess. It was Lady Mendleton's carriage. Dear Lady Mendleton, she was not frightening at all.

Oscar came in with the tea tray and laid it out on the table.

Hemmings soon appeared and said, "Lady Mendleton has arrived, my lady."

Lady Redfield rose. "Dear Louisa," she said, before pausing at the lady's appearance.

She held a bundle wrapped in a fine embroidered silk blanket.

"Goodness," Lady Redfield said. "Is that the baby?"

"Indeed it is," Lady Mendleton said. "Georgiana was perfectly amenable to the idea that our little girl must have some fresh air and I thought your air is as fresh as any. Meet Miss Daisy Louisa Stapleton, daughter of Viscount and Viscountess Langley."

Lady Redfield peered at the baby. Considering how advanced the infant was meant to be, she was rather afraid it might stare at her and say hello.

As it happened, the baby was fast asleep and looked like any other baby she'd ever seen.

"Do sit, goodness, how shall you manage tea?" Lady Redfield asked. "Shall I call Flora to take the baby?"

Lady Mendleton clutched her bundle and practically hissed, "*Take* the baby?"

"No, no, never mind," Lady Redfield said soothingly.

Heavens, the poor lady had reacted as if she'd proposed a kidnapping.

"The Duchess of Stanbury, Lady Heathway, and Lady Easton," Hemmings announced at the door. He followed the ladies in and handed Lady Redfield a note. "This was just delivered, my lady."

As her friends settled themselves, Lady Redfield opened the note with trepidation, praying it was not some directive from Lord Skeffington.

She scanned it and said, "It is from Anne. She sends her regrets, but she cannot attend us."

"Cannot attend us?" the duchess said. "What on earth could take precedence, I wonder?"

Lady Redfield did not wonder, as Anne's note had explained it thoroughly enough. Lady Featherstone was just now studying the facts of a case involving a missing ruby. She thought she would not mention it as it would only irritate the duchess more, and so she folded it and tucked it away.

"Is that the baby," Lady Easton said, "or just a pile of blankets?"

"Of course it's the baby," Lady Mendleton said, pulling the blanket down past the infant's chin.

The ladies peered at the sleeping baby.

"Can you wake her up?" Lady Easton asked.

"Wake her up?" Lady Mendleton replied, her voice full of horror.

"So we can see her do something advanced," Lady Easton said, by way of further clarification.

"This *is* one of the advanced things," Lady Mendleton said. "She never makes a fuss when it would be inconvenient."

"In any case," the duchess said firmly, meaning to draw attention away from the baby's advanced sleeping, "I felt it vital that we meet."

Here it was. Here was the moment when the duchess would condemn her for allowing things to get out of control. At least, she thought they might be getting out of her control.

Lady Redfield braced herself for the onslaught.

"We must begin to make some firm pushes in a sensible direction regarding Lady Arabella."

Firm pushes? What were firm pushes? In what sensible direction?

"It has come to my attention," the duchess continued, "by way of my duke, that Lord Skeffington went to his club last night after dining here. He's putting it about that he is actively courting Lady Arabella and that she is receptive, I presume to warn others off. He also told someone that he had begun to fear for Lady Arabella's comfort, as when he dined here last evening there was very little food and the house was completely bereft of tea leaves. He assumes Lady Redfield has encountered some dire financial difficulties and may no longer be in a position to care for his ward."

"He did not!" Lady Redfield said. She was, for a very short moment, entirely relieved that this meeting had nothing to do with Lord Blackwood. But then, to hear what it *did* have to do with!

"He is a scheming one," Lady Heathway said. "Though, who would ever believe a house had allowed itself to run out of tea?"

"Well I did say—"

"I've known he was a rogue since he first came to Town," Lady Easton said. "Bertridge sized him up instantly and warned me to keep away from him."

"He must be stopped," the duchess said.

"Oh yes, surely," Lady Redfield said.

The ladies paused to hear what Lady Mendleton would say about it, but she was far too engrossed with monitoring the advanced sleeping of the baby.

"The best thing we can do, to my mind," the duchess said, "is arrange some other pairing. Now, I know we all thought of Lord Ryland for Miss Yardley last season. And perhaps thought of him for Miss Wilcox the season before. But, he strikes me as the likeliest candidate. Did anybody notice, did he seem struck with Lady Arabella at the mystery supper?"

Nobody answered, as nobody had noticed.

"Well, if not him, who?" Lady Heathway asked. "Cecilia, has the girl indicated interest in anyone?"

"Interest, well, no more than in the usual way," Lady Redfield said, terrified that the duchess could read her thoughts.

"What has she said though?" Lady Easton asked.

"Said...she did say that Mr. Vance seemed a genial gentleman."

"Vance," the duchess muttered. "If only he had a more seasoned title."

"She seemed to like Lord Ryland well enough, though she did not say anything of interest. Lord Lymington...well...I cannot be certain but I did not think she found him—"

"Lymington," the duchess said. "I had high hopes for him, but the man will not shut up about his horses."

"Perhaps she's said something to Lord Blackwood," Lady Heathway said.

"Why would she say anything to Lord Blackwood?" Lady Redfield asked, her heart pounding in her chest.

"Oh, you know how it is, she might have asked a few innocent questions about somebody," Lady Easton said.

"Indeed, yes," the duchess said. "Why, I remember cornering one of the duke's friends, Lord Frederick, and saying something along the lines of noting how taken the duke seemed to be by Lady Mary Bellington and why should he not be as so many gentlemen were enthralled by her blond curls. Well, I was speedily informed that the duke preferred dark hair and I suppose I patted my dark hair and that was that."

"Theodosia," Lady Easton said, "do inquire into it and find out if Lady Arabella has asked any fishing questions of Lord Blackwood."

"Indeed I will," the duchess said. "I will see him directly after I leave here, as he is so conveniently only steps away."

Lady Redfield did not like the idea of the duchess questioning her son on such a matter. If she were right, if there was something growing between them, might he say something?

A loud wail shattered the direction of her thoughts.

The very advanced baby was awake.

<hr />

LADY REDFIELD HAD sent her to the garden to pick flowers, though it was a task usually done by one of the maids. Arabella knew well enough it was meant to get her out of the way, as she'd overheard Oscar giving William orders about the tea that must be laid for Lady Redfield's closest friends.

She did not mind being sent away and, if she were going to be sent, the garden was ideal. One never knew when Lord Blackwood might decide to stroll through his own garden.

Perhaps they might meet at the top of the wall and examine the stones again.

She'd come out quietly, hoping to hear some sound of him or of Apollo.

Rather, she heard many voices, though none of them were Lord Blackwood's.

"Will you attend the bet between Cackleton and James?" one asked.

"Probably," another answered. "Where will they have it?"

"On Cackleton's estate in Surrey."

A third said, "I'll go, if I can escape. Every time I turn around my mother has devised some scheme to trot out a likely lady for me to wed. She's taken my calendar as her own."

"Blackwood's got the right idea, setting himself up away from the duke."

"But if you go, who shall you bet on?"

"I'll go for Cackleton. He'll be on Swift and he'll be on his own land."

"If I go, I won't bet much. I'm keeping most of my free money by for Skeffington's thing."

"What thing? Skeffington hasn't told me about anything."

"He's hosting a Welch Main. Everybody knows about it. Have you been living under a rock?"

"A Welch Main!"

"Yes, he's already got all the cocks gathered. Ryland told me he's taken over the stables of Mr. Westreth, as he is not in town."

"Westreth? He is just across the square at number thirty-six."

"I wonder if we could go and have a look. Oh-ho, here's Blackwood."

Arabella stayed quiet against her side of the wall, waiting to hear the lord's voice.

"What do you do out here?" he asked.

"We got bored in your drawing room, and deuced uncomfortable too. Why does your butler always scowl at us like that?"

"Never mind him," Lord Blackwood said.

"We were just talking about Skeffington's Welch Main—shall you go?"

"No, certainly not."

"Why not? The duke cannot have you on a rope, you have your own house and can come and go when you like."

"I am on cool terms with Skeffington, if you must know."

"Everybody is on cool terms with the fellow, he's as cold as a block of ice."

"Well, my terms are rather cooler than that."

"Suit yourself. Now let's do be off. Rochester and Blake will be playing piquet at the club and if I'm not mistaken one of them will end fleeing to the continent to escape his debts before the week is out. I'd like to see which."

Arabella sat on the bench as the gentlemen departed. She really wished his friends had left and he had stayed behind.

Flora came bustling down the garden paths and came to a stop in front of her.

"Aye," she said, "I thought I'd help you with the flowers and good that I did, since you don't yet have a single stem in your basket."

"Oh dear," Arabella said, glancing down at her empty basket.

"Come on then," Flora said. "If you're set on daydreamin' you might as well gather flowers while you're at it."

Arabella rose and they strolled down the paths, Flora deciding what ought to be picked and handing her flowers for the basket.

"Flora," Arabella said, "what is a Welch Main?"

"Wherever did you hear of it?"

"Lord Blackwood's friends were in the garden just now and they were talking about Lord Skeffington's Welch Main."

"It's a bad business, if you ask me. It makes me wonder if men have hearts."

"But what is it?"

Flora sighed and said, "I'm not so sure a young lady like yourself ought to know anything about it."

"Flora," Arabella said sternly, "I have grown up in the country, as you have yourself. Neither of us are as delicate as these flowers we are surrounded by."

"Very well," she said. "It's a cockfight, only a rather large one. It starts with thirty-two birds paired up. The winners go on to be paired up again, and then again. It goes on until there is only the champion."

"But—"

"That's right, thirty-one dead and one survived."

"That is beastly!" Arabella cried. "Why would Lord Black-wood's friends involve themselves in it?"

"When it comes to young gentlemen, I suspect they feign interest in whatever manly thing they think they ought."

"I simply do not know how they don't recoil from such barbarism. Skeffington, I can well imagine, he is such a beast, but the others…"

"Put it out of your head, my lady."

"How can I?" Arabella said in a near whisper. "They are all just across the square in the stables of number thirty-six."

"My pa always says, don't concern yourself with what's not your concern. A cockfight most certainly is not a lady's concern."

Arabella nodded and absentmindedly took the flowers Flora handed her. She could not put it out of her mind, though.

There were thirty-two innocent creatures nearby and thirty-one of them would have their lives cut short in a brutal and violent manner.

It was so unfair!

CHAPTER TWENTY-ONE

P EREGRINE WAS MEANT to be off with his friends to see whether it was Rochester or Blake who would prevail at the card table.

However, as he'd been ready to leave the house, the duchess strode into it.

She really was so high-handed! She'd dismissed his friends with the idea that she must have him in conference regarding a vital matter.

Of course, his friends had all marched out like soldiers, none of them having the temerity to cross the duchess.

Now, they were in the drawing room.

"Ah, Mr. Sindu," the duchess said as he supervised Linus laying the tea. "You are looking particularly well these days."

Of course he was. What butler would not look well when he had a commodious bedchamber, a valet, and a library?

"I am careful of my diet and take exercise regularly, Your Grace, as I have advised Peregrine to do too."

"Well, I suppose he does not take your advice, young gentlemen never do."

Mr. Sindu nodded sagely.

It was outrageous, they spoke about him as if he were not even in the room!

Finally, his confounding butler and his footmen departed, closing the door behind them.

"Well, Mother? I am just now missing the destruction of either Rochester or Blake at my club. What is the vital conference?"

"It is about Lady Arabella. There is a problem."

A problem? What had happened? Was she taken ill? He had not really thought she'd had a headache the evening before but perhaps she had and it had since developed into a fever.

"Does she require a doctor?" he said.

"A doctor? Goodness, no. She requires a husband. Lord Skeffington has been putting it about that he is in pursuit and she is not putting him off. He's also hinting that Lady Redfield might not be able to care for her sufficiently. There was some mention of there being little food at table last evening and no tea at all."

"But that was just a ruse, I am certain. Lady Redfield did not wish to make him comfortable."

"No doubt, but he is using it. Therefore, we must counter his schemes with a real match. The ladies and I wondered if Lady Arabella has asked you about any gentleman she may have encountered. Nothing direct, mind. Roundabout questions are what will reveal if she has any particular interests. Anything about Lord Ryland, perhaps?"

Ryland? What did Ryland have to do with it? Ryland and Lady Arabella? No, they would not at all suit.

"Think back. Anything at all that she might have said."

"Why don't you just ask her?" Peregrine said.

As he said it, he noticed that if she *were* asked, he hoped the only person she might mention was himself.

The duchess laughed. "You really are absurd sometimes, my darling. We cannot ask *her*. She will never admit to anything without a declaration on the table. No lady of any sense would set herself up to be known to have disappointed hopes."

Peregrine supposed that was right.

"Well," the duchess said, "keep it in mind. When you have your riding lessons, perhaps do some fishing. If you hear the slightest thing, come to me at once. Or, perhaps I will come by periodically to see if you've uncovered anything."

"No, no need to inconvenience yourself by coming by all the time. I will come to you with anything I uncover."

"You are a dear, Peregrine."

The duchess had kissed his forehead and left, leaving him alone in his drawing room.

So, the old girls wished to push Lady Arabella into a match as quickly as possible.

Why the rush?

Of course, he knew why. It was Skeffington. One could not fathom what he'd try next.

He could not like it. He and Lady Arabella had been going along so pleasantly and now she was to be pushed into a match?

As he sat on the sofa, Peregrine's mind began to drift to those future days that might be ahead of him. He was on his estate, married to some pleasant lady or other, having waited two years to do the deed, just as he'd said he would.

He had employed himself, in those intervening two years, in all the entertainments that the season had to offer. And then, as he'd said he would, he had married.

He could not see the lady's face, but that hardly seemed to matter.

She was well-bred, mannered, and though he could not see her face she was bound to be pleasant to look at. She ran his household in an orderly manner. They were exceedingly cordial to one another.

Now, they were in Town. They had gone to a card party. There was Lady Arabella with her faceless husband.

Lady Arabella with her pert manner and bouncing curls and cheerful mastery of any and all animals within her sphere. Lady Arabella, her lovely petite frame dressed in silks and her charming face upturned to her faceless husband.

Why had he done it? Why had he let such a lady slip through his fingers?

The drawing room door opened and Mr. Sindu walked

through it, bringing Peregrine's mind to the present.

He leapt up.

"There is still time!" he said.

"For?"

"For Lady Arabella. There is still time. The matrons want to push her into a match with God only knows who, but it is not done yet. There is still time."

"Finally, he arrives at the point," Mr. Sindu said. "I have previously suggested Lady Tredwell's masque as being the ideal time and place for a proposal."

"*I* will decide on the time and place, if you please," Peregrine said. "Though that would be a likely time and place. Do find out what she will wear, her maid will know."

⇒⇒⇒⟨⟨⟨

ARABELLA HAD PACED the house all the day long. First in her bedchamber, staring out the window. Though she could not see it on the other side of the square, number thirty-six was there. Thirty-two poor birds were there.

Rusty came to the window twice, looking at her expectantly. He was such a charming little fellow, living his life as he was meant to.

But there were thirty-two other fellows across the square who would not get the opportunity.

She'd since taken to pacing the drawing room. Lady Redfield had gone out and would not be back until dinner, having set off for a meeting with the directors of one of her charities. This dinner really would be only the two of them, and Arabella was grateful for it. She did not think she could make pleasant conversation at the moment.

She'd thought and thought about who might intervene on the poor birds' behalf. Though, she well knew that a gentleman was not likely to interfere with another gentleman's sport.

Arabella had wondered if she might not ask Lord Blackwood, despite his friends' plans to attend the massacre.

She could not though. She dared not cause any more enmity between Lord Blackwood and Skeffington, and Skeffington himself would be delighted to deny any request coming from Lord Blackwood.

Freddy would have been exceedingly helpful just now. Freddy would have no compunction about marching over there and setting the poor creatures free. However, Freddy was in Cornwall and could be no use to her.

Arabella felt helpless. More helpless than she had ever felt. To know there was murdering to come and stand idly by…

No, she could not. She could not stand idly by. If there were no man to step in, then she must do it herself.

She really must. She could not go on living her days always with the idea that she'd known, and she'd done nothing.

Having resolved to free the birds, she must just figure out how to do it.

She'd gone back to her bedchamber to think, and to plan. She could not know if she would find the stables locked, though she thought not. Every animal needed fresh air to survive so there would be half doors open.

Would there be someone there? A guard of some sort?

That was far more likely than finding the place locked up tight.

She would have to get rid of him.

Arabella stuffed some pin money into the pocket of her walking dress. She would tell the guard she'd been sent by Lord Skeffington and she would send him on an errand.

It must be something like that, as she would not be able to overpower whoever she encountered.

But then what? If she rid herself of the guard, then what?

The cocks were bound to be in separate cages, else they'd fight each other to death before the Welch Main ever began.

It was a lot of cages to open. It was a lot of cocks to chase out one by one.

Still, she must try.

Flora knocked and came into the room. "As it gets late in the day, I suppose you'll want to go wanderin' round the square. Are we to casually encounter Lord Blackwood coming out of his own house again?"

"Dear me, no, at least I hope not. Not this day, anyway."

Arabella rose and crossed the room to Flora. She grasped the maid's hands and said, "I will need your help in the next hour and you mustn't tell anyone."

"What's this?" Flora said suspiciously. "You ain't plannin' a run to Gretna Green? Cause I won't keep quiet about it if you are."

"Gretna Green? Certainly not," Arabella said. "It is nothing you can feel ashamed of for assisting. I only mean to save those poor birds."

Flora narrowed her eyes. "What do you mean, *save*?"

"I mean, set them free and allow them to make their way in the world as they ought, rather than murdered for the entertainment of gentlemen."

"You don't have the right to do it, though. They are not your property. You could be hanged for stealing. *I* could be hung for helping you."

"Nobody will be hanged," Arabella said confidently, though her thoughts were not as confident. She had not really considered the stealing part of it, only the saving part of it. Still, she could not turn back now.

"I can't involve myself in this madness," Flora said. "Lady Redfield would sack me."

"Then I must go alone," Arabella said resolutely.

"A young lady out alone when it is almost dusk?" Flora asked. "Anything might happen to you."

"Then you'd best come with me and if anything ever needs to be said about it to Lady Redfield, I will make it clear that you only went because I threatened to go alone. Now, let us set off and I charge you to say nothing to anybody."

Though Flora did not appear entirely convinced, she slowly nodded. "Very well, though this is a terrible idea. Give me a moment to get your cloak, it grows chilly out of doors."

"An excellent thought, and wear your own too," Arabella said. "It will better disguise us if we encounter someone."

FLORA MARCHED DOWNSTAIRS feeling aggravated up to her eyes. What madness were they embarking on, stealing from a lord?

After fetching the cloaks, she rushed into the drawing room and took a sheet of Lady Redfield's paper. Lady Arabella might have ordered her not to say anything, but she'd not forbade her to write anything.

She wrote out a hurried note, folded it and found Oscar in the hall. "Take this to Mr. Sindu at once, Oscar. It is vital he receive it right away."

"Is it from Lady Redfield?" Oscar asked, looking askance at the note.

"It would hardly be from me, would it? She wanted it delivered hours ago and I forgot. Do hurry or she will be very put out about it."

Oscar nodded and took the note.

Just then, Lady Arabella came down the stairs. She donned her cloak and Oscar opened the door for them.

As they passed through it, Flora gave Oscar a warning glance, lest he forget the note in his hand.

It was all she could think to do. She did not dare write directly to Lord Blackwood. Mr. Sindu must alert Lord Blackwood. Lord Blackwood would know what to do.

She prayed Lord Blackwood would know what to do.

ARABELLA HURRIED FLORA through the square. It did not take them long to emerge on the other side, nor to identify number thirty-six.

The house was dark and closed up, just as Arabella had heard when she was in the garden. The owner, Mr. Westreth, was not in town and had only lent his stables to Skeffington.

Arabella took Flora's hand and they crept down the mews to the stables.

At the entrance, a young boy sat on a stool, whistling into the growing dusk.

It was a boy. Thank goodness, the guard was only a boy.

Arabella took a deep breath in and strode up to him. "You are Skeffington's boy?" she asked, forcing herself to sound brisk and confident.

The boy leapt from his chair and swept off his cap. "Yes, mum."

"Excellent," Arabella said. "Lord Skeffington has asked me to deliver you this."

She pulled the coins from her pocket.

"He requires each cock to have precisely one half of an apple, no more and no less. It is essential to build up their strength and energy before the Welch Main."

The boy looked at the coins quizzically. "But where am I to find an apple cart at this time of day, mum?"

"I presume that is your problem, not mine."

"But Lord Skeffington gave me strict orders never to leave the stables unattended."

Arabella sighed deeply. "That is just like him, is it not? Giving two conflicting orders and then leaving this poor boy to sort it out. Very well, I and my maid will stay until you return."

"But...ladies guarding the place?"

Arabella stared sternly at the boy. "I will just point out that my maid is twice your size and, as for myself, I would like to see the rogue who dared cross Lady Amelia Betherington."

"Yes, my lady," the boy said.

THE CHAMPION

"Now, off you go if you are to have any sort of chance at locating a vendor. Do hurry, Lord Skeffington has very particular ideas of how the birds are to be prepared and he shall be furious if it is not carried out exactly as he orders it."

The idea of Lord Skeffington becoming furious seemed to spur the boy on. He took the coins, put his cap back on and ran down the road.

"Lady Amelia Betherington?" Flora said softly.

"Never mind that," Arabella said. "We must hurry."

They entered the stables and came upon an eerie sight.

There were thirty-two cages, each spaced at least two feet from the other. None of the birds slept, but rather seemed alert, their beady eyes all focused on the intruders.

The cages were simple wood-slat crates, each with a leather handle nailed to the top. Arabella did not suppose they could be very heavy.

"If we take two at a time," she said, "we might get them all out in just seven trips. We can take them into the square and down the mews, and anywhere really, as long as they have room to avoid one another."

Flora did not answer, though her expression seemed one of almost terror.

"Come now, the faster we go the faster we are home," Arabella said.

⇒⟫⟪⇐

MR. SINDU HAD taken receipt of the note just delivered by Lady Redfield's household. He presumed it was from Mr. Hemmings, as who else would write him directly?

He was very surprised to see that it was not from Mr. Hemmings. And then further shocked by its contents.

Mr. Sindu—

Please excuse me writing you but this is an emergency. Lady

KATE ARCHER

Arabella is set on releasing Lord Skeffington's cocks he's got for a Welch Main and we are just now on our way to number thirty-six of the square. Lord Blackwood must stop her, as I cannot.

Flora, Lady Redfield's maid

Heaven help them all, what was the lady thinking? Peregrine had been off to his club for some hours. He was expected back any moment, as he had a musical evening he'd promised the duchess he would attend. But he was so often willy-nilly with his plans. For all he knew, Peregrine had sent a note off to the duchess that he would not attend due to some malady and was just now sitting around drinking at White's.

Should he go himself and try to stop the lady? He was not unsympathetic to her cause. The idea of using a cock's innate aggressive nature as a form of entertainment was barbaric. However, he found he was not so sympathetic that he was willing to hang for it. As a foreigner, and he would always be one to these people despite his superior intellect and manners, he would be the first with a rope round his neck.

He was almost never unsure of which course to take, but then he'd never encountered a situation where a lady wished to steal thirty-two cocks from a gentleman.

He heard the clatter of hoofbeats outside.

Mr. Sindu leapt up and raced to the door.

Linus had been on the lookout and had already hurried down the steps to take Peregrine's horse.

"Stop, no," Mr. Sindu said. "Linus, go back inside, Peregrine, get back on your horse."

Both looked at him entirely confused. "Linus, now, if you please."

Linus hurried back inside and closed the door after him.

Peregrine said, "Has there been an accident? My mother or father?"

"No, but there is a calamity in the making," Mr. Sindu said.

He speedily apprised Peregrine of the circumstances.

"Bloody...what?"

"You heard me. She's gone there already."

Peregrine let out a string of curses, some of which Mr. Sindu had not realized he'd known.

Nevertheless, Peregrine mounted his horse and galloped in the direction of number thirty-six.

IT HAD NOT taken them long to make the seven trips in and out of the stables. Flora, in particular, moved like lightning. The maid no doubt wished to be done with this escapade as soon as possible.

They had spaced out the cages and now all that was left was to free the birds, chasing them off in different directions so that they did not brawl.

Arabella began opening cages and shooing them off. Some were perfectly ready to be off, some made a run at another cock and had to be corralled and sent off in a new direction.

Finally, they came to the last few cages.

Arabella hurriedly undid the latches.

She turned to a sound behind her. To her horror, Lord Blackwood appeared through the stable doors.

What was he doing here? Why had he come?

And then, far worse and from inside the stables, she heard a voice like thunder. "What the devil!"

It was Skeffington.

CHAPTER TWENTY-TWO

FLORA FROZE. ARABELLA hurried to her and grabbed her arm, pulling her behind a tree.

Lord Blackwood stood staring at the empty cages. Skeffington raced out of the stables behind him.

"Blackwood," Skeffington said, his voice low with fury. "You'll pay for this. You will pay dearly for this."

Arabella signaled Flora to stay where she was. On no account would she allow Lord Blackwood to take the blame. She could not even guess how he'd got there in the first place.

She emerged from behind the tree and said, "It was me, Skeffy. You know how I detest cruelty to animals."

Flora, though she was meant to remain hidden, hurried to her side and held her hand.

With a small smile, Skeffington said, "You propose to convince me that you have done this, knowing that if I believed you I would immediately send you out of Town to the loneliest and barest cottage I could scrounge up."

"You will do what you must do," Arabella said resolutely. "Just as I have done."

"No," Lord Blackwood said. "The fault is mine. It was only a prank...gone awry. I will pay for the stock."

"Oh yes, you *will* pay," Skeffington said with a small smile. "You have cost me hundreds of pounds and have somehow convinced my ward to take the blame for you. You will pay very dearly for that."

Lord Blackwood did not answer, but rather looked stoically forward.

"I believe," Lord Skeffington said, rubbing his chin, "that since I am the injured party, it is up to me to determine precisely what and how I will be paid."

"Certainly, yes," Lord Blackwood said.

"Very well," Skeffington said. "I will take your horse. The veritable mind reader tied up just outside."

Arabella's heart skipped a beat. No, he could not take Alfie.

The stricken expression on Lord Blackwood's face nearly stopped her heart. "My horse? But surely his price will not cover the cost—"

"No," Skeffington said, "but it will sting far sharper than any amount of pounds and pence."

"This is not right," Arabella cried. "This was all my doing. It was no prank and Lord Blackwood had nothing to do with it."

"Stop your histrionics, Lady Arabella," Skeffington said, "lest I decide to send you packing regardless. The men have come to an agreement." He turned his eyes on Flora. "You, maid, take the lady home and pray I do not tell Lady Redfield that you have placed her in such a dangerous circumstance."

Arabella searched her mind on how to stop this. She could not allow Lord Blackwood to lose his horse. Not his beloved Alfie.

"Come now," Flora said quietly.

"No, I won't. You cannot do this. It is all my fault!"

"Just go," Lord Blackwood said. His tone was dull, as if he were barely living.

What had she done? What on earth had she done?

Had she really traded thirty-two unknown birds for the most beloved horse in England?

Arabella felt a shroud of sadness settle over her shoulders. He would never forgive her. How could he? She would never have forgiven such a thing.

She had just mortally wounded the one gentleman in all the world that she loved.

>>>><<<<

LORD SKEFFINGTON WAS not often taken unawares. At first, there were so many disparate facts coming at him that it had taken a moment to parse them all.

His stable was unattended. Jack had gone off somewhere, though the boy knew well enough the value of what he was supposed to be watching and that he would be sacked. He might just be whipped and then sacked.

Skeffington had slipped down the side of the stable to look through a half-door to survey the situation. It seemed so unlikely that Jack would have dared to wander off that there was the outside chance the boy had been set upon and thieves were inside even now.

Rather than assuring himself that his cocks were in good order, he'd seen the place entirely empty. Racing to the other side, he watched as Lady Arabella and her maid opened cages and chased off birds with abandon.

He'd had the urge to twist her arm and slap her hard. He'd like to choke the life out of her and would be happy to do it if he would not hang for it.

But then, out of nowhere, Blackwood had turned up.

From the look on the fellow's face, he was horrified at what Lady Arabella was doing. Why he'd come, Skeffington could not guess, but he'd not been part of it.

And that was when the answer he'd been searching for had finally arrived.

All along, he had been attempting to figure out how to force Lady Arabella into thinking more of him and thinking less of Blackwood.

But that was never going to work.

Here, though, he had a very unique opportunity to make Blackwood think less of *her*.

For reasons only understood by himself, Blackwood was besotted with his horse.

Let Arabella Berestock be the reason he lost his beloved creature, all over thirty-two cocks.

He would never forgive her.

It was an expensive loss, but Lady Arabella's dowry would more than make up for it.

Now, she was on her way back to the house and he had taken the horse while Blackwood only stared.

Whatever had been burgeoning between her and Blackwood had been stamped out in a moment. Lord Blackwood would no longer stand in his way.

⇶⇇

ARABELLA WAS LED almost blindly across the square, Flora guiding her with a strong hand under her arm.

"What have I done, what have I done?" she whispered.

"Come now, let us just get home," Flora said resolutely. "Perhaps it is not as bad as you think."

"Flora! Not as bad? How could it possibly be worse?"

"Well now, I am sure Lord Blackwood is not happy to lose one of his horses, but he's rich enough to buy himself another without too much hardship."

"It was not just a horse. Skeffington has taken Alfie. Lord Blackwood loves two things most in the world—Apollo and Alfie."

"Shh, now, do not continue to upset yourself. We are almost there."

"I was so obstinate and headstrong and stupid! I did not consider the consequences! I never imagined to see Lord Blackwood there. If only he'd stayed away, why did he come?"

"He came because I wrote Mr. Sindu. You can be angry all you like about it but to my mind you were walking us into danger and I had to alert somebody."

Arabella sniffled and said, "I will not blame you for anything. Nobody can be blamed but myself. Oh, Mrs. Weston would be so disappointed in how I've conducted myself! She thought I might not be ready to be on my own and she was right."

"Now stop the self-recriminations at once," Flora said firmly. "There is the house and let us pray we are getting in ahead of Lady Redfield. I will put you to bed and claim you feel poorly. I shall say nothing else. You will decide what you will say or not say."

Arabella did not answer. She did not know what should be said. She only wished to crawl under her blankets and cry herself to sleep.

She was the worst person in the world.

PEREGRINE HAD STOOD motionless on the road, watching Alfie led away.

It felt as if he were living in a nightmare. It could not be true.

Skeffington had taken possession of Alfie.

What must his horse think, to be abandoned so?

Would Skeffington mistreat him?

Even if he did not, Skeffington had no particular care for animals. He would not understand Alfie as he himself always had.

Peregrine felt a mix of emotions he'd never felt before. He was in a rage and would like to burn the town down to the ground. He was bereft too, as if some vital organ inside him had disintegrated.

He could hardly breathe.

It was as if the bright world he had long inhabited had suddenly gone dark.

He'd stood outside the stables for an hour, maybe more. Carriages passed by him, going hither and thither, their inhabitants unaware of the disaster that had befallen him.

Laughter drifted out of one of them and he wished to shout at them to stop. There was no reason for laughter in this terrible new world.

Eventually, he'd made his way back to the house. The only thing that had driven him there was the idea that there was a brandy bottle inside it.

He would need a lot of brandy.

Mr. Sindu met him at the door. "Did you stop her?" he asked.

"No, I didn't stop her," he said quietly. "And I paid for her crime with Alfie."

Mr. Sindu appeared momentarily stunned. Then he gathered himself. He put his arm around Peregrine's shoulders and said quietly, "Come into the house."

FLORA HAD TAKEN charge and marched Arabella to her room. She'd helped her change into her nightdress and brought her an exceedingly large glass of sherry, which Arabella had drunk down gratefully.

Anything that might help her forget, at least for a few hours, what she had done this night would be welcome.

Flora had blown out the last candle and left her in the darkness.

Arabella had lain there for some time, but she could not still her mind. She'd risen and gone to the window to stare out at the scene of her crimes.

Her breath caught as she saw Lord Blackwood walking toward his house. It had been at least an hour since she had returned home, where had he been?

He walked slowly, all the energy seeming to have been

drained from him.

That was her doing.

Mr. Sindu suddenly ran down the steps and spoke to him.

They exchanged words and then the butler put his arm round his master's shoulders and led him inside.

Arabella got back into bed and wept. Where was poor Alfie now? Was he all right?

She did not know how long she wept or how long her thoughts went in circles, but then the door to her room opened.

Lady Redfield hurried in carrying a candle in a holder.

"You are awake, my dear," she said, "Flora said you did poor-ly and I thought I must see for myself how it was."

Arabella burst into tears and wailed.

"Good heavens," Lady Redfield cried, racing to her side. "My dear, we will call my physician. Sir Henry will know what to do. I am so distressed that you have been in pain while I was out."

"It is only my soul that is in pain, Lady Redfield. I must tell you what I have done, and then you will be so sorry you ever brought me here and will send me away, and I have ruined everything! I am so sorry!"

Lady Redfield appeared stunned and shakily set her candle by the bed.

Arabella poured out what she'd done, and what had hap-pened to Lord Blackwood's horse.

After she ended the tale, Arabella felt an exhaustion over-come her. Lady Redfield patted her hand and made shushing noises.

Arabella said, "You must write Mrs. Weston and tell her to come for me as soon as she can. We must return to Cornwall."

"Oh no, I do not think so, my dear. Now, it is true that Lord Blackwood is very fond of that horse, so that is very much a shame. But it was very good of him to take the blame, it could have ended up a terrible scandal. I do think his actions hint at his regard for you."

Lady Redfield held up her hand as if to stop any objections to the idea. "Oh yes, I have seen something between you developing. Of course, I cannot imagine what the duchess will say to this…however, you are in despair and I find it has quite given me courage."

"It has?"

"Yes, it really has. You see, my boys never have need of me. They tell me nothing and would certainly never cry on my shoulder. But *you* have need of me and I, well, I feel quite up to the challenge. Well, I may still quake when the duchess unleashes what she will upon my head, but I will not fall over."

"I will never forgive myself for Lord Blackwood losing Alfie. I really never will."

"Hmm, I do hope that is not the case. And I think Lord Blackwood will eventually forgive you. Over time, of course."

"No, he never will. He's lost Alfie. He loves Alfie more than anything else. Goodness, at Lord Ryland's mystery supper he even said that anybody hurting Alfie would be his enemy forevermore."

Lady Redfield patted Arabella's arm. "Give him time, my dear. Now, I will minister to you as Flora always does me. I will send up tea and biscuits and laudanum and put a cold cloth on your forehead and things will look better in the morning. You will rise with the sun and it will be a new day and we will put this behind us as best we can."

LADY REDFIELD HAD been as good as her word. She'd insisted that Arabella take tea and eat two biscuits and she'd pressed a cold cloth on her forehead and she'd given her a spoonful of laudanum before tucking her to bed and blowing out the candle.

Arabella had never taken laudanum before. Mrs. Weston had been firm on the idea that such a powerful remedy must only be used in the direst circumstances, such as a broken bone. Arabella found its effects oddly soothing. It seemed to calm her thoughts and even make the pain in her heart fade a little.

Her thoughts, which had been spinning and spinning in grief, began to slow. They began to order themselves and she felt more in control of where they were going.

Along with that settling, came an anger that overlaid her grief.

How dare Skeffington hurt Lord Blackwood so?

She felt vengeful. Very, very vengeful.

She spent some time imagining all the ways that Lord Skeffington could be tortured. Her most satisfying combination was smallpox and gout in both feet.

Arabella suddenly sat up. What was wrong with her? Why had she not realized she could do something? She could fight back! What was she doing, lying here like a defeated woman, wishing smallpox upon a person? She had something more powerful than a disease that might be survived.

All along, she'd had Skeffington's undoing in her possession. She'd found the undoing in his attics in Cornwall and she'd kept it safe. She'd thought she'd use it on her own behalf if she ever needed to. She'd hesitated because she knew it would be dangerous, but she kept it by all the same.

Now, she could use it for Lord Blackwood. She'd use it for Alfie.

She'd get Alfie back.

She would just need to set the stage.

CHAPTER TWENTY-THREE

Peregrine had stayed up with Mr. Sindu and a bottle of brandy, Apollo lazing at his feet, until the early morning hours. When he was finally too drunk to stand, his butler had hauled him up to his bedchamber and rolled him into bed.

He'd slept until the late afternoon and then woke with a pounding head. Mr. Sindu had arranged toast and willow bark tea, along with a large glass of ale.

Now, he still laid in bed, not particularly feeling that there was a purpose to rising.

Mr. Sindu had attempted to convince him that the fault for last evening's disaster could be spread far and wide. Lady Arabella, for coming up with the idea, the maid for writing Mr. Sindu, Mr. Sindu for alerting him to the scheme, and himself for taking the blame.

He supposed that was right, but the whole chain started with Lady Arabella.

Now, he found himself in the odd position of both loving and hating a person.

Just when he'd become fully convinced that there could be no other lady, just when he'd thrown over his plan to wait two years, just when he'd decided to propose at Lady Tredwell's masque…it was all undone.

Mr. Sindu had at least told him one thing that had brought him comfort. He would hire an investigator to look into

Skeffington's stables. What were the accommodations, how were the animals treated? It would bring him some comfort to know that Alfie was well cared for.

There was a sharp rap on his door and before he could answer it, Mr. Sindu entered. He carried a large box.

"Your costume for the masque, Peregrine."

"The masque is this evening," he said. "I'm not going anywhere this evening."

"Of course you are," Mr. Sindu said. "Lord Skeffington took your horse, as opposed to your money, because his aim was to destroy your peace. Do you really propose allowing him to think he has mortally wounded you? Your absence would certainly say so and his victory would be complete."

Peregrine bristled under the idea.

When Skeffington had taken ownership of his horse, he had remained stoic. That rogue had not been able to tell what he thought about it.

He had a mind to keep it that way.

"I believe you may be right," he said.

"I am nearly always right," Mr. Sindu said, "and when I am wrong, it is only the Gods reminding me that I am not a God."

Peregrine did not answer. Mr. Sindu had long held the theory that he was of particular interest to the deity.

"The only revenge you can seek now, Peregrine, is to arrive at Lady Tredwell's house as if nothing is at all wrong. In that way, Skeffington will become convinced that his game was not well-played. He might have recovered the cost of the cocks but has only made off with a horse. I would not be surprised if he does not feel exceedingly foolish."

Foolish. Yes, he would like Skeffington to feel foolish. He would also like him to feel a fever, the gout, the dropsy, and then fall dead on the floor with apoplexy.

"What costume did I choose this year?" Peregrine asked, staring at the box.

"You did not choose, as you never do. I did. You will be

dressed in a simple domino. I had toyed with the idea of Indian Maharajah, but then I realized I was thinking of what would be suited to me, rather than you."

"That sounds about right," Peregrine said, satisfied with the domino. He had no wish to strut around in some absurd costume.

"I will fetch Turnbury," Mr. Sindu said. "It is time to rise and prepare yourself to show Lord Skeffington that he has not defeated you."

Peregrine nodded. He would go to the masque and wear an attitude of indifference. Hopefully, it would set Skeffington's teeth on edge.

As for Lady Arabella, which he noticed Mr. Sindu had avoided any mention of, he would do the same. He would avoid her.

⤜⤜⤜✕⤛⤛⤛

ARABELLA AND LADY Redfield had waited all day to see if there would be some mention of what had occurred.

Each time a carriage rumbled by, they waited for it to stop and deliver a note. Or worse, deliver the duchess herself.

Nobody came, nobody sent word. It seemed that neither Lord Skeffington nor Lord Blackwood was inclined to make the matter public.

There had been some moments of near panic when one of Lord Skeffington's footmen had arrived with a note and insisted on staying for an answer to it.

Rather than any idea of punishment though, it had only asked if they would attend the masque and if so, what would Lady Arabella wear.

Lady Redfield had not wished to say if they went or not, and certainly not whatever costumes they chose. However, Arabella had urged her to confirm that they would go and describe how she would be dressed. She needed Skeffington to be there and she needed him to find her.

"I believe we may be, as the Americans say, out of the woods," Lady Redfield said. "Certainly we would have heard something by now if it were not the case."

Arabella nodded. The nerves in her body had been alive and on fire for the past hours, every second waiting for some dreaded arrival and the ensuing recriminations.

She would not be able to take in a deep breath until Alfie was returned.

"We ought to go up to be dressed," Lady Redfield said. "I do hope you like the choice I have made for you. I had something in mind before I went to Cornwall to fetch you, but then I changed my mind as I got to know you. Can you guess?"

"I cannot be certain, my lady," Arabella said. "But if there is a costume for an obstinate and foolish girl, that must be mine."

"Do not be so hard on yourself, you are not the first young lady to do something rash. Goodness, my sister once dyed one of my father's sheep blue, then found him in his library and said one of the sheep was so depressed it was positively blue. She thought it very amusing, though he did not. I imagine I might have done some rash things myself, had I ever had the nerve."

Arabella smiled over the idea of one poor blue sheep mixed in among the white.

"Now, let us go up. We will be dressed and we will go and I suspect Lord Blackwood will be in better spirits by now and you may make your apologies."

Arabella nodded, though she did not think that was right. It would take Lord Blackwood some time to ever forgive her and the only thing that could hurry it was the return of Alfie.

That was what she must accomplish this night. She must force Skeffy's hand and make him relent. She had copied out the papers and put the originals safely away. She must only have a look at her costume to figure out where to conceal them.

ARABELLA HAD GONE up and Flora had done her hair, though she had been very mysterious on the subject of the costume. Finally, she had gone off and then bustled back in with a large box.

She removed the lid and Arabella saw precisely what had been in Lady Redfield's mind. She would be Diana, goddess of animals both wild and domestic. It was magnificent.

A large bow was accompanied by a hide-covered quiver holding three arrows.

The dress itself was a forest green silk in a modified Roman style, the modification being long bell-cut sleeves. Its drape was straight with no unnecessary volume, which allowed the lively yellow embroidered design to be seen clearly.

All of her animals were there. Mrs. Twitch-nose sat on her shoulder, her extended brood playfully running up a sleeve. The Nightlys occupied the other sleeve, very small and flying in formation as if they were far away. Mrs. Murder and her kittens adorned her waist, their faces all upturned toward the mice. Mr. Prickles peeked charmingly from a stand of bushes. Rusty ran up a tree. Lord Bushwick stood at the hem, appearing suitably fierce.

The mask itself was of the same color green, embroidered with an intricate forest scene.

"How lovely," Arabella said. "Lady Redfield has taken such care in designing it."

"And Lady Featherstone too," Flora added. "They both bore witness to your creatures in Cornwall and described them to the modiste. And a'course, we all saw Rusty and could describe him well enough," she said, glancing toward the window.

"I hardly deserve such courtesy," Arabella said, with a pang that came with the realization that while she had all of her beloved animals around her, another did not.

"Nonsense," Flora said. "What's done is done. Lady Redfield is counting on you to be chin up. She's been chin up herself these days, don't let her down. Do you know, she's styled herself as Latona, Diana's mother, she's that fond of you."

"She is a darling and you are right. I will not let her down. You may go, Flora. I only need a moment to compose myself and then I will go down."

Flora nodded and departed the room, though she paused to have one last look at her handiwork.

After she closed the door, Arabella took out the copies she had made. She folded them up tight and pierced them on one of the arrows, carefully replacing it in the quiver.

She was ready.

LORD SKEFFINGTON HAD confirmed that Lady Arabella would attend the masque. He had not been entirely certain that she would, considering the state she'd been in the night before.

This was to be his chance. Any ideas she'd had in Lord Blackwood's direction were ruined and he had one last inducement. If she would engage herself to him, he would forgo selling off Alfie to a coaching establishment where he would gallop and gallop until he dropped dead of exhaustion and mistreatment. He would be dead in a year, two at most.

That idea might not have worked on just anybody, but it would work on her.

He only must get her alone, and then he would get her consent. His problems with Lord Rendiver would finally be over.

He scanned the ballroom for her. A masque was deuced inconvenient as one could hardly tell who was who. He'd had the foresight to inquire of Lady Redfield what Lady Arabella would wear.

He was, just now, seeking out the goddess Diana.

There were a few he had wondered at, not entirely certain who or what they were meant to be, but matching the height of Lady Arabella.

Then he saw her. The right height, the right hair, and a quiver and bow. He strode through the crowd.

"Lady Arabella," he said, bowing.

"Skeffington," she said.

"Might I put my name down, as a truce from last evening?"

"As you wish," she said evenly, handing over her card.

He wrote his name down for supper.

She glanced at it and then looked away.

He was surprised by her reaction. Or rather, lack of one. He'd expected some complaint about it, but she seemed impervious to the idea.

Very well then. Perhaps his work was half-done already.

He took his leave and moved to the edges of the ballroom.

Blackwood entered the ballroom with his friend Rendridge. He was impossible to miss as his domino hood was thrown back.

He was also laughing and appeared in high spirits.

Why, though?

Skeffington had been convinced that he'd struck a deep blow by taking the man's horse. Why did he seem so jolly now?

Did he have some idea that he would get the horse back? Or worse, was he somehow not holding Lady Arabella to blame?

"Skeffington," Lord Ryland said, coming to his side, "I hear the Welch Main is off and your cocks were stolen?"

"That is correct."

"Worst luck," Ryland said sympathetically.

"No, not really," Lord Skeffington said. "The *worst* luck is death, and I am not dead yet."

>>><<<

PEREGRINE HAD FORCED himself as he never had before. He forced himself to appear cheerful and without a care.

He was not, though.

That Alfie was well and truly gone seemed to hit him periodically. The worst had been when he'd left the house.

Balfour had stood in Alfie's place, waiting to take him to Lady Tredwell's. He was a perfectly good horse, exceptional even. But he was not Alfie.

Now, he would spend an evening in a charade, pretending to be delighted with his circumstances.

Of course, it was not just Alfie he had lost. It was Lady Arabella, too. He loved her, he knew that. But he could not look at her.

"My dear boy," a voice said behind him.

It was the duchess.

"A domino," she said with a small sigh. "Serviceable I suppose, but hardly original."

Though Peregrine knew his costume to be unoriginal, his mother's garb was anything but usual. She was dressed in an elaborate medieval court gown.

He looked at her expectantly.

"Eleanor of Aquitaine," the duchess said.

"I see, and Father is King Louis or King Henry?"

"Henry, of course. Now, my darling, a most untoward thing has occurred. Lord Skeffington has put himself down on Lady Arabella's card. For supper, if you can believe it. He really intends on pursuing this hopeless courtship. Has she not said anything at all about who she might prefer? Nothing about Ryland, perhaps?"

"No, nothing," Peregrine answered.

Why was Skeffington intent on taking Lady Arabella into supper?

He must have some plan or scheme in mind.

Peregrine's heart began to pound in his chest. Of course he had some sordid scheme in mind. He planned on blackmailing the lady. He would threaten to advertise just who it was who had stolen his cocks unless the lady submitted to his plans.

That tale would undo any lady. Slipping out with a maid and stealing a gentleman's property? It would not just come off as wrong, and bold, and unladylike. It would sound insane.

What family would be prepared to overlook the endless talk about it? What family would be prepared to believe that a serious lack of judgment such as that would not occur again?

She would be cornered.

All along, Peregrine had been comfortable in the knowledge that whatever Skeffington might do, it would all end in eleven months. She would be in her majority and free of him.

But what use would freedom be if she were ruined?

He could not allow that to happen because…well, because…

He loved her. He still loved her. Hated her, also, but still loved her.

Perhaps he could not propose himself. At least, not until he could bear to look at her once more. But he would not allow her to be ruined.

What was he thinking? Of course he could propose to her. If he did not, somebody else would come along. Then, when he was ready, it would be too late.

He must forgive her now. He must forgive her in his heart.

As if the intention were a balm, he felt his heart soothed. This was only one moment in time, a terrible time as it happened, but it would not last. The pain of it and the memory of it would fade.

When that happened, he must have Lady Arabella by his side.

Somehow, he must keep Skeffington far away from her side. He would keep a close watch on Skeffington.

He would keep his card clear of a supper engagement and sit himself down beside them. If Skeffington tried anything, he would step in.

"Goodness," the duchess said, "you are off in the clouds, Peregrine."

"Sorry, I was thinking of something else."

"Clearly."

ARABELLA WENT THROUGH the dances in nearly a trance. Her thoughts, her focus, and her aim was on one outcome only—force Skeffington to return Alfie.

That he had put himself down for her supper had been very convenient.

She could not ignore that Lord Blackwood had not come near her. She'd seen the duchess speaking to him and looking in her direction, but he did not look. He did not come.

It pained her, and yet it gave her courage also. She might, if she did everything just right, be able to put his heart back together again.

Then, he might forgive her. Perhaps.

Skeffington came to collect her for the dance before supper. She would be neutral and noncommittal. She would not give away her contempt for him. Not yet.

As they moved through the changes and she willed herself not to recoil from his touch, he said, "I believe last evening's events have somehow caused a new maturity in you, Lady Arabella. Am I correct in thinking you have been chastened?"

"Yes, of course," she said, though she'd really prefer to retrieve her bow and quiver left at the edges of the ballroom and shoot him through.

"Excellent," he said.

They went on wordless after that, for which Arabella was grateful.

Of course she was chastened. Did he take some credit for it or somehow think she appreciated the comment?

He might just. He was looking supremely confident at the moment.

The dance blessedly ended and there began a surge of couples leaving the ballroom to cross the great hall to the dining room.

Arabella had looked around carefully when she'd arrived and knew there to be doors to a library just outside the ballroom doors and to the right.

As they reached those doors, Arabella looked at them and said, "You are hardly subtle, Skeffy. I am convinced you have something to say to me in private and equally convinced I'd like to get it over with."

Skeffington appeared surprised, but nodded, and they slipped into the library as couples streamed by them.

It would probably have been noticed by somebody, but Arabella hoped it would not cause talk as Skeffington was, after all, her guardian.

He closed the door behind her and she said, "Well?" As she did so, she moved behind the desk to put distance between them.

"As you are so eager," Skeffington said, "I propose an engagement. Immediately. We may leave here and deliver the happy news."

"You are forever a goose, Skeffy. I will never marry you and God help the poor woman who ever agreed to it."

Skeffington appeared annoyed, but not put off. He said, "I did not come unarmed, Lady Arabella. If you do not agree, I fully intend to send Lord Blackwood's horse into the carriage trade. You, animal lover that you are, will be well aware of what the rest of his short life will entail."

If Arabella had at all wavered or felt frightened, that was all gone now. He was a beast.

"You may be surprised to know that I also did not arrive unarmed."

She reached behind her and pulled the arrow from her quiver, the copied document still securely on its tip. She notched the arrow in her bow and aimed, firing it off to pierce the bookcase a foot from Skeffington's head.

"Have you lost your mind?" he asked.

"You had better read that paper, Skeffy. Then we'll see whose mind is lost."

She watched with satisfaction as he yanked the arrow out of the wood and wrestled with the paper until it was unfolded.

He grew white as he read it.

"Where did you get this?" he asked.

"It was in your attic in Cornwall. Did I not ever mention that I am a snooper?"

"This is nothing," he said, crumpling the paper in his hand.

"Nobody would believe any of it."

"Really? Because there is a lady just now locked up in a private madhouse. Through these documents, which are copies by the by, and the various letters I found, I was able to piece together your depravity. Ten years ago, you eloped with an actress named Mary Huffman. Your parents were furious, of course. Though, your father is very like you, as it turns out. He invited the happy couple to visit, then he locked you up for a few days and Mary disappeared.

"You asked about her, of course, and your father eventually explained that a doctor had been paid and Mary had been committed. It had been easy enough to do—she was an actress who was living under the delusion that she'd married a nobleman. She insisted on being addressed as Viscountess. Naturally, with the vehement denials from the family, she was not believed.

"Now, you carry on as if you are a single gentleman. You have even dared to declare your intention of courting me. Though, if you were to marry, you would be a bigamist."

"What do you want?" Skeffington said. His eyes were narrowed and his fists balled up. Arabella was certain he would beat her to death if he thought he could get away with it.

She took a deep breath.

"Three things," she said. "You will transfer ownership of the Cornwall house to Freddy, you will return Alfie to Lord Blackwood, and you will not object to whoever I decide to marry, should I do so in the next months. Otherwise, I will make this public and your family will be utterly destroyed."

Skeffington took a step toward her. In one swift movement, Arabella reached for another arrow and notched it, aiming at his head.

"I wouldn't," she said.

The door burst open behind him.

Lord Blackwood strode in.

⇶⤛⤛

PEREGRINE HAD KEPT Skeffington and Lady Arabella in view in the middle of the crush to get to the dining room.

At least he had, until he hadn't.

They seemed to have disappeared into thin air.

He'd pushed past people to get into the dining room, but they were not there.

Where had they gone?

Rendridge came up beside him with Lady Elizabeth on his arm. "What now, old boy? Has your supper companion made a run for it?"

"Have you seen Lady Arabella?" he asked.

"Her guardian has just waylaid her in the library, probably going to scold her over some matter. You know how guardians are."

Peregrine might not know how all guardians were, but he certainly knew what this one was like.

He turned and pushed his way back out of the room. Reaching the library's doors, he threw them open, not daring to imagine what he might find.

"Skeffington. What do you do in here?"

At the same time as he said it, he realized Lady Arabella was aiming her arrow at Skeffington.

"What has he done?" he asked Lady Arabella.

"What he always does," she said, "made himself exceedingly unpleasant."

Peregrine turned to Skeffington. There nothing for it now, he'd have to challenge the rogue to a duel.

Skeffington gripped some sort of paper in his hand and pointed at Lady Arabella. "Say nothing."

"I shan't say a word, as long as we are in agreement regarding the terms," Arabella said.

Peregrine could not fathom what they were talking about.

Before he could think what was to come next, Skeffington turned and fled the room.

He rushed to Lady Arabella's side and she dropped her bow. He towered over her; her face upturned to his.

"Has he hurt you?"

"Not at all."

"I was afraid he had some scheme…"

"Oh yes, he always does."

They stood there for some moments, only the sound of their breathing heard.

"I did not think you would ever speak to me again," Lady Arabella said softly.

"I thought it myself, for a few hours. But it will not do! Yes, you heard me, it will not do."

"It will not?"

"Certainly not," Peregrine said. He wished he had thought through what he might say at such a moment.

"I am glad it will not do," she said.

"Well, we could hardly marry if I were not speaking to you. It's not the done thing."

"Ah," Lady Arabella said, her face flaming purple.

He supposed his own was just as burgundy. At least, it felt as if it just now housed a thousand suns.

"What *is* the done thing? If we are to marry?" she asked.

"The done thing is to kiss the lady you love, I am sure of it."

Peregrine bent down, and it was a very long way down. He kissed her soft lips and she pressed them firmly to his. She wrapped her arms around his neck and he picked her up and sat her on the desk.

They kissed again and he began to feel time slip away. They should always remain in this attitude. It suited them both exceedingly well.

She whispered in his ear. "You must well and truly forgive me."

"I have already, my little darling."

"I'm glad. Also, Alfie should be returned sometime tomorrow."

Peregrine pulled away. "What? How?"

"Never mind the what and the how. You'd better kiss me again."

And so he did, deeply, her petite person fitting so nicely in his arms.

He supposed they remained in the library for quite some time, though it was difficult to measure. She was so enchanting, it was as if a petite sorceress had taken over his thoughts.

They might have remained there all the night long, had not a search party been sent off to look for them.

The library door crashed open and a screech shattered the quiet of the room.

"Peregrine!" the duchess cried.

CHAPTER TWENTY-FOUR

PEREGRINE PEERED THROUGH Arabella's rolling curls to see his mother and Lady Heathway standing at the door, their mouths agape.

"Not again," Lady Heathway said. "It's as if we never learn."

"Peregrine," the duchess repeated. "Stop that...what you are doing. At once!"

"I pray you are engaged," Lady Heathway said, "considering this display."

It occurred to Peregrine that he'd not actually asked the question. Of course, he could not imagine that Lady Arabella went round kissing gentlemen she did *not* intend to marry.

He untangled himself and lifted her back to the floor, setting her on her pretty little feet.

"Lady Arabella, if you agree to do me the highest honor of becoming my wife, I will promise to...well, I will be a very good husband. I'm sure of it. I will not even complain if I discover there is an injured hedgehog living under a table or a rabbit living in the nursery, or I don't know what else."

Lady Arabella stood on tiptoes and kissed his chin, as that was as far as she could reach, and said, "But no badgers. As my very stern husband, you must draw the line somewhere."

"Then you do say yes?"

"A hundred times over."

"We must only wait another eleven months and you will be

out from under Skeffington's control."

"I am out from under now. We need not wait—send him a note, he will not object."

"I shudder to think what you've threatened him with to achieve all this."

"As you should, and I will tell you all about it in time."

"My daring little sorceress."

"Excuse me! What happened to Lady Constance, if you do not mind my inquiring?" the duchess said, staggering to a chair.

"I was never going to marry Lady Constance, Mother. It was just a ruse."

"A ruse," the duchess said quietly. "A ruse on your own mother?"

"It was necessary, I'm afraid," Peregrine said.

"Necessary," the duchess said thoughtfully. "I see. It was done to protect me, of course it was. *Protect* from what? How should I know, I've been protected from it by my devoted son."

Lady Heathway looked at her friend as if she'd gone mad. Peregrine did not think she was mad, exactly. Just determined to maintain the fantasy that she was the proud owner of the most devoted son in England. He was perfectly happy to comply.

"Lady Arabella," the duchess said softly. "Well, it could be worse, I suppose."

Lady Redfield hurried into the room. "They are found, thank the heavens."

"And engaged," the duchess said. "Cecilia, did you know things were going in this direction?"

"Well I suppose I did, Theodosia. You may rail all you like about it, but I did and am not sorry to say it."

Lady Heathway peered at Lady Redfield, seeming to wonder who this stalwart lady was.

"I have no intention of railing, Cecilia. I happen to view it as a very good match. Surprising, but good all the same. There have been things going on behind the scenes. Things I have been protected from, you see."

It was clear enough that Lady Redfield did not see what things the duchess mentioned. Still, she appeared very relieved. "I quite agree, it is a very good match," she said.

"It is an *excellent* match," Peregrine whispered into Arabella's ear.

"Most excellent," Arabella replied.

ALFIE WAS BROUGHT back to Grosvenor Square the morning after Lady Tredwell's masque ball.

It was difficult to say how he viewed his trip away from home, but he very graciously accepted an apple from Peregrine so he did not seem any worse for it.

If there were anyone as delighted as Peregrine and Arabella regarding their match, it was Lady Redfield. That lady was filled with a new confidence and further buoyed by the idea that her dear Arabella would always be her neighbor in Town. Her days began being filled with daring. At least, daring by her own yardstick. In an audacious frame of mind one morning, she ordered all of the baron's Indian furniture up to the attics and retrieved her staid old English furniture. She was exceedingly gratified by her five sons' incredulity when they became apprised of these changes.

Of course, Mr. Hemmings was delighted with the match for entirely different reasons. Mr. Sindu, a butler just like himself, had decided who his employer should wed and Mr. Sindu had prevailed. It seemed as if anything were possible in this brave new world.

Arabella and Peregrine arranged to be married by special license as, just as Arabella predicted, Lord Skeffington speedily gave his consent.

Mrs. Weston came to town for the wedding and arrived with her own news. It had transpired that her sister's brother-in-law, the Bishop of Bath and Wells, had been very genial indeed. They were to marry and Mrs. Weston would become mother to his young daughters. When the girls got older, Arabella supplied them with generous dowries, as a small payment for all of Mrs. Weston's kindnesses during the lonely years in Cornwall.

When Arabella and Peregrine set off for their wedding trip, they left the distinct impression that they were traveling to Italy. That was not where they went, though.

They traveled first to St. Albans to see the physician overseeing the private madhouse where Mary Huffman had been confined for the past ten years. Arabella brought copies of all she had collected to prove that Mary had always spoken the truth, and then pointed out the evidence that the doctor had taken payment to receive the lady. It turned out he had taken payment every month since.

Faced with exposure, the physician had speedily acquiesced to their demands. The first being, to have a private interview with Mary.

They found her subdued, and suspicious of why they had come. Over the course of an hour, Arabella was able to convince her of their sincerity in wishing to help her.

Arabella had wondered if Mary would wish to confront Skeffington and see him punished, or to demand her rightful place as the viscountess. If she did, Arabella was not at all certain how they should proceed.

Mary did not wish to do either of those things, though. What she wished for was to be reunited with her sister, and to have a quiet cottage by the sea where they could live in peace.

They packed her meager belongings and took her away that very afternoon, traveling on to Ramsgate. After speedily renting rooms, they spent the first week of their wedding trip finding just the right cottage for Mary. At the third property, they all knew they had found it. It had a long drive, its entrance not obvious from the road, it had three bedchambers as well as a small servants' quarters that could accommodate a cook and a maid.

But most of all, it had a lovely view of the ever-changing sea.

They hired a maid and a cook, the maid doing extra duty as a companion of sorts. Peggy would prove to be just what Mary needed. She was youthful and engaging and treated Mary as the viscountess she actually was.

It would not be long before Matilda, Mary's sister, was located in a rather dingy set of apartments in London and apprised of the situation. She promptly relocated with her young son, leaving her wastrel of a husband to fend for himself.

There, by the seaside, the two sisters lived quietly on the generous disbursements Peregrine had arranged, occasionally sending Arabella a note about how they got on.

Skeffington would eventually discover Mary's release, but not where she'd gone. He was left with the understanding that others knew his secret and that he could never dare marry. He eventually paid off Rendiver by mortgaging his estate.

Once Mary was settled into her cottage and properly cared for, Peregrine and Arabella set off on a tour peculiarly their own. With no bearing reins in sight, Bullford drove them up to Scotland to a small fishing lodge Peregrine had inherited from an uncle.

It was a compact little place with no servants as such. A grumpy fellow came by each day to restock the wood pile and care for Alfie and Bonny Betsy. His wife brought in provisions and straightened the place, always frowning at how they had left things.

For the most part, they lived on ham sandwiches and ale and a tea kettle on the hob. On fine days they rode the wild highlands, coming back exhausted and falling into each other's arms in front of a cheery fire that drove off the night's chill. When it rained and the wind howled, they simply stayed under a blanket in front of the fire all the day long.

Under that blanket might also be found a juvenile hare with a sore paw. Arabella had spotted it lurking by a stand of trees near the cottage and patiently lured him in with the lettuce from the ham sandwiches. The problem had been easily enough remedied, a thorn was removed and the hare should have been on its way. It stayed around for a full three days though, being a bit of a malingerer.

They would eventually drag themselves away from this small slice of heaven, though they would return to it often. As the years went by, their children would grow to love the place, even though they were all crowded in together and the caretaker remained as grumpy as ever.

Upon returning to London, Arabella became more closely acquainted with Lord Blackwood's household. As she had so often done with the woodland creatures she had rescued, she took Mr. Sindu's measure carefully. She never told him what he ought to do, only wondered about the proper course. He was rather generous with doling out advice, all of which she accepted gratefully.

It was in this careful approach that she was eventually able to convince him that they must have a housekeeper. Perhaps pointing out that it should give him more time in his library and that he should make the final decision on which woman ought to be hired had helped too.

Mrs. Radisson proved to be a treasure. She was competent and organized and understood perfectly well that Mr. Sindu must be treated with the utmost respect.

When summer came, they retreated to the duke and duchess' estate in Somerset. It was not three weeks later that a certain solicitor named Mr. Robins arrived with extraordinary news. He had been tasked with searching for Mr. Amandeep Sindu and had been doing so for years. He had only been able to track him to an alms house in Somerset over twenty years before, and then the trail had gone cold.

While they had all been aware that Mr. Sindu's parents had died of influenza, they had not known of any extended family. It turned out, he had an uncle who had never given up looking for him. That uncle had died several years before, but had left provisions for the search to continue. Amandeep Sindu was the sole beneficiary of his uncle's now liquidated estate. Mr. Sindu was suddenly a very rich man.

As might be imagined, he took the news in stride. He promptly resigned his position and bought a house on Grosvenor Square. He would go on to set himself up as the arbiter of good taste and proper views on things. He had a natural advantage over the *ton*, as he was not opposed to stating his opinions forcefully, with no care over how they would be received.

He began to be respected, and even feared, as he delivered his judgments on all he saw around him. He was often heard to claim that English habits were barbarous, though he had been raised an Englishman himself.

His salons were well-attended and he was known as a rather urbane figure. He partnered with Arabella to found *The Society Against Bearing Reins*, though this was not at all well-known. They kept things quiet as they understood that it was no easy task to convince people, especially young gentlemen, that their horses ought not be inconvenienced just for appearances. Rather, they hired an army of street boys and paid them for every bearing rein they brought back, most of them cut away with a knife.

Mr. Sindu judged that these boys were better employed at the task than pickpocketing, which is what they would have been doing. The newspapers often reported tales of the "Rein Bandits" and young gentlemen became more cautious of where they left their carriages when they employed a bearing rein. They took to hiring a nearby boy to keep watch, and that boy was often one of Mr. Sindu's own, who would demand payment up front, and then cut off the rein anyway.

Mr. Sindu did not only concern himself with the *ton* though. Over the years, he kept in touch with his friend Mr. Hemmings.

Hemmings had gone on to found the mysterious secret butler's society that had supposedly already been in existence. He had no trouble at all attracting members, as every house in Town desperately wished to claim their butler a member in good standing in the esteemed society.

They met on Wednesdays at four o'clock during the season, having taken the lease of a small house on St. James and modified it for their purposes. There was no sign on the door, as there was no name to the society, thereby maintaining its mystery.

The tenancy of the place was afforded by a generous donation from their only patron—Mr. Sindu. Having been a butler himself, albeit a very original one, he was not just considered the society's patron, but its advisor too. It was not at all unknown for Mr. Sindu to stroll in with the others on a Wednesday and fill their heads with terrible notions.

Many a lady of the house was left shaken by an idea rising thither. And yet, if the society decreed that apples must never be served after March, no matter how well they had been stored, then that was that. Any lady not following the directive would only be giving away that her butler did not belong to the society—her household had somehow failed to measure up.

Mr. Sindu's own butler, Mackay, most naturally began to have his own ideas. Mr. Sindu was perfectly amenable to them, as they only amounted to an extra half-day off and a specially built smoking room in the servants' quarters.

Freddy went on very well, having taken over Lord Skeffington's Crookhill Manor in Cornwall. Peregrine funded a stint at the Royal Veterinary College, which gave Freddy a foundation in the sciences, though his instincts served him just as well as any facts or theories. His expenses were low and he lived comfortably on the fees he collected for treating horses and livestock. But of course, he was especially known for his ability to heal the smaller creatures of his sphere and he was beloved by the children in the neighborhood as they knew they might turn up with a kitten's runny nose or a bunny's lack of appetite.

Mrs. Murder and Mrs. Twitch-nose continued their game of cat and mouse, though there were always far more mice than cats about the place. The Nightlys went on unmolested in their wing of the house. Sir Slippery finally heard the call of the river and moved off. Mr. Prickles never did venture much past the drawing room, he seeming to realize that though the forest might have its charms, it did not have biscuits.

In his proposal to Arabella, Peregrine had sworn he would not complain should she bring the forest creatures into the house. He did not, though there were times he might have liked to. It was very hard to hear the hunt gallop past in the distance and note the bushy tail of a fox in his drawing room.

His children seemed to be equally enthusiastic about dragging animals in from everywhere and they'd lost a few governesses over what small and darting creatures might be lurking in the nursery.

He could not remain piqued at his children, however, as whenever they were caught out, their faces flamed afire like so many tomatoes in the summer sun, just like their mother and father.

In any case, whenever Peregrine was surprised by the swish of a tail under a table or a bird suddenly found perched on the sofa, he could count on Apollo to be just as alarmed. It was often a reliable clue as to where a wild animal might be to note where Apollo was not.

Following the season when cocks were set free on Grosvenor Square, Lady Featherstone received a frantic missive from the Earl of Copeland. She could hardly make heads or tails of it, but for understanding that his daughter must come to Town, his gout could not manage it, she was accused of jilting Lord Luckstone, and she had certainly not jilted anybody.

There was some mystery surrounding these strange circumstances.

The last lady in London who could resist a mystery to be solved was Lady Featherstone.

Whether she should have resisted remains to be seen.

The End

About the Author

By the time I was eleven, my Irish Nana and I had formed a book club of sorts. On a timetable only known to herself, Nana would grab her blackthorn walking stick and steam down to the local Woolworth's. There, she would buy the latest Barbara Cartland romance, hurry home to read it accompanied by viciously strong wine, (Wild Irish Rose, if you're wondering) and then pass the book on to me. Though I was not particularly interested in real boys yet, I was *very* interested in the gentlemen in those stories—daring, bold, and often enraging and unaccountable. After my Barbara Cartland phase, I went on to Georgette Heyer, Jane Austen and so many other gifted authors blessed with the ability to bring the Georgian and Regency eras to life.

I would like nothing more than to time travel back to the Regency (and time travel back to my twenties as long as we're going somewhere) to take my chances at a ball. Who would take the first? Who would escort me into supper? What sort of meaningful looks would be exchanged? I would hope, having made the trip, to encounter a gentleman who would give me a very hard time. He ought to be vexatious in the extreme, and *worth* every vexation, to make the journey worthwhile.

I most likely won't be able to work out the time travel gambit, so I will content myself with writing stories of adventure and romance in my beloved time period. There are lives to be created, marvelous gowns to wear, jewels to don, instant attractions that inevitably come with a difficulty, and hearts to break before putting them back together again. In traditional Regency fashion, my stories are clean—the action happens in a drawing room, rather than a bedroom.

As I muse over what will happen next to my H and h, and wish I were there with them, I will occasionally remind myself that it's also nice to have a microwave, Netflix, cheese popcorn, and steaming hot showers.

Come see me on Facebook! @KateArcherAuthor